All about the author...
Kate Hewitt

KATE HEWITT discovered her first Harlequin® romance novel on a trip to England when she was thirteen, and she's continued to read them ever since. She wrote her first story at the age of five, simply because her older brother had written one and she thought she could do it, too. That story was one sentence long—fortunately, they've become a bit more detailed as she's grown older.

She studied drama in college and shortly after graduation moved to New York City to pursue a career in theater. This was derailed by something far better—meeting the man of her dreams, who happened also to be her older brother's childhood friend. Ten days after their wedding they moved to England, where Kate worked a variety of different jobs—drama teacher, editorial assistant, youth worker, secretary and, finally, mother.

When her oldest daughter was one year old, Kate sold her first short story to a British magazine. Since then she has sold many stories and serials, but writing romance remains her first love—of course!

Besides writing, she enjoys reading, traveling and learning to knit—it's an ongoing process and she's made a lot of scarves. After living in England for six years, she now resides in Connecticut with her husband, her three young children and, possibly one day, a dog.

Kate loves to hear from readers. You can contact her through her website, www.kate-hewitt.com.

* * *

"Hewitt's couple shines in her intensely emotional tale, spiced with shamelessly funny dialogue and sensual, explosive love scenes."
—*RT Book Reviews* on *His Brand of Passion*

"Hewitt's heartwrenching Corretti drama is an all-encompassing second-chance romance that's mired with loss and misery. It's pure magic how she turns regret into hope and despair into everlasting love With breathtaking landscapes, over-the-top luxury and ultra-sensual and emotional lovemaking, this is a love story not to be missed."
—*RT Book Reviews* on *An Inheritance of Shame*

"Hewitt's excellent second-chance romance will thrill readers with its angst-filled dialogue, incredible characters and exquisite love scenes."
—*RT Book Reviews* on *The Husband She Never Knew*

"Hewitt gives romance addicts everything they need for a fix, including an over-the-top storyline, memorable characters and a timeless romance set on a picturesque island."
—*RT Book Reviews* on *Santina's Scandalous Princess*

"Hewitt's romance is touchingly haunting, and her realistic characters will humble readers with their acts of forgiveness and love in the face of loss."
—*RT Book Reviews* on *The Darkest of Secrets*

The Fifth Avenue series

AVENGE ME Maisey Yates
SCANDALIZE ME Caitlin Crews
EXPOSE ME Kate Hewitt

Other titles by Kate Hewitt available in ebook:

A QUEEN FOR THE TAKING? *(The Diomedi Heirs)*
THE PRINCE SHE NEVER KNEW *(The Diomedi Heirs)*
AN INHERITANCE OF SHAME *(Sicily's Corretti Dynasty)*
HIS BRAND OF PASSION *(The Bryants: Powerful & Proud)*

KATE HEWITT

expose me

HARLEQUIN PRESENTS®

Recycling programs
for this product may
not exist in your area.

ISBN-13: 978-0-373-43039-0

EXPOSE ME

Copyright © 2014 by Harlequin Books S.A.

Special thanks and acknowledgment are given to Kate Hewitt for her contribution
to the *Fifth Avenue* trilogy.

This edition published by arrangement with Harlequin Books S.A.

For questions and comments about the quality of this book, please contact us
at CustomerService@Harlequin.com.

Printed in U.S.A.

expose me

Chapter One

Alex Diaz leaned forward in his seat as the limo pulled to the curb of Seventy-Second Street and West End Avenue. The luxury high-rise building was all soaring modernity and tinted glass, and exactly the sort of place he'd expect Chelsea Maxwell to live in.

His lips curved in an ice-cold smile of anticipation as he pressed the intercom to speak to the driver. "Just wait a few minutes, please."

"Very good, sir."

His gaze flicked to his watch and he brushed a near-invisible speck of lint from the crisp sleeve of his tuxedo. Seven twenty-five. The party started in five minutes, but naturally Chelsea Maxwell would be fashionably late.

As would he, since he intended on giving her a lift.

Outside the lights of Manhattan gleamed in a wintry darkness and people hurried past on West End Avenue's wide pavements, heads bent against the cutting wind that funneled down the street. It was early February and New York was caught in a stranglehold of cold unrelieved by the softness of any snow.

The weather, bitter and relentless, suited Alex perfectly.

Tonight was the beginning of his personal revenge on Jason Treffen, much anticipated and long overdue. They said revenge was a dish best served cold and if so Jason was going to enjoy every icy mouthful.

And for that he needed Chelsea Maxwell. Or at least her television show.

Seven twenty-seven. Had she decided to skip the party? He let out his breath in an impatient hiss. Tonight's party was a birthday bash for Chelsea's boss Michael Agnello, and if rumor had it, the man with whom she'd slept her way to host of the number one daytime talk show. She had to be going.

Seven twenty-nine. Alex shifted in his seat, suppressing a flare of irritation. *Where was she?*

Then the tinted glass doors of her building swooshed open, and she stepped out into the freezing night, her body swathed in a long, elegant coat of ivory cashmere. Her chestnut hair was pulled into an elaborate up-do, and diamond chandelier earrings sparkled and swung against her jawbone. Alex saw her gaze flick toward his limo, and then her face tightened in annoyance, and he knew she was irritated that the driver hadn't come out to open the door for her. She thought his limo was hers when in actuality hers hadn't arrived.

Because he'd called and canceled it.

His mouth curling in a smile of pure, predatory anticipation, Alex pressed a button to roll down the window. He leaned out, a blast of wintry air ruffling his hair, as Chelsea started toward the limo, all confident, glittering purpose.

"Ms. Maxwell?"

She stopped, eyes narrowing, as he leaned a little more

forward so she could see him. "Alex Diaz," he said, though she had to know who he was. They'd only met at various media events a handful of times, but most people in the industry knew him and in any case, Chelsea Maxwell didn't seem like someone to forget a face. "Am I right in thinking we're both headed to the same place?"

"I suppose that depends where you're heading." Her voice was low and throaty, attractive yet decidedly cool, and her eyes were still narrowed. Curled up on one of her trademark pink velour sofas on her talk show, Chelsea Maxwell was all wide eyes and husky sweetness. In real life she was harder, sharper, but then Alex supposed you didn't get where Chelsea Maxwell had by being stupid or soft.

"Michael Agnello's fortieth birthday party?" he prompted, and she just cocked her head, waited.

Normally he wouldn't have bothered going to a party such as this one. He had no time or patience for the petty scheming and schmoozing that was the trademark of such industry events. But he'd known Chelsea would be going, and he needed to talk to her. Find out what she knew, what she planned on doing.

To use her, or at least use her show.

He opened the door of the limo just as another gust of icy wind blew Chelsea's coat around her long, slim legs. "May I offer you a lift?"

She hesitated and Alex waited, adrenaline and impatience rushing through him even though he remained completely still. He hadn't considered what he would do if she said no. He never thought about failure.

"Thank you," she finally said, and slid in next to him in the limo. Alex moved over a bit, but her thigh still nudged his and he inhaled the scent of her perfume, something expensive and understated.

He stretched one arm along the back of the seat as the limo pulled away from the curb, and she turned to him, a knowing little smile curving her lips. "So why did you steal my limo?"

He felt a flare of surprise, a glimmer of cool amusement. So she wanted to work a little flirt? Fine. He could play that way, too. He arched an eyebrow, smiled back. "Do I look like someone who would do that?"

She gave him a deliberately thorough once-over, her gaze sweeping him from head to foot and lingering unapologetically on certain places. His body reacted to her assessment, groin tightening, gut plunging. There was, he acknowledged, something incredibly erotic about her confident perusal of him. "I'd say so."

He shook his head mockingly. "So suspicious."

"Isn't everyone in this business?" She dropped the light tone and leveled him with a hard look. "So, why the cloak-and-dagger routine? What do you want?"

He just smiled and arched an eyebrow. "What makes you think I want something?"

"I wasn't born yesterday, Mr. Diaz."

"Call me Alex."

"I'd be delighted to." Her smile was flirtatious and yet her eyes were cool. Amazing eyes, really. Gray-green fringed with thick, dark lashes. "So, Alex," she said, her voice dropping into a purr. "I hire a limo for tonight but I find you in one instead, offering me a lift. Coincidence?" She raised her eyebrows, two thin arcs of incredulity, that knowing smile curving her mouth—quite an amazing mouth, too, now that he was looking at it. Full and lush even when her lips had been pursed. "I don't think so."

Alex almost smiled, despite the fact that Chelsea Maxwell's ability to see straight through his paper-thin ploy should have alarmed, or at least annoyed, him. This wasn't going to be as simple as he thought. Not nearly. Good thing he enjoyed a challenge. And good thing he intended to publicly ruin Jason Treffen no matter what the cost, or who paid. The fact that he could do it on live television just made it all the sweeter.

He shrugged slightly, relaxed back in his seat. "Fair enough. I do want something, Ms. Maxwell."

She did not, he observed, tell him to call her Chelsea. She just waited, eyes still narrowed, that cool little smile playing about her mouth.

"How long have you been at AMI?" he asked, naming her network.

Surprise flashed so briefly across her features he almost missed it. Chelsea Maxwell was good at hiding her emotions, Alex suspected. Working on TV would do that to you. "Ten years."

"And you've had *Chat with Chelsea* for—"

"Nearly four." She cocked her head, one elegant eyebrow still arched. "And you're asking this because...?"

"I'm interested in your show."

She didn't so much as blink. "You don't seem like the type to watch celebrities spill their guts on afternoon television, but I suppose everyone has their secret vices."

He laughed softly, enjoying this unexpected repartee. He was used to people sucking up to him, and the respite was surprisingly pleasant. "It's the number one daytime talk show on any network," he pointed out, and that lush mouth curved just a little more.

"I know."

"I'm not interested in your daytime talk show," Alex said after a second's pause. He needed to be careful now, needed to consider how much to reveal. How honest to be. He wasn't about to give Chelsea any more information than necessary—not until he knew what she'd do with it. "I'm interested in the hour-long interview you're doing with Jason Treffen on prime time in March."

"Really." She crossed her legs, the coat slipping open, and he saw the thigh-high slit in her silvery-gray gown, revealing a hell of a lot of slim, tanned leg. His libido stirred again and Alex gave it a hard shove back. He wasn't about to complicate this with sex. Not unless it served a purpose, anyway.

"Really," he answered.

She cocked her head, her gaze sweeping over him slowly, in that same thorough assessment that had his groin tightening again. So maybe he did want things to be complicated. Sometimes sex was a means to an end, and with Chelsea it would undoubtedly be an enjoyable one. He wondered what she was like in bed. Wild and unrestrained, or coolly controlled? He suspected the latter, but he'd like to see her certainty slip a bit, her coolness replaced by fire.

"Are you making me an offer?" she asked, and there was no mistaking the teasing innuendo in her voice, rich with laughter and full-bodied flirting. Was this what Michael Agnello hadn't been able to resist? Alex could certainly understand it.

He stretched the arm he had draped over the seat so

his fingertips barely brushed her shoulder. The cashmere was cold and soft under his fingers. "No, just telling you I'm curious."

"You went to quite a lot of trouble for mere curiosity's sake, Mr. Diaz." She smiled, shaking her head slowly, her earrings sparkling as they moved. Even though she was acting friendly, flirtatious, Alex knew she was nobody's fool.

And neither was he.

"Waiting in a limo isn't that much trouble," he told her, and she tilted her head again, eyes bright, her mouth still curved in that smile he didn't know whether he wanted to kiss or wipe off her face. It both annoyed and intrigued him, how coolly certain she was about everything. How unfazed by him.

He realized he had been expecting a little breathless flattery, a little dazed gratitude. He didn't like anyone kissing his ass, but he'd assumed Chelsea would jump at the carrot he dangled in front of her: the possibility of working on Diaz News. But now that he'd spoken to her he didn't think Chelsea Maxwell jumped for anyone.

Except she obviously had for Michael Agnello. And damn it, she would for him.

"I'm in contract with AMI for the next three years," she said and he nodded.

"I know."

"So…?"

Alex glanced out the window; they were approaching Columbus Circle and would only have a few more minutes before they arrived at the party, and Chelsea was swept up into Michael Agnello's glittering circle of close friends.

"Let's talk over dinner."

She let out a soft, throaty laugh. "I wasn't aware there was anything to talk about."

"Don't play games with me, Chelsea." His voice came out hard as he turned to look directly into her eyes, but instead of seeing anger or annoyance or better yet, regret, in those hazel depths he saw something that jolted through him so he nearly rocked in his seat.

Desire. Lust. It was gone as soon as he'd locked his gaze with hers, but he still felt its aftershock reverberate through him. Felt the desire he'd seen in her eyes harden his groin.

He wanted, suddenly and quite fiercely, to sweep his hand up that long, lovely expanse of leg. To slip his fingers under the silvery, slippery folds of her dress and see just what it was hiding. And it seemed like Chelsea wanted it, too.

Well, wasn't that interesting. Complicated, perhaps, but definitely interesting. Maybe he didn't need to pretend he wanted Chelsea on his network. Maybe he could just show that he wanted her in his bed.

And maybe complicated could become simple.

"You think I'm playing games?" she queried, her expression completely veiled now. "You're the one hiding out in a limo, acting like you're James Bond." She shook her head, laughed softly. "When you want to talk straight with me, Diaz, I'll listen." Her smile curved deeper and she gave him another up-and-down, her gaze resting briefly on the bulge in his trousers. "Maybe."

Alex nearly swore. He felt like a horny teenager, unable to control himself, and the absurdity of it annoyed him. When had he lost control with a woman, with anyone?

The limo pulled up to the curb of The Mandarin Hotel. A doorman stepped forward to open the door and Chelsea fluttered her fingers. "But thanks for the lift," she added, and then she was gone.

Alex leaned back against the seat, furious, frustrated and yet still buzzing a little bit from the conversation. So Chelsea Maxwell was going to be a little bit more of a challenge than he'd anticipated.

Although if the awareness he'd seen in her eyes was anything to go by, maybe not. Maybe he could play this differently than he'd planned.

His plan, or so he'd told Hunter and Austin when they'd brainstormed together how to bring Treffen down for good, was to dangle the possibility of a show on Diaz News so Chelsea let him work with her on the interview with Treffen. It had seemed simple; she clearly wanted to prove herself as a serious journalist, and as CEO of the country's top news network he could make that happen. He'd tell her the truth about Treffen when he could be sure what she'd do with it.

Whether he actually offered Chelsea something on Diaz News was another matter entirely.

Revenge was a costly business. A price had to be paid. He'd certainly paid his.

Even now the memory of the last time he'd seen Sarah made his insides freeze with icy determination. He would avenge her, and every other woman Jason Treffen had used and abused. And he'd do whatever it took to accomplish it, Chelsea Maxwell be damned.

"Sir?" The driver peered into the dark interior of the limo and with a nod Alex climbed out.

He didn't give up that easily. He wasn't done with Chelsea Maxwell. He'd promised Hunter and Austin; they'd done their part, and it was time for him to do his, whatever it took. Smiling grimly, he headed into the hotel.

Chelsea slid off her coat and handed it to the young woman at the coat check, barely aware of taking the ticket or getting in the elevator that would take her up to the thirty-fifth floor where Michael's party was being held. She closed her eyes, breathed in deeply.

That impromptu meeting with Alex Diaz had left her dazed and breathless. A little buzzed, too, and a lot wary. She'd learned too many lessons the hard way not to wonder when a man wanted something.

And Alex Diaz definitely wanted something.

Adrenaline pumped through her as she thought of the way he'd filled the space of the limo, arms stretched out along the back of the seat, legs casually sprawled. Fingers brushing her shoulder. Even through the thick cashmere of her coat she'd felt it. And Alex had too; no way had that little caress been unintentional. It had taken everything she had not to shiver.

She didn't like being so responsive to a man, any man, but especially one like Alex Diaz. He was overwhelmingly, inarguably male, potent and primal. And her body had responded even as her mind had raced from his words, the obvious implication.

I'm interested in your show.

Not her chat show, but the prime-time interview she'd worked her ass off to get. Ever since she'd started *Chat with Chelsea* she'd known she wanted more. She wanted to be taken seriously as a journalist, and that wasn't going to happen as long as she sat on a pink velour sofa and interviewed weepy country singers and washed-up soap stars. It might be popular and it might have made her rich, but it sure as hell didn't mean anyone actually respected it...or her.

She knew what people said about her and Michael; she was neither stupid nor deaf. But even Michael couldn't give her an hour-long interview with a serious subject. If she nailed the interview with Treffen, if it became the iconic interview of the decade as she hoped and planned, that wouldn't be up to Michael.

It would be up to her. And everyone would know it.

She let out a long, slow breath. And if the interview with Treffen led to something on Diaz News? Anchorwoman, or even her own serious interview slot? Her stomach tightened and her mind started racing again.

No, she couldn't think like that. Not yet. Not till she knew what Diaz really wanted. She thought of the bulge she'd seen in his trousers before she'd left the limo, left him hungry just as she'd intended. He was attracted to her; that had been, at least to him, painfully obvious. She wasn't above using that attraction. Hell, no.

But life had taught her to be a skeptic, a cynic. To watch her back. And she wasn't about to jump into bed with a man like Alex Diaz, not even for a job.

Especially not for a job.

Even so just the thought—the remote possibility—of being on Diaz News made her heart beat harder and her fingers curl into determined fists. Diaz's news network was the most respected on TV, and was the only one that managed to rise above the petty, political squabbling and scaremongering of other networks. "Facts, not opinions" was Diaz News's motto, and made it the most-watched news channel on television.

And she could be on it, as a serious, respected journalist...

Her mouth twisted cynically. Or maybe Alex Diaz just wanted her in bed.

Which wouldn't be such a bad a place to be...

Maybe not, but Diaz was so not her type; he was too arrogant and controlling. She liked her men a little meeker. They were meant to do her bidding.

But if she could get Alex Diaz to do her bidding...

Now her smile curved in anticipation. Wouldn't that be satisfying. Alex Diaz in front of her, on his knees. Begging.

As she once had.

But never again. She didn't beg, plead or even say please. When it came to sex, she took.

But she needed to stop thinking about sex.

Chelsea took another deep breath and then raised her chin a notch as the elevator stopped at the thirty-fifth floor.

If Diaz did have something legitimate in mind, he'd seek her out again. *Legitimately*. She wasn't about to go running to him, asking for favors.

The party was in full swing as the elevator doors opened onto the private room with wraparound views of Manhattan, Central Park an oasis of darkness amidst the endless lights of the city. Chelsea stepped into the room, head held high as she nodded at a few acquaintances. People who would say they were her friends, but Chelsea knew better. She knew a million people like that, but nobody knew her. She didn't give them the chance.

Still, she worked the room, laughing and chatting, air-kissing and waggling her fingers. The effort was exhausting, but that was something else nobody knew.

In any case, most people at the network were jealous of her meteoric rise to talk show host by age twenty-eight, and the rumors that she'd slept her way to that position still swirled around her four years later, although she ignored them with the airiness of someone who didn't give a damn. And she didn't. Wouldn't.

That route to success might have worked for her once—or not—but she was a different woman now. Harder. Smarter. And nobody's fool—or plaything.

"Chelsea." Michael came toward her, hands outstretched. Chelsea took them and leaned in as Michael brushed his lips against her cheek. She could feel people watching them, eyes narrowed, ears pricked for some overheard salacious snippet. Not that they needed any; they could just make them up. She never denied anything. Denying rumors put you on the defensive, and ended up just stoking the fires of gossip higher. Let people wonder. Let them smirk. She'd still come out on top.

"Your hands are cold," he said, and she laughed lightly.

"It's freezing outside, Michael." She slipped her hands from his, suddenly conscious of someone watching them. She didn't need to look to see who it was. She'd felt his gaze on her ever since the elevator doors had pinged open after her, had felt his presence, dark and forceful, even though she'd refused to look at him even out of the corner of her eye.

Alex Diaz was there. And she *felt* him.

Michael leaned back, studying her for a moment, concern making his eyes narrow and the dignified crow's-feet at their corners look more pronounced. He was always worried about her, even though Chelsea told him not to be. Pretended as if she didn't need someone's concern or care, because admitting to that was both weakness and need and she never showed either.

But she did need Michael. He'd discovered her when she was twenty-two: desperate, damaged and determined, and she'd told him more about herself than she had anyone else, even her sister. Yet she still hadn't told him everything, and never would.

"You look tired," he said, and she laughed again.

"Thank you very much."

"And gorgeous, of course," he added with a smile. "It goes without saying. But I hope you're not working too hard."

"Don't fuss." Despite only eight years between their ages, Michael tended to act like a father toward her, or perhaps a big brother. Protective and just a little bit bossy. They'd never been romantic, not even close, but as always Chelsea had done nothing to dispel the rumors. Neither had Michael, at her request. It was always better to hold your head high than to trip over yourself explaining what people were determined to believe anyway.

And in any case, they had good reason to believe it. Or they would, if Chelsea wasn't so good at hiding her past. Hiding herself.

"All right." He smiled, his teeth blindingly white in his tanned face—he'd been skiing in Aspen last week—and Chelsea was reminded just how charismatic he was, how good-looking and good-natured. If she'd ever wanted a sure bet for a relationship, she would have chosen Michael. He almost made her feel safe.

But she'd never wanted a relationship; men were for the occasional satiation of physical needs only. And for some reason that thought made her think of Alex Diaz. Damn.

She couldn't keep her gaze from seeking him out; she knew right where to look, even though she'd been determinedly not looking at him for the past fifteen minutes. He stood in the center of the room, breathtaking in a tuxedo, his gaze narrowed even as he smiled at a passing acquaintance, everything about him dark and powerful and just a little bit intimidating.

He was, Chelsea acknowledged, an incredibly attractive man. Michael Agnello had charisma, but Alex Diaz had something more powerful, primal and raw. Sex appeal, pure and simple. Muscles rippled under his tuxedo jacket, his body seeming to take up so much space the huge room suddenly felt small. He had to be at least six-three, Chelsea decided. She was an inch under six feet and in her three-inch heels—she never conceded to flats because of her height—she was still an inch or two shorter than him. She liked a man who didn't make her feel like a giraffe, she acknowledged, and then banished the thought.

She didn't like men. She used them.

And she wondered then what it would feel like to use Alex Diaz.

Dangerous.

And almost as dangerous was the realization that he was coming straight toward her. She felt a frisson of anticipation, mixed with just a little alarm. Something about Diaz felt…off. There was too much grim focus in his gaze, too much predatory intent in his measured walk. If he wanted her for his network, he'd be easygoing, friendly. He'd have gone through her agent and set up a dinner at Le Cirque with them both. It would have been all insider jokes over five bottles of wine, not this hooded, hawklike look as if she were a baby squirrel who had just tumbled all soft and downy from her nest.

She straightened her shoulders, turned to him with a glittering smile. *No baby squirrels here, sucker,* she thought, still smiling right into his narrowed eyes.

He had beautiful eyes, deep brown with golden glints, and lashes that were incredibly thick and full. His hair was ink-black and cut very short, but it still made Chelsea wonder how it felt, if it would be soft as she threaded it through her fingers.

And as for his body…a confident, rangy power in every limb and muscle. She yanked her gaze away from his thighs, curved her mouth into a flirty little smile. "Hello again."

"Hello, Chelsea." How did he manage to inject a simple salutation with so much intent? So much…sex?

Or was her libido going into hyperdrive because she hadn't felt this magnetic tug of attraction in a long, long time?

Maybe ever.

"May I get you a drink?" he asked, coming to stand close enough so she could breathe in the woodsy scent of his aftershave, feel that almost irresistible pull toward him. She stepped back. Resisted. She wasn't about to jump into bed with a man like Alex Diaz. That wouldn't just be foolish, it would be insane. Not with her track record. Not when he wanted to talk business.

She'd learned that much, at least.

"Seltzer water, please."

"Of course."

She watched him head toward the bar, admiring the muscular back, the trim hips and taut butt. Yes, he was an attractive man. That had clearly been established. *Moving on.*

She took another deep breath and willed the knots of tension in her shoulders to untangle, or at least loosen a little. She hated parties, had for ten years, and now she felt that first prickle of anxiety at being in a crowd and resolutely forced it back. Alex returned with her glass of seltzer in one hand, a beer bottle in the other. "Here you go," he said, and gently but with clear purpose, his hand coming around her back, he steered her toward a private space near the window. She didn't resist, but as soon as possible she stepped away from him, gave herself a little needed distance.

"Amazing view," Alex commented, the beer bottle raised to his lips. "I never get tired of it."

Chelsea didn't even glance out the floor-to-ceiling windows. She had virtually the same view from her penthouse apartment, and her eyes were on this man. "So why are you interested in my show, Alex?" Might as well spell it out. Spit it out, no needless sugarcoating.

His lips twitched in something close to a smile. "You're good at what you do."

"Which is?"

"Seeming sympathetic while slipping a dagger between the ribs."

She blinked, surprised, and then smiled because yes, that was definitely one description of what she did. Cozying up to celebrities so she could make them confess and cry. But they liked it; they needed the absolution her show seemed to provide.

"And you like that?" She hadn't meant to load that question with sexual innuendo, of course she hadn't, yet somehow it came out anyway, and she saw Alex's pupils flare, felt that same hard kick of attraction she'd felt in the limo. *Painful.* Unwanted.

"I like people who are good at what they do."

"Still, it doesn't seem like the type of thing you'd feature on your network, if you are in fact implying you'd want to go somewhere with this."

"No, it doesn't." He took a sip of his beer, and Chelsea kept her face neutral. Waited—but for what?

She could still feel the aftershock of attraction, like pins and needles on her skin. She knew Alex felt it, too, and wondered just how complicated this would be.

She didn't do complicated. Didn't mix business with pleasure, or sex with emotion, or sex with anything. Not anymore. She kept sex in the same mental box as annual physicals or biannual dental cleanings. Sometimes it was fun, and sometimes it was very fun, and sometimes it was just boring. But necessary, no matter what, to good health.

Alex lowered his beer bottle, gave her a considering glance. "How did you end up getting Treffen to agree to a prime-time interview with you?"

She bristled, because he sounded so incredulous. As if

he couldn't imagine how a ditzy used-to-be-blonde like her had been capable of it. "I worked hard."

"Treffen's never done a television interview before."

"I realize. I did do my homework, you know." Inwardly Chelsea winced. She sounded defensive. Pathetic. And she didn't do either.

Alex's mouth curved, and Chelsea felt her pulse skyrocket. The man had the sexiest smile she'd ever seen. Just the twitch of his lips made her shift where she stood, feel a rush of warmth she tried to ignore. "So tell me," he said in a low voice that rolled over her like a wave of honey. "How did you do it?"

"I was patient." The words came out clipped, because now terseness was her only defense against the tide of desire that was washing over her, wrecking her resolve like castles in sand. "I spent a year getting to know him, making sure I was at the same parties he was, admiring his work—"

"Sucking up."

Chelsea drew back, startled by the scorn in his voice. And a few seconds ago she'd been semicontemplating having sex with this man. "He's an incredible person," she said shortly, "who has done a world of good for women's rights—"

"I know what he's done." Alex smiled coldly, and the eyes she'd thought were so amazing with their golden glints now looked like chips of black ice. "But I wonder if you do."

"What's that supposed to mean?"

"Are you going to put him on your sofa? Have him spill his secrets and make him cry?"

His voice was a low purr but Chelsea still heard the sneer. Felt it. "It's not that kind of interview," she answered coolly. "I'm not interested in shock value with Treffen. But frankly, I'm not really sure why you care."

"Because I care about Treffen."

"You sound like you hate the man."

"*Hate* isn't the right word. But I'd like to see what he does with an interview. What you do with it." He raised his beer bottle to his lips again, his mouth still curved in a cool smile, his eyes still hard.

Chelsea decided she'd had enough of his innuendo and snark. So he didn't like Jason Treffen. Considering the lawyer and human rights activist was lauded as a modern-day saint, that was a little strange, but it had nothing to do with her.

Except maybe it did. Because she was interviewing the man, and if she wanted to make it as a serious investigative journalist, she needed to know. Needed to dig.

But not right now. Not when Alex Diaz was making her feel so weak, both from his mockery and the attraction she still, damn it, felt. It coursed through her relentlessly, a river of want that carried her will right along with it.

Almost.

She straightened, flashed him one of her glittering smiles. "Well, stay tuned, then. It airs live on March twentieth."

And without waiting for a response, she turned and walked away from him, her shoulders thrown back, her chin held high.

Alex raised his beer to his lips as he tracked Chelsea's movements around the room. For a moment there he'd considered telling her the truth about Jason Treffen, but then he'd thankfully thought better of it. It was hardly cocktail party chitchat, and he didn't know her well enough to trust her with that particular powder keg. Not yet, anyway.

She was ambitious, he got that, and tough. He was pretty sure she had the balls to bring down Treffen on live television, if she wanted to.

The question was, did she? Could he convince her? He possessed a savage need to see Treffen with his world crumbling around him, and everyone else seeing it, too. No longer would the man fool everyone into believing he was such a damned saint. They would know him not just as a sinner, but a devil.

Austin had already exposed Treffen to his family, with the help of Sarah's sister, Katy. Hunter was working on ousting Treffen from his law firm. And Alex had been charged with confronting the man on national television, showing the world what he really was: a monster who used the women he said he was saving. Who damned them to lives of shame, scandal and sin. Everything in Alex ached to see Jason publicly exposed—and he would do whatever it took to make it happen.

Including use Chelsea in whatever way he could. The woman was cold; she'd slept her way to the top. He didn't feel so much as a flicker of guilt for using her. Sleeping with her, if it came to that.

But he did feel a certain amount of frustration. *Sexual* frustration. Never mind Treffen, he wanted Chelsea Maxwell in bed, beneath him, those gray-green eyes turned to molten silver with desire. He wanted her haughty little smile to become a desperate, begging kiss, to turn her tinkling laugh into a breathy sigh of pleasure and need.

He wanted to be the one to do it. To shatter her icy control and make her melt. For him.

He glanced at her walking away from him, her dress flowing over her like mercury. The front might have been high-necked and as chaste as a nun's habit, but the back plunged right down to the tempting curve of her butt. Alex had always considered himself more of a breast man, but the sight of Chelsea Maxwell's back, golden and perfect, made him reconsider.

He watched her glide away from the crowd and then instinctively followed, curious as to why she was leaving the party so soon. He stopped when he saw she was just heading toward the narrow hall that led to the ladies'. What the hell was wrong with him?

He was letting this woman lead him around by the balls, and she didn't even know it.

Or maybe she did.

Chelsea checked her makeup in the mirror of the ladies' toilet and took a deep breath. And another, because parties like this—and exchanges like the one she'd had with Alex Diaz—brought her to the brink of an anxiety attack. Not that she'd ever show it. Ten years on and she'd learned not just to live with it, but to hide it.

She stared at her reflection in the mirror, willed the color to return to her cheeks, her heartbeat to slow and her palms to stop tingling. *You're better than this, Chelsea. Stronger. Will it away.*

A breath. Another. She continued to stare at her reflection, her face composed, her eyes hard. And finally, finally, the color returned and the tingling went away and she breathed deeply, her heart rate normal.

There. See?

Taking one last breath to steady herself, she turned from the mirror and left the ladies' room.

Twenty minutes more and she'd call it a night. The thought brought an almost painful wave of relief. Her exchange with Alex Diaz had made her feel particularly edgy, everything just a little too close to the surface even though she knew, intellectually at least, that it was all still well hidden away.

Thank God.

Even Michael didn't know how hard these occasions could be for her. When you had a high-profile career in television, you could hardly admit that socializing sometimes made you almost cripplingly anxious. That people scared you.

People like Alex Diaz.

She'd continued to feel his eyes on her as she'd moved around the room, and while his attention hadn't scared her precisely, it had made her wary. Wary and aware, because even from fifty feet away he had the power to affect her. Make her ache. And that was too much power for one man to have.

She turned away from the mirror and headed back out to the party, stopping suddenly when a familiar bulk blocked the narrow hallway.

Paul Bates, AMI's leading news anchorman and a complete ass. A drunken ass, judging from the fumes Chelsea could smell from ten feet away, and the way he lurched toward her. She took another deep breath and started to move past him.

He grabbed her arm, fingers digging in, nails snagging onto the slippery fabric of her dress. "Where you going, beautiful?" he slurred, and the whisky fumes now hit her full on the face. Chelsea didn't move, didn't pull her arm away. She knew better than that; men like Paul Bates liked a little resistance. Or even a lot.

"Back to the party, Paul," she answered calmly. "But I'd suggest you remove your hand from my arm unless you want to be slapped with a sexual harassment suit."

"Oh, come on, Chelsea." She could get drunk off his breath alone, Chelsea thought dispassionately. "You could be a little friendlier to me, you know," he continued, his voice turning both insistent and wheedling. "I could help you the way Agnello does."

As if. She'd seen Paul eyeing her at the studio before, had ignored a few thinly veiled insults, some offensive innuendo, but he'd never actually come on to her before. He'd never touched her.

"Oh, I'm sure you could, Paul," Chelsea murmured, tossing in a throaty chuckle for good measure. He made a clumsy grab for her hand and started drawing it to his crotch. Chelsea let him, felt his rather unimpressive hard-on. And smiling sweetly, she squeezed his balls hard enough for him to choke.

With a gasped curse he released her hand.

Chelsea moved past him, stopping abruptly when she saw another figure blocking her exit.

Alex Diaz.

He was gazing at her with narrowed eyes, his mouth twisted into something like a smile.

"And here I was about to charge to your rescue," he murmured.

"Watch out you're not next," Chelsea fired back, keeping her voice flirtatious, and she heard him laugh softly.

"I'd better move out of the way, then."

He moved to the side and Chelsea slipped past him, her breasts brushing his chest. Her breath hitched and she tilted her head up, gave him a slow smile. "Although maybe you'd enjoy it," she murmured, and he gazed back, his face expressionless now.

"Maybe I would."

She felt her heart lurch inside her. Why was she doing this? Alex Diaz was dangerous, and exactly the wrong kind of man for her.

And that was exactly why she was doing it. Because playing with fire proved you were strong and smart enough not to get burned—or at least not to mind a few singed fingers.

Still smiling, she dropped her hand and let her fingers brush against the front of his trousers. He didn't so much as twitch, but she could still feel his arousal and answering desire arrowed through her. She leaned forward so her earrings grazed his jaw, and he still didn't move. "I don't need rescuing, Diaz," she murmured into his ear.

Alex turned slightly so his lips brushed her cheek, less than an inch from her mouth. Everything in Chelsea clenched hard. "You sure as hell don't, Miss Maxwell," he murmured back and before she lost it completely she stepped away and walked back into the ballroom.

She felt his gaze on her back all the way to the elevators.

Chapter Two

Alex watched Chelsea Maxwell walk away and shook his head slowly. The woman was incredible, and he wasn't sure he meant that in a good way.

Although maybe he did. A certain part of his anatomy certainly did, because when she'd brushed against him with her fingers he'd had to resist the urge to grab her by the arms and push her against the wall, kiss her until they both were senseless. And more.

Which didn't make him all that different from Bates, who was still bent over and wheezing from Chelsea's smiling squeeze of his balls.

The woman was no victim. No Sarah, used and abused by men with power, and the thought gave him a strange, savage satisfaction because that was the kind of woman he needed.

But first he had to get her to agree.

His gaze narrowed as he saw her heading for the elevator. Was she leaving the party already? For a moment he considered following her, but then decided against it. He'd laid the groundwork tonight; he needed to think about the best way to handle Chelsea Maxwell before he spoke with her again. And he also needed to get a handle on the obvious attraction he felt for her. He didn't like feeling out of control, especially not when it came to sex. Men started making stupid decisions when they let themselves be led by their dicks.

And Alex had no intention of letting that happen. If he slept with Chelsea, it would be on his terms, because it served a purpose.

Even if he suspected it would be incredibly enjoyable.

The elevator doors opened and she stepped inside, head held high, her chin tilted at an almost defiant angle. She looked haughty and magnificent, the ultimate ice queen—and then Alex noticed one hand clenched in the folds of her gown. That little, telling action surprised him, and he wondered just what it revealed. Was she angry with the drunken idiot who had come onto her? She'd seemed no more than coldly amused when Bates had stumbled up to her.

From behind him Alex heard Paul Bates mutter a wheezy curse.

"What a bitch," he mumbled and Alex glanced at him in derision.

"You're just saying that because she got you in the balls."

"Like I said—"

"And you deserved it." Alex shook his head, taking in the man's golden good looks that were now on the wrong side of forty, with broken veins and bloodshot eyes—not to mention a sizeable paunch—revealing a lifetime of reckless living.

"You know she's Agnello's tart, don't you?" Bates demanded, and Alex just shrugged.

"She's not yours, at any rate," he said with deliberate mildness, and walked away with Bates still gasping behind him.

The next morning he headed to his office on Hudson Street, scanning the headlines on his smartphone as he took the elevator up to his penthouse office.

He stepped into the soaring room of glass and steel, glanced again at his phone as he powered up his computer, and wondered whether to call Chelsea now. He needed to think carefully about his next move, and yet he couldn't deny he was looking forward to sparring with her again, craving the little buzz conversation with her had given him. There weren't many women like Chelsea, he mused: ruthless, ambitious, and sexually confident.

Yes, she would definitely be a match for him in bed. And no matter what happened with Treffen, he decided, he was going to find a way to get her there.

But first he needed to think about Treffen. That little curl of anticipation he'd felt low in his belly now soured into a churning mix of regret and resolve.

Jason Treffen was lauded far and wide as an advocate for the downtrodden and oppressed, especially those who were women. He'd gained a reputation for mentoring smart, driven young women who'd gone to the Ivy League schools on scholarship—with no one knowing that he was actually coercing them into committing the most sordid of acts.

His gut roiled as he remembered what Austin, Jason's son and one of Alex's best friends, had discovered from Sarah's sister Katy just before Christmas. All those years ago after Sarah's death they'd assumed it had been a sadly simple case of sexual harassment. Then they'd learned the truth in all of its incredible horror when Katy had approached Austin with the information that Treffen hadn't just been coming onto his young female employees, he'd been roping them into a high-end prostitution ring.

Sarah hadn't just been harassed by Jason, she'd been forced into servicing his clients. The thought still had the power to bring bile to Alex's throat. Since that night, the tenth anniversary of Sarah's death, when Austin had lobbed that grenade into their usual desultory chat about work and women, they'd discovered more of the grim truth. Not only had Jason run a prostitution ring, he'd blackmailed the clients, men of power and position who got off on having a desperate and upwardly mobile young woman on her knees.

Austin had revealed the truth to his family, alienating his father from his wife and children. Together he and Hunter, along with Katy's help, had begun the process of ousting Jason as partner in his law firm.

So far Treffen had managed to retain his public image. His separation from his wife had simply and sorrowfully been explained as being caused by stress from his high-powered job. Austin's mother had been too ashamed to admit the truth.

Hunter was working on getting Treffen to step down from his law practice, but so far the man was clinging to his credentials. To his saintly reputation. Alex wouldn't be satisfied, and neither would Austin or Hunter or now Katy Michaels, until Jason Treffen was completely and publicly ruined. Until the truth was known, and Sarah's memory avenged.

And the perfect way to do that was on Chelsea's live television show, watched by thirty million people.

Yet after talking to her last night, Alex wasn't ready to trust Chelsea with the truth. *I'm not interested in shock value.*

What Treffen had done was the ultimate in shocking.

He just had to convince Chelsea of it—and of the need to take the man down.

Alex reached for his phone.

He dialed American Media Industries, Chelsea's network, and within a few seconds was connected to her assistant, who told him that Chelsea was in a meeting and would call him back.

Alex wondered if she really was. Chelsea definitely seemed the type who would keep him waiting just because she could. His mouth thinned into a hard line. She might think she had all the control, but he looked forward to proving her wrong. To taking it away from her...both in bed and out of it.

Impatiently he drummed his fingers against the polished teak of his desk. He might look forward to stripping away Chelsea Maxwell's arrogant certainties—as well as a few other things—but right now she was the one who was calling the shots. All he could do was get on with his work and wait for her to call.

Eight hours later he'd left his office and headed uptown to meet his friend Jaiven Rodriguez for a beer. He and Jaiven had known each since childhood in a Dominican-dominated neighborhood in the Bronx; while Alex had escaped on a scholarship to Walkerton Prep, an exclusive boarding school in Connecticut, Jaiven had stayed in the Bronx and had earned his way out by his sweat and his fists.

The first time Alex had come back from Connecticut, Jaiven had punched him in the face.

Alex still smiled to remember the belligerent look on his friend's face, and his own slack-jawed shock at his split lip and swelling eye.

"If you're going to turn into some preppy asshole," Jaiven had said, "don't bother coming back here."

The words had gone deep. He'd been putting on airs, Alex had realized, without even being aware that he was doing it. Collar up on his polo shirt. Rolling his eyes when Jaiven had started talking about their old friends. Dropping names of rich, entitled boys who went to his school, boys who'd relished humiliating the half-Dominican scholarship kid from the Bronx, who wore secondhand uniforms and came to school not in a chauffeured Rolls but on the public bus. And he'd been pretending to Jaiven that they were his friends.

Even now he felt the burn of shame at how quickly he'd lost the sense of himself, even if he'd only been fourteen. How he'd wanted to fit in rather than claim who he was.

Never again. He never would forget his roots, never wanted to pretend he hadn't worked hard and earned everything he had. It hadn't been given to him on a silver platter, the way it had for just about everyone else at Walkerton, and then later, Harvard.

That had been what had initially drawn him to Sarah; they'd shared a freshman business class and he'd seen the same hungry ambition and hard-won hope in her that he'd felt in himself. They'd been best friends, even after Sarah had started dating Hunter, a football quarterback and, along with Austin and Zair, his freshman roommate. He'd had no time for what he saw as three over-privileged trust fund babies until Sarah had softened him, shown him that rich kids were real people, too. After college Zair had gone back to his home country in the Middle East, and he, Austin and Hunter, and Sarah, too, had been damn near inseparable until her death.

After she'd died he'd focused solely on work, on building a news network that promised honesty. He was known throughout the industry for telling it straight.

So maybe he should tell it straight to Chelsea.

He hesitated, let that thought roll around in his mind for a little while. No, not yet. He might have founded his career on honesty, but revenge, revenge on Treffen, was something else entirely. If the end had ever justified the means, it was now.

Now he stepped into the bar in the Bronx that was one step down from a dive and looked for Jaiven. His friend was parked in a booth of ripped vinyl in the back, a beer bottle already in front of him. "Hey." Alex slid in across from his friend and hailed the waitress for his own beer.

"You look like shit," Jaiven remarked.

"Thanks very much." With a murmured thanks Alex took the bottle from the waitress. "As it happens, I didn't sleep much last night."

Jaiven cocked an eyebrow. "Good reason for that?"

"Not the one you're thinking." Alex thought, briefly, of Chelsea. Chelsea naked, that silver dress slithering off her like a snakeskin. Her hair down, long, wavy, mussed. Her mouth parted, lips rosy and swollen—

Damn it. He was getting a hard-on just thinking about her. Alex shifted in his seat, forced his gaze back to Jaiven who chuckled knowingly, the sound rich and deep. "What, the great Alex Diaz didn't get lucky? Unbelievable."

Alex smiled coolly and shook his head. "I wasn't trying."

"Sure you weren't." Jaiven stretched out in the booth and drained half his beer. "So were you out at some swanky media thing?"

"A birthday party."

Jaiven just shrugged and took another swig of his beer. Although Jaiven's fortune rivaled Alex's own, his friend steadfastly refused to rub elbows with the people he still considered snobs and he never attended any society parties or events.

He'd quit school at sixteen and started his own shipping business with nothing more than with a strong back and a beat-up van with expired plates, and in the fifteen years since then he'd built it up into a multimillion-dollar shipping enterprise. In all that time he'd never left the Bronx behind.

He still lived there, admittedly in a much nicer place, and he was proud of where he'd come from, who he was and always would be. He often told Alex he'd punch him in the face any time he started acting like an ass again, and Alex took him at his word.

"But there is a woman, right?" he asked now, and Alex lifted one shoulder in a shrugging answer.

"There might be."

"What, she's playing hard to get?"

"Not exactly."

Jaiven shook his head, let out another laugh. "Whoever it is, she's got you by the balls, my friend. You're looking like you need to get laid."

Alex smiled grimly. "Maybe I do." He and Jaiven had always shared the same approach to sex and love: one-night stands, the occasional week-long fling, and absolutely no expectations of anything else. He was honest about that as he was about everything else; he made sure a woman knew the rules before he'd so much as got her bra off.

Except he doubted Chelsea Maxwell was looking for a relationship. No, he was pretty sure she'd view sex the same way he did. Mutually enjoyable for an evening, and no more.

He felt his insides clench with anticipation. That would be plenty.

Chelsea stared at the little pink slip with Alex Diaz's name scrawled on it and wondered again just what the man wanted.

He'd called two hours ago, and she wasn't about to trip all over herself to call him back. No, let him wait. Let him wonder. She tucked the slip in her purse—no need for anyone to know Alex Diaz was calling her—and reached for her laptop.

"Chelsea? Do you have a minute?"

She looked up to see Michael Agnello entering her office. "Of course." She shut her laptop, pushed her chair away from her desk and crossed her legs. "Just answering some emails."

"I wanted to talk about the Treffen interview."

"All right." Seemed like everyone did, she thought. Coincidence? Probably not. Probably everyone, even Michael, was surprised she'd actually scored a prime-time interview with Treffen. Everyone but her. She'd worked hard for it, and she'd earned it, and she fully intended to have it make her career.

"What about it?" she asked as Michael sat down across from her.

"Treffen and his lawyer want to meet with you before the interview to go over exactly how it's going to proceed."

Chelsea frowned, even though she wasn't really all that surprised. "That seems a bit counterproductive. I'd like to have our conversation progress naturally."

"Treffen wants a little more control."

"Why?"

Michael shrugged. "Why not? The man has a reputation, Chelsea, and it's not to sob on a pink velour sofa."

Annoyance prickled, even though she knew Michael had a point. "You know this interview isn't going to be like that."

"I know, which is why you should meet with him. It makes sense."

"Maybe."

In the past week she'd taped two shows, one with a disgraced Olympian who'd had to give back her bronze medal after a doping scandal, and another with a country Western star trying to resurrect her career after several album flops and public meltdowns. Chelsea had brought them to tears both times.

But her interview with Treffen was going to be different. No sordid secrets, no noisy tears. Just honest, respectable journalism. Treffen, after all, wasn't a washed-up has-been trying to resurrect his career.

I know what he's done.

She thought suddenly of the hard look on Alex Diaz's face when he'd spoken about Treffen. No matter what he had or hadn't said, he clearly didn't like the man.

And now, Chelsea realized, she wanted to know why. She needed to know, especially if Treffen intended on imposing his control over the interview.

"I'm happy to meet with him," she told Michael. "But he'd better not expect to dictate all the terms of the interview."

"He just might," Michael warned her with a shake of his head. "And if you want Treffen to do this interview, you just might have to agree."

Chelsea pressed her lips together in silent, if unwilling, acceptance. Nothing could jeopardize this opportunity to interview Treffen, to finally make her career. Rise above the rumors she had always refused to deny. Nothing—not even the man himself.

Chapter Three

Several hours later she was still mulling over the upcoming meeting with Treffen, set for next week, when her administrative assistant buzzed through. "I've got Alex Diaz on the line."

Chelsea felt a surge of satisfaction. So he'd called. Twice. A smile of anticipation on her lips, she reached for the phone. "Alex."

"Hello, Chelsea."

Her insides contracted at the sound of his husky murmur. His voice seemed to steal right inside her and wrap around her soul. It wasn't fair, to be affected by a voice so much.

More importantly, it was stupid. And Chelsea was never stupid about men. Not anymore. She'd ignore that kick of attraction for now. Play it businesslike. Smart. *Safe.*

"What can I do for you?" she asked briskly.

"Interesting that you ask," he answered, and that soul-stealing voice took just a little bit more away from her.

"And why is it so interesting?"

"Because what you can do is go out to dinner with me."

Heat flared. He made it sound like a date. And maybe

it was. "Why would I do that?" she asked, and this time she kept her tone on the wobbly line between challenge and flirt.

"Because I'd like to get to know you a bit better," he answered, and it was impossible to tell what he meant. Personally? Professionally? Chelsea had no idea, and she was pretty sure that was how Alex wanted it.

"Interesting," she drawled, "but I'm not sure it's mutual."

Alex laughed softly, the sound strangely, stupidly intimate over the phone. "Are you sure about that, Chelsea?"

The sound of her name on his lips made her feel weirdly exposed, especially considering it wasn't even her real name. "I never said I wanted to get to know you," she answered flippantly. "Now, if you're offering something else…" She dropped her voice suggestively, wondered what he'd do with her innuendo. What she would.

"And what would you like me to offer?" Alex asked after only a second's pause, his voice still a sexy rumble.

"You know, I don't think I've made up my mind."

"Then let's discuss it over dinner."

She hesitated, her hand suddenly slippery on the phone. It was just dinner, she told herself. *With a very sexy man.* And something about Alex Diaz, about his cold sense of purpose…well, *scared* wasn't quite the word. But close to it.

He was a man, she realized, who would take absolute control. And she was the one who needed to be in control, who insisted on it in all of her relationships, no matter if it was the man who fixed her dishwasher or the one she took to her bed. She called the shots. Always.

Somehow she didn't think Alex Diaz would play by her rules, with her in charge.

And yet she wasn't ever one to back down from a challenge. "All right," she finally said. "I have a standing reservation at Le Bernardin—"

"Very nice, but we'll do this my way. See you tomorrow."

And then, to her immense irritation, he hung up on her. Chelsea stared at the telephone receiver for a full ten seconds before slamming it back in its cradle. She cursed aloud. He'd only hung up on her because he knew exactly what she was trying to do—and he wouldn't let her do it.

Her irritation turned to amusement, even a grudging admiration. Maybe she'd finally met her match.

Twenty minutes later she received a text on her phone: Your place. 7 pm.

She wondered how he'd got her private mobile number, but then realized that Alex Diaz could probably get any information he wanted. He owned the most respected news network in the country. She suppressed the twinge of alarm that thought caused. She had far too many secrets to have a man like Alex Diaz curious about her.

It would, she acknowledged reluctantly, be safer to nip this one in the bud. Say no to dinner, no to any possible opportunity on his network, and definitely no to sex.

How would Alex Diaz be in bed? As arrogant and assured as he was in person? She pictured those strong, capable hands on her body, that mobile mouth on her skin. He would dominate in the bedroom, she thought, but he would do it so wonderfully that the woman in question wouldn't care.

Desire coursed through her in a hot rush, doused quickly by the ensuing icy shock. Just what the hell was she thinking, getting excited by a man like Alex Diaz? He was arrogant, controlling, and he could potentially be her boss. Three strikes against him already. And yet she couldn't deny that she wanted him, and she wanted him the way he was: in charge. Commanding. *Dominating.*

Good Lord.

Slowly Chelsea shook her head, disgusted with herself. Had she learned *nothing* in ten years? Hadn't three years of humiliation and heartache, not to mention a significant stint in intensive care, been enough?

She might consider working for Alex Diaz, she decided, but she definitely wouldn't think about sleeping with him.

Or perhaps vice versa.

Shaking her head, annoyed with her own flip-flopping thoughts, she opened her laptop and turned back to her work.

The next evening she stood in front of the floor-length mirror in her bedroom and inspected her reflection. She'd put her hair back in a tight, sleek bun, and wore discreet pearl studs in her ears. Her makeup was smoky but understated: nothing *come hither* about just a touch of mascara and lip gloss. And the dress was definitely on the modest side, while highlighting her assets. Made of cream cashmere, cinched at the waist with a gold link belt, it covered her up from neck to knee. It looked subtly sexy, but still professional. And that's what she needed to be tonight... because she still wasn't sure what Alex Diaz wanted with her, or what she wanted with him.

In the twenty-four hours since their phone call, she'd

thought about canceling their dinner, just not going in that direction at all. As tempting as the possibility of working for Diaz News was, and possibly having a respected news show on his network, she also knew Alex wasn't promising anything and it would be far safer, far *saner* to stay away from a man who already affected her too much. But walking away was weakness, and Chelsea never let herself be weak.

No, she'd go to dinner with Alex Diaz, find out if he really was considering her for something on his network, or if, like so many other men, he was just trying to talk her into bed.

And if he was?

Well, maybe she'd take him up on it. The thought made alarm and excitement churn inside her, an unsettling mix. Alex Diaz was so, so different from the men she normally took to bed.

But that made him exciting. A challenge. If she could control him, make him weak with wanting her…

Hell, if that wasn't the most potent aphrodisiac in the world.

The phone connecting her apartment to the lobby rang, and answering it Chelsea told the doorman she'd meet Alex in the lobby. He wouldn't come upstairs unless she invited him.

This evening, like everything else in her life, would be on her terms…no matter what Alex intended or thought.

Alex was inspecting a modern sculpture on display in the lobby when she came out of the elevator. Dressed in a charcoal business suit, cheeks flushed with cold and a faint five o'clock shadow drawing attention to the hard line of his jaw, he was too gorgeous for words, damn the man.

"What do you think this is supposed to be?" he asked and Chelsea tore her gaze away from him to glance at the twisted iron-and-copper monstrosity she'd never bothered to notice before.

"I don't know. A tree?"

"Some tree."

Her lips twitched in a sudden smile. "Not a fan of modern art?"

"Not this kind." He swept his gaze over her, leaving warmth in its wake. "But I am an admirer of the art of understatement." His gaze lingered on her figure in its close-fitting cashmere dress. "Definitely that."

She tingled. Everywhere he looked, she felt her body treacherously, wonderfully respond. Melt and ache and want.

She smiled coolly, forced all those feelings away—and almost succeeded. "So where are we going, if not Le Bernardin?"

He placed his hand on the small of her back as he guided her out of the building. "Le Cirque."

Chelsea slid into the limo idling at the curb, every nerve ending tingling from his light touch. Alex followed her inside, stretching his arm out along the back of the seat so his fingers just barely brushed her shoulder, as they had the last time she'd been in his limo. He looked completely relaxed and barely aware of what he was doing, but Chelsea knew right down to her bones that the little touch had been intentional. And it had had, she suspected,

Alex's intended effect. She felt edgy and aching, restless and uncertain.

Not the way she wanted to start the evening.

"Le Cirque?" she repeated. "Now, that's a bit predictable."

He glanced at her, his expression inscrutable in the dim interior of the car. "How disappointing for you. I suppose I'll have to try harder next time."

"You don't strike me as the type to try hard at all," Chelsea answered flippantly. "I'm sure you expect women to fall at your feet."

He arched an eyebrow, clearly amused. "They're not much use to me there."

"Oh?" She let her gaze sweep over him in lingering assessment, and felt a fierce stab of satisfaction at the sight of the heat flaring in his eyes. "Where are they of use to you, Alex?"

"Oh, in a variety of places. And positions."

Chelsea arched an eyebrow. "How intriguing. Care to specify?"

His lips curved in a cool smile, his gaze locked on hers. "Not at the moment."

"Perhaps later?"

"Perhaps."

She smiled, even though inside she was seething. Whenever she tried to turn the tables on him, he turned them right back at her. Made her feel desperate, not just with desire but this need somehow to prove herself to him.

She wasn't *like* that. Not anymore.

Except with this man, it seemed she was.

"It's not polite to stare, you know," he said softly, and

she realized she had been openly, hungrily looking at him. Damn it. She'd stopped talking, stopped thinking, because her brain had snagged on the sight of him: long, lean legs stretched out, his hard jaw glinting with that sexy five o'clock shadow, those ink-black lashes feathering his cheeks. Long lashes and lush lips on the most masculine man she'd ever encountered.

How was that even possible?

She slowly lifted her gaze to his. "Just checking out what's on offer," she answered, and his mouth kicked up at one corner.

"I never actually said what was on offer."

"Care to clarify, then?"

He didn't answer, just waited, his eyes glinting in the darkness as the awareness stretched and tautened between them. Chelsea had to remind herself to breathe.

"I guess not," she said softly, and made a show of sorrowfully shaking her head. Alex just smiled. Nothing fazed him. Nothing shocked him. Nothing made his precious control slip, and it infuriated her because hers was skidding all over the place.

Alex Diaz had been in the driver's seat of this relationship from the moment he'd waited outside her apartment in his limo, no matter how many times she kept trying to take the wheel.

"So let's talk business," she said, recrossing her legs and making her voice brisk. "Do you really want me for Diaz News?"

Alex's gaze didn't falter for a second as he answered. "No."

Chelsea blinked. She kept her face neutral, but only

with a lot of effort. After several fraught seconds where she scrambled for something to say, she finally pursed her lips and stated coolly, "So you are just dicking me around."

"No. Interesting choice of words, though."

"Very amusing." She narrowed her eyes, crossed her arms. She wanted to go on the attack, but she felt defensive. Raw. Exposed.

So he didn't want her for his stupid network. It shouldn't surprise her. It shouldn't *hurt*.

"Why did you ask me out to dinner, Alex? Are you just trying to get laid?"

"If that were my sole purpose, there would be far simpler ways to accomplish it," he answered calmly.

Annoyed and still smarting, she snapped, "I'm sure there would be. Just cruise down Forty-Second Street—"

"Don't be childish, Chelsea."

"Don't patronize me—"

"I'm not. I'm just stating facts. I'm not interested in having you on my network, but I am interested in your prime-time interview."

"Treffen." She spat the word, and Alex remained calm, unruffled.

"Yes."

She shook her head, feeling angry and vulnerable, needing to lash out but knowing it would just reveal her all the more. She took a breath, let it out slowly and forced herself to calm. "You don't like him."

"Not particularly."

"Why not?"

"We'll get to that."

"All in good time?" she mocked. "I don't like being used, Diaz. Or manipulated."

"A few moments ago you called me Alex. And if anyone is planning to manipulate you, it's Treffen."

She thought of the meeting next week with Treffen and his lawyer. There might be some truth to what Alex was saying, but she still didn't want to be his, or any man's, pawn. "I won't have my interview sabotaged."

"That's not my intent."

Looking into those dark, fathomless eyes, she didn't believe him. Didn't believe for a moment that he wouldn't sabotage her interview or even her whole career to get what he wanted.

And yet, even now, especially now, she felt her body ache and pulse for him. No matter how hard or ruthless Alex Diaz was, she still wanted him. Maybe because he *was* so hard and ruthless. Maybe because the thought of him wanting her, needing her, made her blood surge and her heart sing. She wanted this man to bend for her. To break.

No matter how many petty shots Alex called now, *that* would really show who was in control.

"We're here," Alex said and let his hand drop from the back of the seat onto her shoulder, his palm warm through her coat and cashmere dress, his fingers almost brushing her breast.

His golden-brown gaze locked with hers and she felt as if she were trapped in a vise. Barely able to breathe. She slipped from the limo and away from his hand, wondering how on earth she was going to get through this evening.

Alex watched Chelsea, her back straight, her hips swaying slightly as she preceded him into the restaurant. Every exchange they'd had was loaded with innuendo, heavy with intent. But he had her. He could tell he had her; she was curious as well as ambitious and hungry. She would do what he said, and sex would be a sweet way to seal the deal. To celebrate it. He'd seen the desire in her eyes, the hunger, even though she would never admit it.

He'd make her admit it. He'd bring her to her knees, sobbing out his name, begging for his touch. The thought made him smile.

It also made him hard.

Shifting to ease his discomfort, he followed Chelsea into the restaurant.

"So tell me about yourself," he said once they were seated, menus open before them and linen napkins placed in their laps. "I don't know anything about you except the bullet points of your résumé."

Her eyes narrowed like a cat's, and he could see her debating the merit of a snappy comeback. Finally she shrugged and took a sip of water. "There's not much more to know beyond that. I've pretty much lived for my career."

"As have I, but that doesn't mean you could compress my personality into a single sheet of paper. What do you like to do in your spare time?"

She looked surprised, as if no one had ever asked her such a thing before. "Hobbies?" she said, leaning back in her seat. "I work out. A lot."

"I could have guessed that."

"Oh?"

"You're a control freak."

She cocked her head. "Takes one to know one."

"Absolutely."

He felt the clash of their wills as if a metallic clang had reverberated through the room. It was going to be so good to take her to bed, he thought. And then leave her there.

"I foresee a problem," she said, glancing down at her menu so her long, chocolate-coloured lashes feathered her cheeks.

Alex leaned back in his seat. "Which is?"

"We can't both be in control."

"Definitely not." He felt heat unfurl in his belly as he saw her eyes flare. Knew what they were both thinking of. Knew then, with an absolutely solid certainty, how this evening was going to end.

The air between them seemed to snap and crackle with electric tension. Alex could almost hear the sizzle.

Time to bring it down a notch. He wanted to make it through dinner, at least. "In any case, I don't believe you. Everyone's got a hobby."

"All right then, what's yours?"

"Scuba diving."

"That's not something you can do everyday."

"No. Holidays only."

"So what do you do to relax on a daily basis?"

"Besides the obvious?"

Her mouth curved. "I'm not talking about basic needs."

"I also swim," he said, and her mouth curved wider, drawing Alex's attention to it. It was delicious, full and lush. He wanted to feel it against his own.

"Doesn't that count as working out?"

"So does fulfilling my, ah, basic needs."

She laughed softly, the sound no more than a breath. "So you must be *very* fit."

"You'll have to judge for yourself."

"Is that a promise?"

"More just a statement of fact."

Her smile widened, revealing a dimple in one cheek. "Does it relax you?" she asked and for a second he thought she was talking about sex. Then he remembered what they'd been at least pretending to talk about. *Swimming*.

"I've learned to let it relax me."

"What does that mean exactly?"

"I didn't learn to swim until I was in high school." Alex paused; suddenly he could almost smell the chlorine and sweat of Walkerton Prep's pool. Could feel the hard shove on his back.

"Alex." He glanced up, blinking, and saw Chelsea giving him a teasing smile. "Whatever you're thinking about, it feels like a bit of a buzz kill."

He inclined his head in acknowledgment. "Maybe, but it motivated me to learn how to swim." She raised her eyebrows, waiting, and he continued. "I got a scholarship to Walkerton Prep. You know it?"

"The boarding school in Connecticut? Who doesn't? It seems like everyone with money is trying to get their kid in there."

"Exactly. I fulfilled their diversity quotient, I guess. Half-Dominican kid from the Bronx."

"I didn't know that," she said, and her voice had turned thoughtful, her head tilted to one side as she gazed at him.

"Which part? Dominican or the Bronx?"

Her mouth curved again in a small smile; she really did

have the most amazing lips. "Both, I guess. But you were telling me how you learned to swim."

"We had to take swimming at Walkerton. The first day one of the kids in my class pushed me into the deep end of the pool, when the coach was in his office." Alex swallowed; he could still remember the feel of the water closing over his head, filling his mouth and nose as he choked and flailed and a dozen preppy boys watched him dispassionately.

"Did he know you couldn't swim?"

"Oh, yeah." He'd had the naïve idiocy to share that little nugget of information before he'd been pushed. He shook his head, managed a wry smile even as surprise rippled through him that he was telling this to Chelsea Maxwell. He didn't talk about his years at Walkerton Prep to anyone. He didn't like to remember the lonely boy he'd been, desperate to fit in, to matter. He would have sold his soul then, just to belong. Thank God Jaiven had snapped him out of it with a right hook to his eye. Thank God he'd learned to be harder, tougher, and to stamp all over spoiled, entitled kids like that. "Fortunately the coach returned before I deep-sixed it. But I think those kids would have let me drown."

"That's awful." Chelsea was quiet for a moment, her expression serious and yet somehow closed. "But I believe it," she added, and there was too much understanding in that statement, too much experience. He almost asked her about it, and then decided not to.

If he thought sex might complicate things, some kind of emotional connection would screw it up completely. He didn't go there. Ever.

"Well, like I said, it motivated me. I learned how to swim and I ended up on the varsity diving team. I ended up being captain my senior year, which infuriated the guys who tried to drown me. Sweet revenge."

"I bet."

"In college I learned how to scuba dive, and now I spend a lot of time in the water."

"Do you like it?" she asked, and he saw a gleam of shrewdness in her eyes that jolted him. No one had asked him that before.

"Do you think I'd do it if I didn't?" he asked back, and she tilted her head as her gaze swept over him.

"You're a control freak, right? Absolutely. Anything to feel in control."

He laughed and held up his hands in mock defeat, even though her insight made him feel a little more exposed than he'd have preferred. "Well, you're right, Miss Maxwell. I still hate the water. But I do it."

She nodded slowly. "I understand that."

Her tone was heartfelt, and again he wondered. Wanted to know what she hated and still did. Her show? He knew she was hungry to prove herself professionally but did she actually dislike going on the pink sofa with those washed-up stars?

Something else he wasn't going to ask. He didn't actually want to *know* this woman. He just wanted to use her.

In more ways than one.

"Shall we order?" he asked and she nodded again. After the waiter had come and gone he decided to steer the conversation onto safer ground. Keep it innocuous, at least for the moment.

"So you're from Alabama, right?" And just like that she tensed right up, her expression closing like a fan. Interesting. Strange, but interesting.

She took a sip of water and then slowly, carefully put the glass back on the table. "Yes," she said, and even that seemed like more information than she was comfortable imparting.

"You've lost your accent."

Her face was utterly blank as she gazed at him. "Yes."

Alex leaned back in his chair. "Why do I get the feeling you don't like to talk about your past?"

"It's not very interesting."

"And if I'm interested?"

"Somehow I doubt you actually are. But you can read my bio online."

"I have." He'd read the question-and-answer interview with her on her show's website. He'd started out as a journalist; he did his homework, just like Chelsea. According to her bio, she'd an idyllic childhood in Alabama, all homemade cookies and trips to the state fair, and then she'd joined AMI as an intern when she was twenty-two. There was the inevitable list of awards and charities she supported, and that was it.

Pretty bland, really, and she obviously liked it that way, for she shrugged now, the movement invariably drawing his gaze to her breasts, their round shape outlined in cream cashmere. He wanted to slowly peel that dress off her, and soon. "Then you know all there is to know."

He raised his eyebrows as well as his gaze. "Which is nothing."

She just shrugged again, and he felt a sharp spike of curiosity again. *Who was this woman?*

Better not to wonder. Not to know.

Their appetizers came then and they didn't talk about anything more alarming than industry gossip and news for the rest of the meal, which suited Alex fine. He was at a good restaurant with a beautiful woman, and he intended to enjoy it for a little while.

And then he intended to enjoy a whole lot more.

What was it about this man, Chelsea wondered, that made her say things? Feel things? She'd told more about herself to Alex than she had to any other person, except for Michael and her sister Louise. And she barely knew the man. Admittedly, what she'd told wasn't that much, but she still felt exposed. He could dig into her history now, search Alabama records, and knowing him, he'd find something. He'd find too much.

Her insides iced and she told herself she wouldn't say another word. She'd keep it professional or physical, one or the other, but no more of this *talking*.

Damn it, she was not that kind of woman. She didn't let men get close. She didn't tell them things. She used them for business or sex and that was it. That was how it had to be.

And she intended on using Alex in one way or another. Hell, maybe both ways. After their charged, innuendo-laced conversation she knew he wanted her. She wanted him.

That, at least, could be simple.

As for business? He'd deliberately not mentioned Treffen

for the entire meal, and that suited Chelsea fine. She wasn't ready for that conversation, didn't want to be wrong-footed.

But no matter what happened between them, she'd keep it from being intimate. Emotional.

Except it already felt emotional. Already she felt a hard tug of sympathy for that boy perched on the edge of the pool, flailing in the water. God knew she understood how that felt. Everyone enjoying watching you fail. Smiling as you were humiliated, laughing when you were hurt.

No, she had to stop thinking like that. Wanting to know more about this man, cracking open the window of her soul to let him in just a little.

Sex would cure her, she thought. Sex made things simple. A bodily function, a basic transaction, and when it was over she invariably moved on to someone else. She'd never slept with the same man twice, not in ten years.

Sex would get him out of her system.

She smiled at him, pushed away her coffee cup and barely-touched dessert plate. She'd chosen fruit sorbet, the lowest calorie item on the menu, but she'd only eaten a mouthful. Television was unforgiving on a figure. Now she smiled, arched her eyebrows in obvious expectation. No innuendo in her voice, just simple fact. "Ready to go?"

Alex gazed back at her, gold flaring in the depths of his brown eyes. He slid a black credit card that she recognized as an exclusive, invitation-only card from his wallet and dropped it carelessly onto the table. "Yes," he said. "I'm ready."

They left the restaurant, Alex's hand low and sure on

her back. He had already texted the driver and the limo was waiting by the curb.

He guided her inside, his thigh nudging hers as he slid next to her on the spacious leather seat. She suppressed the urge to lay her hand on that hard muscle, slide her palm upward…

Her hand jerked of its own accord and she pulled it back into her lap. Would his skin be hot or cool? Smooth or rough? Her hand jerked again.

Belatedly she realized they were heading downtown. She turned to Alex. "Where are we going?"

"My apartment."

"What?" She shut her mouth with a snap. "Aren't you Mr. Manners. I don't recall you asking me to go home with you, Alex."

"I didn't."

She stared at him; he looked so unruffled she would have thought he was bored, save for the magnetic gleam in his eyes. She felt a tangle of emotions: fascination, frustration, even a little fear.

And she was more excited, more aroused, than she'd been in a long, long time.

Which showed how screwed up she really was.

She folded her arms across her chest. "Do you think the caveman tactic is attractive?"

"No, I simply prefer to cut to the chase. You knew we'd be sleeping together from the moment you agreed to dinner, Chelsea."

"A foregone conclusion, was it?" Her voice, thankfully, came out dry.

"We're attracted to each other. We both view sex as—what did you call it? A basic need?"

"So?"

"So of course we'd sleep together." He shrugged, as if the matter were of no consequence. "It *is* a foregone conclusion."

"You're very romantic," she said, and her voice had taken on an edge. "Lay on the violins and roses, why don't you?"

"I thought you'd appreciate my plain speaking."

And normally she would, because that was how she always approached sex. She just didn't like him approaching it that way. *She* was the one who told men how it was going to play out, and then she kicked them out the door when she was done.

She never went home with them. She never let them call the shots. She was always in control, always on top. Literally. And she usually didn't even take off all of her clothes.

At least not her shirt.

The limo slowed and she saw they were already downtown, somewhere in Tribeca, near the Hudson River. And as amazed and aroused as she was by his sheer arrogance, she knew she wasn't going to go into his apartment.

She wasn't that stupid.

"Sorry, Diaz," she said, "but I have my rules. I'm not going home with you."

His gaze locked with hers, and his expression didn't change. "Fine," he answered. "Who said we needed a bed?"

A thrill ran through her, jolting her to her core. Why, she wondered distantly, was that sexy? Was it just because he was so incredibly good-looking, that she ignored his arrogance?

But no, it was his absolute assurance that made her weak with want. Thrilled and excited her. And considering her past experience, that made her one sick puppy.

Still she didn't move. Didn't speak. And neither did he. The chauffeur waited in the driver's seat, separated by a soundproof, tinted window. Chelsea had no illusions that the man would know what they were up to. Maybe he'd done this before. Waited for Alex to finish his business.

Her palms went damp and she resisted the urge to wipe them against the side of her dress. Alex's expression didn't so much as flicker as he said in a low, sure voice, "Come here, Chelsea."

Of course she shouldn't move. Shouldn't obey that absurd command. No way. Absolutely not. In fact, she should tell him just what he could do with his ridiculous, arrogant attitude. Shove it up his—

And yet she felt herself move, as if her body had a will of its own. She slid across the seat, her dress and coat whispering against the leather, her gaze glued to his. She couldn't have looked away if she'd tried, which she didn't. She could hear her own breath, almost a pant, loud in the utter silence of the car. So revealing, and yet she was unable to stop herself.

Alex put his hands on her hips and in one easy, fluid movement he pulled her onto his lap, slid her legs wide to straddle him, her dress hiked up to her hips, her feet braced on the seat.

Chelsea closed her eyes. She could feel his arousal pressing against her even though he didn't move. He didn't need to. Even just that little bit of contact felt achingly, painfully exquisite. Her breath hitched and instinctively she pressed against him, felt a surge of feeling mixed with a primal satisfaction. His breath had hitched, too.

She opened her eyes. Alex was gazing at her, his eyes burning gold, his face still strangely expressionless. Chelsea pressed again, harder this time, and his hands locked on her hips.

With slow, deliberate intent, he slid his hand along her thigh, under her dress. He reached the elastic of her tights and slid his hand underneath, his gaze never moving from hers, his inscrutable expression never changing.

She held her breath, her heart seeming to still completely as he slid his hand lower, to the damp heat between her legs. He pressed, and she shuddered.

Her hips began to move, her body caught in a pulsing rhythm. She felt a sob start in her chest, a cry of longing and need. She wanted more. She wanted more from him, more hands and lips. More skin.

He brought his other hand to the back of her neck, his fingers tangling in her hair. She felt her careful, tight chignon come undone, pins raining around them as he drew her face down to his, his lips a whisper away from hers.

"Kiss me," he said, another command, and yet she heard the edge of desperation, of need, in his voice, and without even thinking or questioning it she obeyed.

She pressed her lips to his and breathed in the scent of him before he took control of the kiss just as he'd taken control of everything else. He slid his tongue into her mouth, his hand still curved around her neck, their bodies pressed to each other in every way possible.

Almost.

Chelsea arched against him, still wanting and needing more. His hand pressed back against her and then her foot slipped onto the seat and she suddenly lurched sideways, her head hitting the window with an audible thunk.

It would have been funny, all that intensity turned into clumsiness, if she'd been a different woman with a different kind of past. In a different world, a different life, she would have laughed. He would have asked if she was okay, then taken her by the hand and pulled her back onto his lap. Maybe he would have kissed her head.

But this was her life, with her memories, her experience and anxiety and fear. She blinked, reeling as if the collision with the window had nearly knocked her unconscious. Her head didn't hurt, but her heart did. Her body burned not with desire or need, but with shame.

What had she been thinking?

Alex, she realized, didn't help her up. He simply watched her, sprawled as she was against the seat, her head pressed awkwardly against the window, her dress still rucked up about her hips.

Tears of humiliation and rage stung her eyes and she blinked them back. Jerked down her dress.

"Now that's a classy move," she drawled, thankful her voice didn't shake. She reached for her purse.

Alex didn't say anything. He barely even looked at her. The hurt she felt was so thick and hot she could choke on it. She fumbled with the handle of the door, her fingers near to trembling.

Alex wrapped his hand around hers. "Let me take you home," he said quietly. "We're in the middle of nowhere."

"We're in Manhattan," she snapped. Anger, she knew, was her best defense.

"The middle of nowhere for Manhattan, then," Alex answered calmly. His hand remained on hers, and somehow, strangely, she found it comforting.

Still she shrugged it off, sat back in the seat opposite him. "Fine," she said coolly, and purposely, as if she was as bored with him as he obviously was with her, she stared out the window as Alex leaned forward and told his driver to head uptown.

Chapter Four

Alex gazed unseeingly into the darkness of the limo and wondered what the hell had just happened. One second Chelsea had been on his lap, his hands in her hair, his mouth so gloriously on hers, and the next—

She'd been sprawled on the seat, her eyes twin mirrors of horror and hurt. Even in the taut silence of the limo now speeding uptown he could hear the hard thunk of her head against the window. A stupid accident, certainly a badly timed one, and yet somehow the way she'd looked at him had made him feel...sleazy.

No, worse than that. She'd looked at him as if her falling off his lap was his fault. As if he'd pushed her. Used and abused her, the way Treffen had countless women, including Sarah.

Wearily Alex rubbed a hand over his face. He had to be reading way too much into this. Into one shocked look. Hell, she'd probably just been embarrassed. Chelsea Maxwell wasn't a woman who seemed ever to take a misstep, so falling right on the floor had to have really got up her nose.

It had certainly killed the mood.

Moments ago he'd been on the brink of losing his precious control. He'd started out strong, had made sure Chelsea knew they were playing by his rules. And then he'd felt her on his lap, her body pressed against his, her mouth warm and soft and lush and every thought had emptied out of his head. Every thought but one.

More.

It was just as well it had ended the way it had, Alex decided. Sure, he'd wanted Chelsea in his bed. Or in his limo, as the case would have been. But he wanted revenge against Treffen more. And judging from that one look—and maybe he *was* reading too much into it—sex with Chelsea was going to be a bit more complicated than he'd thought.

No, it was definitely better this way. It was just too bad his libido didn't agree.

The limo pulled to the curb outside of Chelsea's building, and Alex realized they hadn't spoken in nearly fifteen minutes. Now Chelsea reached for the door handle, wrenched it open. She turned to him, her lips still swollen from his kiss, her hair half tumbled about her shoulders. The smile she gave him was blade-sharp and mocking. "And you said you didn't like women falling at your feet," she said. She shook her head once and then without so much as a goodbye she slid out of the limo.

He watched her head into her building, the doormen springing to attention, her coat swirling about her tall, slender figure.

Then he leaned back against the seat, felt a tide of utter weariness wash over him.

"Where to now, sir?" Eric, his driver, asked and Alex closed his eyes.

"Right back downtown again, Eric," he said, and sighed.

Chelsea's heart pounded and her body ached with need, but her mind was cold and clear as she walked away from the limo.

That had been close.

She'd almost been incredibly stupid…again. Almost slept with a man who wanted to control her. Who had. And she had let him.

Thank God she'd slipped, as stupid as that had been, and hit her head. It had served as her wake-up call.

So maybe she wasn't strong enough to take on a man like Alex Diaz. Maybe she'd learned that when a man like Alex, charismatic and powerful and arrogant, crooked his finger, she still came running. Or crawling.

She remembered the way she'd slid across the seat, let him pull her onto his lap. He could have asked anything of her, and because she'd been so dazed by lust, she would have done it.

She almost had.

And it brought back every bad memory she'd ever had, and bile to the back of her throat.

Never again.

By the next morning she'd come up with a plan. That was what she did, what she always had done when life spun crazily out of control, as it had for most of her childhood. *I'll be very quiet. I'll sleep under the bed. I'll pretend I'm invisible, and maybe no one will see me.*

Unfortunately none of those plans had worked, but this one would. She'd completely ignore Alex Diaz. She wouldn't see him again, wouldn't take his calls, wouldn't attempt to find out what he knew about Treffen. Hell, she was a journalist. She'd find out for herself.

From this moment on, Alex Diaz ceased to exist in her reality. How was that for a bit of efficient relativism?

Except that plan wasn't working either, because all through the filming of two shows, several corporate meetings, and a brainstorming session with her creative team, not to mention her usual drill of beauty appointments that kept her looking as airbrushed as possible, she still thought of him. The way his eyes had simmered and burned. The way his mouth had been both hard and soft. The feel of his hand, strong and firm, wrapped around the back of her neck.

Come here, Chelsea. Kiss me.

And she had, oh, she had.

She still wanted him. And more than that, she wanted to redeem herself in her own eyes—and his. Wanted to make him crawl, instead of being the one to do it.

As if that would ever happen.

But if it could…

Then maybe she'd let Alex exist again, for as long as she had use of him.

Three days after her dinner with Alex, Chelsea left work at five to meet her sister Louise for dinner, an occurrence that still felt strange enough to unnerve her.

After the train wreck of their childhood, she'd lost touch with Louise for nearly fifteen years. Then a couple of months ago Louise had seen her on *Chat with Chelsea—*

had recognized her despite the name change, the hair dye, the cosmetic surgery, and reached out.

They met for dinner once a month, which was about as much emotional intimacy as Chelsea could handle. She didn't like to remember her childhood, not the bleak moments hiding under the bed, or the constant uncertainty and fear and the bone-deep belief that she was only worth something if she was beautiful. It had taken years for her to get over that one, and sometimes she wondered if she still believed it. Some part of her did, anyway. You couldn't work in TV and not believe that on some level.

They met, as always, in a quiet restaurant on the Upper West Side; Louise was already waiting, a sheaf of essays in front of her. She'd been given tenure at Columbia University last year, one of the youngest professors to do so. Her normally stern face, all hard angles and strong lines, creased into a hesitant smile as Chelsea approached.

"Aur—Chelsea."

Chelsea smiled, but it felt tight. Uncomfortable. "You're never going to get my name right, are you?"

"Sorry. Old habits die hard, I guess."

Louise stood, and Chelsea hugged her, barely. They both sat, stared at each other.

Louise shook her head slowly. "We've been doing this for nearly six months and it still feels weird."

"I know."

"Maybe it's because you look so different now."

"That was kind of the point."

Louise nodded, her mouth turning down at the corners. Chelsea had told her just a little of her past: that there had been a man, and he hadn't been nice. The way her sister had seemed to understand so quickly made her wonder what secrets she might be hiding. What kind of pain. Perhaps their childhood had led them both to make some bad decisions.

"So, anything new going on in your life?" Louise asked, all brisk brightness now. She swept her pile of essays off the table and into the messenger bag by her feet.

"Not really."

"Not really?" Louise arched an eyebrow, waited, and Chelsea shrugged. She had a sudden urge to talk about Alex, which was absurd considering how awkward these dinners with her sister were. They had trouble talking about the weather, for heaven's sake. She wasn't about to unload her angst on this near-stranger, even if she still remembered the way Louise had rocked her to sleep when they were children, both of them lonely, afraid and desperately unhappy.

"What about you?" Chelsea asked, her tone holding that over-bright note that always sounded so false. She deserved an Oscar for the way she cozied up to celebrities, but she couldn't be real with her sister. "Anything new in your life?"

Louise smiled wryly and shook her head. "Lectures and research. Not much else goes on in my life."

"And you like it that way?" Chelsea asked, suddenly curious. She lived for her work, and she wondered if her sister was the same.

"I do." Louise's mouth twisted a little. "Easier all round really, isn't it?"

Chelsea nodded, and they both stayed silent for a moment. They hadn't really shared much of anything, and yet it was still more than they ever had before.

Louise toyed with her salad for a moment before she looked up, a surprising glimmer of mischief in her eyes as she said, "So that 'not really' has nothing to do with the photo I saw of you and Alex Diaz?"

Chelsea went utterly still. "What photo?"

"In a gossip magazine—"

"You read those things?"

Louise shrugged, her eyes positively dancing now. Chelsea had never seen her sister look so animated. It softened the stern lines of her face, lit her up from within. "When they're lying around. This one was left in the student union—"

Chelsea sighed and shook her head. "That was fast."

"So are you seeing him?"

"No. It was just a work thing."

Louise bit her lip, her eyes still glinting, but she didn't say anything. Their relationship, Chelsea knew, had never had this kind of repartee, not even when they'd been kids. "What is it?" she finally asked, exasperated, for Louise's face still held the glimmer of a smile.

"You're blushing."

"No, I'm not—" She *never* blushed. And yet even as she issued the denial she felt the heat in her cheeks. Just thinking about Alex made her face warm, her body heat. Her heart hurt. She took a sip of water and willed her color to recede. She could talk on national television about an aging Hollywood star's impotence problem with nary a blush but when she thought of Alex Diaz in even the most generic terms she burned right up.

What was *wrong* with her?

"Sorry," Louise murmured. "I shouldn't tease you. We don't really know each other well enough anymore for that."

No, they didn't. Although Louise had never really teased her when they'd been little. Held her, rocked her, sometimes pushed her away. But life had been too precarious for jokes, too precious for bickering. "Tit for tat, then," Chelsea finally said. "Tell me something I don't know about you. About a man."

Louise shook her head. "There's nothing to tell."

"You must have had a boyfriend or something," Chelsea said lightly. "In the last fifteen years?"

Louise's expression darkened, all the glimmer gone. "No one," she said flatly. "Not in a long time."

Chelsea knew better than to press.

They hadn't really been close as children; Chelsea, with her blond curls and show-off attitude, had endured her mother's attention and ambition while shy, stammering Louise had been dismissed and ignored. Both of them had suffered.

Their mother, Diane, had died when Chelsea was sixteen and Louise just eighteen months older, and they'd gone their separate ways. Social services hadn't been interested in two trailer park teens. Sometimes Chelsea wondered how her life might have turned out differently if they'd stuck together. Helped each other. She didn't let herself dwell on such possibilities for too long, though. There was simply no point.

In any case, they'd shared enough today. Maybe too much.

"Well, let me know when that changes," she told her sister, and Louise just shook her head.

"It won't."

Chelsea gazed at her sister, took in her firm jaw, her shadowed eyes. She wondered what had happened to Louise in the past fifteen years that had made her wary of relationships, just as she was. Neither of them had talked about those missing years, just as they hadn't talked about their childhood.

Neither of them wanted to remember all that uncertainty and anger and fear, their mother's endless parade of drunks and layabouts that served as boyfriends and, according to Diane, hopeful father figures. *As if.* Chelsea didn't remember every sad sack her mother had brought home, but the ones she did sure as hell hadn't been interested in being her *father.*

No, not when she'd been dolled up by her mother for another child beauty pageant. Dressed in tottering heels and a too-tight dress glittering with sequins, her face made up like a hooker's and all of six years old, what drunken no-hoper of her mother's could resist her? Some hadn't.

Thank God for Louise. Her older sister had tried to protect her from the lecherous advances of one of her mother's boyfriends on more than one occasion, and she'd succeeded. Mostly.

Afterward though, she'd always shoved her away, as if she was angry with her.

No, they hadn't really been close. But they'd needed each other. Maybe they still did.

Alex clicked his mouse on Pause so the video froze on Chelsea's face. Some starlet was sobbing on her pink velour sofa and Chelsea was gazing at her with patent sympathy, her mouth turned down at the corners, tissues in hand. But her eyes were steely.

She was good at what she did, Alex had to admit. Really good. She had a warmth and vibrancy to her that he'd seen in the flesh. People were drawn to her, lured onto her sofa and into her confidence. And just when they felt understood, accepted, she cut them to the quick with her razor-sharp questions.

And that's when you had the affair?

Was stealing just too much of a temptation?

Would you say you had a drinking problem?

Always delivered in a tone of compassion, of sincerity, as if she were promising them salvation. Absolution. They trusted her, they loved her, even as she raked them over the coals of their own sins.

She was a professional, but could she handle Jason Treffen? Would she even want to?

She'd as good as admitted she didn't want Treffen's interview to be the soap opera everyone else's was. But would she want it to be an exposé? It could make her career as a serious journalist, but it would kill it at AMI. Treffen might even take her to court; he would undoubtedly have her sign something agreeing to ask only pre-approved questions before they ever went on air. In any case, Alex didn't know her well enough yet to trust her with the truth. To give her any control.

Sighing, he let his gaze flick back over the screen shot of Chelsea. She wore a crisp white blouse and gray pin-stripe pencil skirt, her long, slim legs neatly pulled to one side, leaning forward as if hanging on every word of—who was it again? Some Hollywood hopeful who had been caught in one too many compromising situations.

Chelsea looked crisp and professional, but in his mind's eye he was remembering her as she'd been in the limo right before she'd fallen off his lap. Eyes wide, pupils dilated with desire, lush lips parted. She'd wanted him, been ready for him, and somehow it had all got ruined.

His phone buzzed with an incoming text and Alex glanced down at it. It was from Austin, checking on his progress with Chelsea. Update?

He thumbed back a quick text. Working on it.

Frustrated in more ways than one, Alex spun in his chair. So he hadn't got it on with Chelsea Maxwell. *Get over it.* All he should be thinking about was Treffen. About Sarah. About finally avenging her death.

As for Chelsea Maxwell? He really couldn't give a damn.

It was Sarah who mattered, Sarah whose memory drove him. Hunter and Austin, he knew, felt the same. So did Katy; she was Sarah's sister, after all. So many people who wanted and needed to see Treffen brought to justice. He'd lost his family already, and he was on the brink of losing his job, but Alex knew that wasn't enough. The man needed to pay. Publicly.

He still remembered the first time Sarah had tried to talk to him about it. He'd been blathering on about some article he wanted to write—a profile of some corporate hero—and with her mouth twisting downward and her hair sliding forward to half hide her face, she'd said, *Sometimes those corporate heroes aren't so perfect.*

He'd had enough intuition to sense she was talking

about someone specific. *Yeah, they've all got skeletons in their walk-in closets. Who are you thinking of?*

She'd just shrugged then. *Maybe Jason Treffen isn't the paragon he seems.*

And he'd laughed. He'd actually thought she was joking.

Had Treffen reeled her into his select circle of call girls by then? He could see how it might have happened. *You're so sweet, Sarah. I've got a client who needs a woman's touch. Just butter him up a little bit for me, take him out to dinner...*

By the time she realized what was going on it would have been too late. She would have been too ashamed and afraid to protest. To seek help.

Except she *had* sought help, from Hunter. From Austin. From him, one of her best friends. And it hadn't done her a single bit of good.

But it would now. He couldn't bring Sarah back to life, but he could avenge her death. He could ruin Treffen.

With Chelsea's help.

He needed to see her again. They hadn't talked Treffen over dinner, and maybe that had been a mistake. Maybe if he'd stopped thinking about how he could get into her pants he would have her on his side now, instead of angry at him for God only knew what reason.

But he'd redeem it. He'd have to. And with a sudden, clarity, he knew how.

He'd been so damn intent on showing Chelsea he was in control, he'd lost sight of his goal. Stupid, he saw now, and short-sighted, but no longer. The next time he saw Chelsea he'd be calling the shots—and she wouldn't even realize it.

★ ★ ★

Three days after her dinner with Alex, Chelsea was standing on the edge of the *Chat with Chelsea* set, reviewing her question cards as one of the show's producers attempted to coax the day's guest out of her dressing room. Apparently she'd got cold feet after arriving at the studio this morning. Chelsea wasn't surprised; more than one guest had had a last-minute panic attack about going on air and spilling secrets.

"Hello, Chelsea."

Chelsea tensed, nearly dropped one of her cards. She turned around slowly, took in the sight of Alex Diaz in an elegant suit of dark gray silk, his hands in his trouser pockets, a faint smile on that inscrutable face of his. He looked too damn sexy for his own good—or hers.

"What are you doing here?"

"Watching your show, of course."

"What for?"

"Because I thought I'd like to see it live. See you in action."

She didn't actually hear any innuendo in his words, although she still wasn't sure she believed him. Why had he sought her out again? And why did she have to feel so excited about it?

She flicked her fingers to the rows of seats in front of the stage. "The studio audience sits over there."

"I thought I'd watch from here."

Chelsea's gaze narrowed; backstage was a personnel-only area. "Who let you in?"

"I batted my eyelashes at security."

She almost laughed at the image that conjured up, but

suppressed it at the last minute. Couldn't keep her mouth from twitching, though, and Alex noticed.

"José was the most susceptible to my charm."

José was six foot five and weighed nearly four hundred pounds. The laughter came again, like a bubble rising inside her, determined to escape. She clamped her lips shut. Alex was dangerous enough already, without adding charm to the mix.

"Why do you want to watch my show, Alex?" she asked, keeping her voice cool, even cold. "Is this about Treffen?"

He stepped closer, close enough for her to smell his aftershave and feel that now-familiar wave of lust threaten to pull her under. She could drown in it, just like Alex almost did in his old school pool.

"I want to watch your show because I'm interested in it," he said, his voice a low hum for her ears only. "But I came here really to see you."

She shook her head, not sure what she was saying no to. Him. Him here. Him wanting to see her. "No."

"No, what?"

Weary now as well as wary, she just shook her head again. "I don't know, but just no, Alex. No to everything." Hardly the most eloquent or even coherent of responses, but sadly she didn't have better.

"I also came to offer an apology."

Now *that* was unusual. "What for?"

"Good question. I'm not sure. Something scared you when we were in my limo, and—"

"I wasn't *scared*."

"Unnerved, then," Alex amended calmly.

She just shook her head. Again. Where was her flirty

banter, her devil-may-care attitude? She needed it back. Now. "I just changed my mind, Alex. I suppose that's got to happen to you once in a while."

"No, actually, it doesn't."

She rolled her eyes. "Okay, super stud. Sorry to disappoint you, but I decided I didn't want to be your little lapdog after all."

"Lapdog? Who said I wanted that?"

She nailed him with a hard look. "It's all about control for you, isn't it? I'm sure some women find that incredibly sexy, but I don't." *Liar.* She had, and he knew it.

He didn't tell her as much now, though. He simply gazed at her, his expression unreadable, his mouth slightly pursed.

"We're on in five, Chelsea."

She nodded at the production assistant as someone from makeup darted forward to do some last-minute touches.

"Is Tanya out of her dressing room?" she called to the assistant who gave her a fleeting, nervous smile.

"Almost."

"Who's your guest today?" Alex asked. "The lingerie model who took it all off?"

"That was yesterday," Chelsea answered. She turned around, glad to have her composure retouched along with her makeup. "Try to keep up. Today is Tanya Hart, kiddie star who was charged with a DUI."

"That's not too scandalous, is it?"

"She's only fourteen."

"I see."

She smiled, hard and bright, knowing it didn't reach

her eyes. "I'm about to go on air, Alex. Thanks for coming to the show. I hope you enjoy it."

"I'm sure I will." His eyes burned gold as he took a step closer to her. "You think I've got a thing about control, Chelsea? You know you do, too."

She stilled, save for the thudding of her heart. It felt like thunder. "Which is why I'm not into your little games."

"Then maybe we'll turn the tables. Maybe I'll let you order me around."

She drew in one quick, sharp breath. "You'll *let* me?"

"Yes. I'll let you."

So he'd still be in control. He'd just give her a little of it. Thanks, but no thanks.

Unless…

Unless she could really make him lose it. Beg, just as he'd almost had her begging. On his knees, crawling to her—

"Turns you on, doesn't it?" he murmured, and she gave him a tight smile.

"A bit."

"Two minutes till air, Chelsea."

She waved away the assistant and stared hard at Alex. He gazed back, unperturbed, and yet even so the air crackled between them with tension. Sexual tension, so every nerve ending Chelsea possessed tingled with a powerful intensity she'd tried to deny. But perhaps denial wasn't the way to go. She'd swum down that river for too long, anyway. She'd admit it, deal with it and move on.

She'd make Alex beg.

She took a deep breath and nodded once, her jaw bunched. "Fine. Meet me here after the show."

He raised his eyebrows in acceptance. "I'll be waiting."

Anticipation mingled with the alarm and anger she already felt. Nodding again, she turned and walked onto the set.

Tanya was already seated on the couch, eyes wide and tissues in hand. She was ready to cry, ready to confess and be absolved by Chelsea, forgiven by the public. That was how her show worked: cry and be cleansed. Going on *Chat with Chelsea* was the fastest way to polish a tarnished public image.

Ironic, that.

Chelsea sat in her usual seat across from Tanya, trying to blink the world into focus as she was miked. Her brain was buzzing, her body tingling. Tanya offered her a wobbly, uncertain smile, and Chelsea smiled back. At least she hoped she did. Everything inside her felt electric and alive, and yet fragile, too. Breakable. *Breaking*.

She needed her strength back, her sense of control, and she'd get it by sleeping with Alex. He might say he was letting her take control, but she'd turn the tables on him once and for all. She'd make him beg. Plead. Writhe. *Want*.

And *that* would break this awful hold he had on her.

She took a deep breath and let it fill her lungs slowly. She closed her eyes as she exhaled, willed her muscles to loosen. It was a relaxation exercise she'd learned ten years ago, after the attack, when she'd been so anxious she'd actually started losing her hair. That, along with the scars, had made her feel pretty damn ugly.

But she'd crawled back from that dark place. She'd worked hard to become less anxious, more confident. She'd learned self-defense. She'd had reconstructive surgery. She'd met Michael, who had given her the chance she'd needed, and she'd worked her ass off for ten years.

And she was not going to risk any of it by giving in to someone like Alex. Playing his little submissive obey-me type games and making her feel like the desperate, pathetic people-pleaser she'd once been.

Never again.

And tonight she'd prove it.

"Thirty seconds."

She opened her eyes and smiled again at Tanya, listened to the opening music of the show and felt her reconstructed sense of self take hold of her, like slipping on a mask, a familiar and needed disguise.

Chelsea Maxwell was on the air.

Chapter Five

As soon as the show finished Chelsea stalked off the set. Her beautiful face was set into lines of grim determination, which made Alex curious about just what she intended— and also made him incredibly turned on.

There was something about her hard-ass attitude that he really liked. He'd wanted to see her lose her control the other night, but now he wondered what it would be like when she had it.

Or at least thought she had it.

He'd see how long he let this little game go. If it got what he wanted—her trust—then it would be worth it. It also might be surprisingly interesting…and enjoyable.

She stood in front of him, a tiny bit of ivory lace cami-sole peeking out from underneath her crisp white blouse. She wore a narrow pinstriped pencil skirt and sky-high stiletto heels in black patent leather. If she'd been decked out in red lace lingerie she couldn't have been sexier.

She narrowed her gaze, lips pursed, hands on hips.

Alex raised his eyebrows in silent query.

"Let's go," she said and he nodded his assent, amused

by her transparently bossy attitude. He wondered how far she'd go with it. How far he'd let her.

Because he might be giving Chelsea some control, but he was still *giving* it to her. He still fully intended to be the one in charge. Always.

"Where to?" he asked as he followed her out of the studio.

"My apartment."

"Good choice."

They didn't speak as they left the building, but Alex felt the tension in the air, the tension in himself. This was a new experience for him, and it made his nerves feel electric, everything in him charged and tingling. How long since he'd felt this way, this *alive?*

He couldn't remember. Didn't want to.

Outside AMI's head office in midtown Chelsea hailed a cab, one slender arm raised, her face still set in lines of rather grim purpose.

"You don't look like you're enjoying yourself," Alex remarked as a cab screeched to the curb and they both got inside.

Chelsea gave him a smile of acid sweetness. "Trust me, I am."

Alex smiled back. "Well, I'm enjoying myself."

"Good to know."

She took out her phone and scrolled through her messages as they rode uptown. Alex watched her, amused. So she was taking care of one business before moving to another.

He rather liked that in a woman. No worries about messy emotions or sudden tears with Chelsea. He was careful with his bed partners, but sometimes he made a mistake. Slept with a woman who thought she was in a *relationship*.

And Alex didn't do relationships. He'd seen the mess of his mother's, the heartbreak of Sarah's. Sex was sex with him: essential, enjoyable and ending at dawn. Usually before.

He was pretty sure Chelsea felt the same as he did, or nearly.

Ten minutes later they were at her building, and then up into the elevator.

"Penthouse?" Alex asked as she pushed the button marked PH, and she just nodded. No words as they soared toward the top floor, and the doors pinged open and Chelsea stepped into a black-and-white checkered marble foyer that opened into a living room decorated entirely in stark black and white.

Alex paused in front of a huge white canvas with jagged black lines along the bottom of it.

"I'm not sure I think much of your taste in art."

"That canvas is a collector's item," Chelsea answered as she shrugged out of her black wool trench coat and hung it up in the closet; no mad passion in this moment, at least. He wondered if she ever let that precious control slip even just a little.

It had in his limo. He'd told her to come to him and she had, her eyes glowing, her mouth parted, everything in her wanting and wanton. He wanted to see that happen again, never mind who was in control.

But for now he'd run with this. He had too much at stake to gamble on passion.

"It's worth over a hundred thousand dollars," she informed him, and Alex glanced again at the six feet of white space.

"Hate to say it, but I think you've been ripped off."

"I'll be the judge of that." She stood in front of him, arms crossed now, gaze sweeping over him in cool yet thorough assessment. Alex raised his eyebrows, waited for her verdict.

"Take off your clothes, Alex."

He laughed, surprised and yet also still incredibly turned on. "Not very imaginative, Chelsea, but I'll indulge you."

"You certainly will." She stepped forward and loosened the knot of his tie. Her fingers moved briskly to undo it with dispassionate expertise and yet Alex still felt himself respond. He kept his expression amused as she slid the tie away from his shirt.

"I thought you wanted me to take off my clothes. I'm happy for you to do the job yourself, though." He stood still as she slid his suit jacket from his shoulders. "Quite happy."

"Just helping you along," she murmured.

"Mind hanging that up? If we're going to be business-like about this?"

She glanced down at his hand-stitched jacket and then tossed it across the foyer. Alex laughed aloud.

Her eyes narrowed in annoyance and he waited, his jacket and tie gone but otherwise still dressed. He didn't want to piss her off, but he couldn't help himself. She had a lot to learn about control. She was like a child, stamping around, grabbing all the toys.

And yet he had to admit it was still incredibly sexy.

"Now what?" he asked because she was just staring at him, eyes still narrowed.

"Shirt."

"Fair enough." He undid his shirt, watched her gaze follow the path of his fingers, her pupils flaring as he reached the last button and shrugged it off. He tossed it to join his blazer. "Happy?"

"Not yet."

"I think I can guess what's coming next."

"I bet you can."

Smiling he undid his belt buckle. The snick of the leather as he pulled it from his trousers made Chelsea's pupils flare again. Her breath hitched.

And she actually thought she was in control. Alex wrapped the belt around one hand, arched an eyebrow. "What do you want me to do with this?"

"You can add it to the pile," she answered shortly, and he saw she'd gone tense. Interesting. He tossed the belt, and she relaxed again, her shoulders lowering a tiny fraction.

"And now?"

"Keep going, Diaz."

He unbuttoned his fly, his fingers brushing his own arousal. His little striptease was clearly affecting both of them. He pushed his trousers down and they puddled around his ankles. Not the most sophisticated look, but at this point he hardly cared.

"So I guess you don't feel the need to create a mood?" he asked and she looked up from her perusal of his tented boxers with a wicked smile.

"I am creating a mood."

He inclined his head in acknowledgment. "Can't argue with that."

"Boxers next."

"You don't want to do the honors?"

"I'll leave that to you."

He glanced down at his feet. "There seems to be a problem with mechanics," he remarked. "Shoes."

Chelsea paused, and he knew the exact nature of her hesitation. She didn't want to go on her knees in front of him to take them off. Such an act would be a relinquishing of her control, a sign of submission.

"I suppose it's easily fixed," he murmured, deciding to humor her, for now at least. He kicked them off along with his trousers. "But I might need help with my socks."

Her eyes glittered as she stepped forward and tugged down his boxers. "You can keep your socks on."

He kicked off his boxers as her hand slid down the length of his erection. Her skin was cool and soft, her fingers wrapped around him. Alex felt himself go even harder.

"Impressive, Alex."

"Thank you very much."

She stepped back and he waited. He was sporting nothing but a pair of socks and a massive erection, and he felt more turned on than he ever had in his life.

He nodded toward her crisp blouse and skirt. "You going to take those off?"

"All in good time." She folded her arms, watching him, and he smiled equably back. So this was her little show of control. Fine. He could take it.

"All in good time," she repeated softly, and started unbuttoning her crisp white blouse as she walked toward him. Nothing about those slender fingers moving through buttonholes should be that erotic, and yet somehow it was. Incredibly. Alex's whole body jolted as desire surged through him like an electric current, strong enough to short-circuit his senses.

She shrugged out of her blouse, and he saw she wore a white lace camisole with thin straps underneath, cut high across her breasts, leaving just about everything to his imagination—and oh, he imagined. The sweet curve of her breasts begged for his palms to cup them, feel their fullness. He wanted to slide that silky camisole up and over her head, toss it aside and slide his hands over her bare, bare skin, control be damned.

He restrained himself, remained still as he watched her undo her pencil skirt, the sound of the zip as loud as a screech in the taut silence of the foyer. The skirt slithered down her stocking-clad legs to the floor and she stepped out of it, that knowing little smile on her lips.

Alex swallowed. Audibly. She wore a pair of white silk boy shorts, sheer stockings, and garters. *Garters.* And her heels. He didn't think he'd ever seen a sexier woman, and judging from that flirty little smile she knew it. She was loving this.

She stepped closer to him, heels clicking on the floor, her breasts brushing his chest, the silk of her camisole whispering against his skin.

She ran one fingernail down the length of his chest and Alex shuddered. He couldn't help it. Her smile widened and she raised her eyebrows.

"You like that?"

"I like you touching me."

"How about this?" she purred, and she wrapped her fingers around him, squeezed with just the perfect amount of pressure. Alex nearly groaned. He did close his eyes, and didn't even realize it until he opened them again.

"Yes, I like that, too," he murmured.

His hands ached to touch her; his palms itched to feel the softness of her skin. To make her as crazy as she was making him. Still he resisted. Control now meant letting her stay in charge. Seeing where she went with her little show of power.

Gaining her trust—and preferably not disgracing himself in the process.

She ran her hand up and down his length and then stepped closer to him so he thrust his hips forward instinctively, his body aching to bury himself inside her. She laughed softly and for the first time Alex seriously considered stopping this game.

Chelsea was enjoying this just a little too much.

"Now, now, Alex," she murmured. "Patience."

Her voice, he heard, was just a little ragged, her breathing just a little uneven. She was as turned on as he was, and that kept him still, waiting for her next move.

She walked around him and then pressed a hand in the small of his back. "Bedroom."

"Glad to hear it," he answered, and walked into her bedroom, her hand still on his back.

He stopped in front of a king-size bed with white satin sheets, the city visible all around them with floor-to-ceiling windows on three sides. Chelsea pushed him so his knees hit the bed and he would have fallen if he hadn't twisted around, grabbed her hand and taken her with him.

He lay on his back, Chelsea sprawled on top of him, and grinned. "Now that's better."

She was annoyed, but she hid it well. "Isn't it," she murmured, and rose to her knees in one fluid movement so she was straddling him.

His mind glazed over as he felt her against him and he arched off the bed, driven by a need so basic and elemental he could neither hide nor deny it. He didn't even want to.

She laughed softly, tantalizing and teasing him as the sides of her knees pressed his hips and she hovered above him so he could only just brush against her.

"Almost, Alex," she soothed and he heard her pant as he arched again. She wanted this as much as he did, even if she was pretending otherwise. Alex nearly swore. He was going out of his mind, and he wanted to do nothing more than flip her over and plunge inside her.

Clucking softly, she shook her head. "Patience, remember."

"I remember," he answered, his teeth gritted. Sweat broke out on his brow. *Hell.* He was so close to losing it.

She leaned over, her breasts brushing his face, making him groan aloud, and retrieved a condom from her bedside table. He reached up to grab her shoulders, but she twisted out of his grasp, pushed his arms down on the bed.

"What, I can't even touch you?"

"Oh, you can touch me." She ripped the condom packet open with her teeth and slowly, languorously, rolled it over him. Alex shuddered. "And I can touch you," she murmured and slipping her shorts aside, she sank onto him.

"Chelsea…" Her name fell from his lips, a moan, a plea as she moved over him, his body deep inside hers even as he angled his hips for better access.

"Almost there, Alex," she murmured, and he heard the satisfaction as well as the desire in her voice, knew she had him where she wanted him. Underneath her, writhing and begging.

Fine. He'd beg. This once, he'd beg, at least with his body. He grabbed her hips, anchoring her to him as he thrust upward.

She rocked faster, and he heard her breath hitch as she threw her head back, her hands braced behind her. He knew she was as close to losing control as he was, but their little power play had ceased to have any meaning for him.

Then he stopped thinking about anything but the exquisite sensation of being inside her as he gasped out his climax, and her own breathing broke on a cry she quickly swallowed. She lowered her head, her hair brushing his chest, as her breathing slowed.

Before the last wave of pleasure had even subsided, she was rolling off him, adjusting her shorts with trembling fingers, her eyes glittering with defiant triumph.

"You know where the door is," she said, and without so much as a backward glance she left him there, sated and naked on the bed, and headed toward the bathroom.

Alex lay there for a single stunned second before he tossed the condom aside and rolled off the bed in one sinuous movement. He reached for her wrist, her skin smooth and cold under his fingers.

"Interesting idea, Chelsea, but our evening doesn't end there."

She eyed him with haughty disdain even though he could feel her tremble. "It does for me."

Alex smiled and shook his head slowly, his gaze nailed to hers, his fingers still encircling her wrist. "Not even close."

"I don't do pillow talk."

He widened his smile, his gaze never leaving hers. "Neither do I."

She pulled her wrist away from his grasp. "So we're done here."

He caught her by the shoulder as she tried to turn away, forced her to face him. "No," he said, "we're not."

Chelsea stared at the determination on Alex's face and felt a thrill of something she couldn't name. No, she could name it; she just didn't want to.

Excitement. Pure, unadulterated, sexual excitement. So he wanted a little control now. And damn it, she wanted to give it to him.

She'd got what she wanted. She'd had him begging, writhing. And his seeming submission had given her the most mind-blowing orgasm she'd ever had.

Yet she still wanted more. And so did Alex.

How frightening was that?

She lifted her chin, tried to stare him down but he wasn't even blinking. "You sure you're up for round two, champ?" she mocked and he gave her a smile that was positively feral.

"Definitely."

Chelsea didn't answer. Stupid of her to challenge him. Idiotic to feel this thrill, this sudden need, even deeper and fiercer than before.

"Fine," she said, feigning a boredom she didn't remotely feel. She dropped back down onto the bed, and lay there, supine. "Ready?"

He laughed softly. "You are a piece of work, Chelsea. But you've had your turn. Now it's mine. Get up."

She didn't move, even though she wanted to. Even though everything in her ached to obey him. *Stupid, stupid, stupid.*

"I told you I wasn't going to play your little games, Alex."

"Everything with you is a game. But you want to lie there on the bed and pretend you're bored? Fine. I can work with that."

Damn. She was in big trouble. Chelsea sat up, scooted away from him. "Sorry, but I don't actually do repeats."

Smiling lazily, he reached for her hand, pulled her up to him, and damn it, she went. "This isn't going to be a repeat."

He pulled her to stand next to him, and she trembled as she felt the scorching heat of him. "You get off on this, Alex? This whole controlling thing?"

"You just did," he remarked. "But don't worry, Chelsea, I'm not going to make you do anything you don't want to do. I'm not that kind of man." He studied her thoughtfully. "But you're scared—"

"I'm not *scared.*"

"Pissed, then. Pissed off that I'm going to make you want to do things you don't want to do. Aren't I?"

"Just try," she snapped, all bravado. She knew very well he could do exactly that, and the fact that he knew it made it all the more dangerous. More terrifying.

"Oh, I will." He shook his head sorrowfully. "You didn't even want to climax, Chelsea. You practically fought it. What was that about?"

"I enjoyed myself," she answered tersely. How had he, in the midst of his own orgasm, seen so much? She'd always hated the vulnerability of letting go that much. She wasn't a prude; she enjoyed sex. But she ended it quickly. Yet with Alex she hadn't even had a choice. Her body had simply taken over, in overwhelming response to his.

"I want you to lose yourself," Alex told her, his words both threat and promise. "I want you to lose your mind. Anything else is an insult to my manhood."

"Oh, please." She looked away from him, tried to claw back some of her cool composure, haughty disdain. It was nowhere to be found.

"I like that," he murmured, his hand on her shoulders now, holding her in place. "I like it when you say please."

She turned back to him, her lip curling even as her body thrilled to his touch. "So this is an ego trip?"

"Is it an ego trip to want you to come? Fine, then yes, it is."

"I had my pleasure, Alex. It was watching you beneath me, helpless and begging. Trust me, I'm fine."

He gave her a cold smile. "You really like to lay down the gauntlet, don't you?"

"Just stating facts."

"I can do that, too," he murmured, and covered her mouth with his own.

Just a kiss, and yet it was a shock to her system, like diving straight into cold, clear water. Suddenly every sense was alive, electric. She stood still beneath his touch, mind and body reeling under the onslaught of his mouth and tongue.

And it was a practiced, expert onslaught; the man knew how to kiss. It was only with the very last ounce of her self-control that she kept herself from reaching for him, putting her arms around him and drawing him closer. Everything in her yearned to feel the hard press of his body against every aching point of her own, and yet still she resisted. Out of pride. Out of fear. Out of a desperate need to keep herself from giving—and losing—everything to this man who affected her like no one she'd ever known.

Alex lifted his mouth from hers and Chelsea almost gasped aloud at the loss. "You want me to work for this, don't you?"

Somehow she found a smile. "Would you expect any less?"

"Never."

And work he did. He kissed her again, sliding his tongue along the seam of her lips before plunging inside, making everything in her pulse with that same electric shock of awareness. Intense. Painful. And yet so very alive.

Still she remained still, her hands clenched at her sides, her mouth barely parted under his. She wasn't about to make his conquest easy, and she'd never let him know how much she wanted this. *Him.*

But of course he knew. She knew he could feel the heat coming off her in waves, the shudder that ripped through her despite her every effort to suppress it. And belatedly she realized the mewling little gasps that broke the stillness in the bedroom were coming from her.

"You really are resisting this," he murmured against her

mouth as he slid his hand down her body to the juncture of her thighs. "What's so scary about an orgasm, Chelsea?" he asked, and there was a new, surprising tenderness in his voice that she couldn't bear. Not giving in, she realized far too belatedly, was more revealing than surrender would have been.

Why hadn't she seen that?

He pressed his hand against her, and she heard the sound she made. Then he took his hand away and touched her chin with his fingers; she opened her eyes. "You want me to stop?"

She said nothing. She couldn't admit that she didn't, and she wasn't strong enough to say yes.

He smiled as he stroked her again. "I think that's a no." One finger slid beneath her shorts. She gasped aloud. "Is that a yes, Chelsea?"

And then she broke. "Damn you," she gasped even as she fought the waves of pleasure that coursed through her, the pressure building.

"And you said you didn't do pillow talk."

She let out a sound that was half laugh, half sob, because this man amazed and affected her, and he made her body sing. She steadied herself, her hands on his shoulders as he touched her. "I'm going to make you pay for this—"

"I look forward to it."

He took away his hand and she gasped, every sense in her body screeching to a shocked halt. "Don't—"

"Don't what, Chelsea?"

She just shook her head. She wouldn't say it. She *wouldn't*. But he would.

"Don't what, Chelsea?" he asked, his voice soft, his

gaze hard and burning. "Don't stop? Is that what you were about to say? To beg?"

She leveled him with a look, or tried to. "I never beg."

"Maybe not, but your body does. Your body is begging me to touch you. To finish what I started."

And she knew he was right. She shifted restlessly, the ache in her pelvis insistent, intense, and still tried to stare him down.

"I really should take pity on you and end this," he murmured. "But I'm a hard man, Chelsea. I'm going to make you work for it."

She let out a choked laugh. "What do you call this?"

"Desire isn't weakness, you know," he said quietly and she just glared at him. She wouldn't tell him that for her it was. It always had been. "You want me to be the one to beg?" he asked, a ragged edge now tearing his voice. "You want me to be weak, Chelsea? Fine. I want you. I was inside you moments ago, and I still want you again. And I want you to want me, to admit it not just with your body but your mind. Your mouth. Tell me you want me, Chelsea."

And she almost did. She'd never had a man ask that of her, and yet when she opened her mouth nothing came out. Nothing could.

Alex's gaze turned to glitter as he kissed her again, hard, demanding, and still she wouldn't give. He was destroying her, crumbling away years of carefully-constructed defenses, and he didn't even realize it, didn't see the rubble around her heart. She'd never let him know.

His mouth still on hers he propelled her across the room,

until her back came up hard against the floor-to-ceiling window.

Then he sank to his knees in front of her and her fingers clenched in his hair as he pulled down her shorts and put his mouth to her. Her knees buckled. He was on his knees and it should have made her feel strong but instead she felt weaker than ever, overwhelmed with emotion and need as his mouth moved over her and her head came back against the glass as she shut her eyes and finally gave in to it, powerless now to resist the tidal wave of sensation that rose up to flood her, overwhelm her with feeling.

She was splayed out against the window, all of Manhattan behind her, but it was the man in front of her on his knees that made her feel exposed. Vulnerable. And she had no strength left to fight it.

With her jaw clenched, her breathing hitched, tears of pure emotion starting in her eyes, she came.

Her climax rolled over her in an all-encompassing wave, obliterating everything but a pleasure so intense and exquisite it hurt. Her hands clenched harder in his hair and she pulled, wanting him to feel just a tiny bit of what she was feeling. Pleasure. Pain. *Too much.*

He stood up, sliding his hands over her body, and while the aftershocks of her orgasm were still frying her brain and making her whole body strain and quiver, he slid those clever hands under her camisole and slipped it over her head, leaving her incredibly, unbearably bare.

Even through the daze of her desire she saw the smile leave his face, the shock dilate his pupils.

"Chelsea," he said, and his voice was hoarse. "What the hell happened to you?"

Chapter Six

Alex stared at the long, jagged line of torn flesh on Chelsea's left breast in shock. She didn't cower or cover up, just lifted her chin a notch as he was starting to realize was both her default and defense and met his gaze full-on with an unyielding one of her own, even as her breath continued to come out in ragged gasps.

"I fell out of a tree when I was a kid."

"And onto what? A chainsaw?"

"Fine, it was a car accident. A metal sign came through the wind shield and I was on the receiving end of its edge." She shrugged, but her eyes flashed fury and her jaw was as hard as granite. And just moments ago she'd been molten under his mouth, sobbing out a climax she'd tried so hard to fight.

"Had a good look?" she drawled and Alex realized he was still staring at the scar on her left breast. It had long since healed over, but the raised, puckered flesh told of a serious, life-threatening wound.

"Sorry," he said. "I didn't mean to embarrass you."

"You didn't." She retrieved her camisole and then slid it back on. "But now that you've had what you wanted, you

can go." And without another word, without even looking at him, she stalked to her bathroom. He heard the audible click of the lock turning and he sank onto the edge
of the bed, the satin sheets barely rumpled from their time
on them, and wondered just what the hell had happened.

Sex was meant to be simple. That was how he liked
it—no emotions engaged, just basic physical pleasure. And
Chelsea's attitude had seemed to mesh with his own in
that regard, yet somehow the whole thing had spiraled way
out of control and his emotions seethed inside him, a hot
tangle he didn't have the energy or resources to unknot.

It had started as a game of control, something he thought
was merely amusing, and it had turned into something else.
Something deep and complex and emotional.

He didn't do any of that. Neither, he knew, did Chelsea. So how had they got here? What had happened? And
what was he going to do about it?

He knew Chelsea was expecting him to be gone by the
time she came out of the bathroom, and he also knew that
would be the easiest option. Get the hell out of there before it became even more complicated.

He didn't move.

He couldn't leave it like this. He couldn't leave it at all.
No matter what had just happened between them, and
hell if he knew what it was, this was still about Treffen.

About Sarah.

He couldn't forget that ever, not even now. Especially
not now.

Chelsea waited for nearly an hour before she left the
bathroom. She'd showered, washed her hair, brushed her

teeth: all useless attempts to get the scent and taste of Alex off her.

It didn't matter if her mouth now tasted of mint and her skin smelled of almonds. He was still imprinted on her brain, seared onto her soul. The man had reached her the way no one else ever had, and she couldn't bear it. Couldn't bear how weak and exposed he'd made her feel, how much he'd seen. How much she still wanted him.

At least she wouldn't see him again. He must have left by now, and she had absolutely no intention of ever so much as smiling at the man again.

She knotted her ivory silk robe tight at the waist, pulled her damp hair into a ponytail and drew in a deep, calming breath. Then she opened the door of the bathroom and stopped short when she saw Alex sitting on the edge of the bed. At least he'd put his clothes back on. Yet with his tie left undone and his hair still rumpled, he looked just as appealing as he had when he'd worn nothing but his socks. Chelsea had a mad urge to push him back on the bed and instead of straddling him, curl up next to him. Feel his arms around her, holding her close.

She pulled the knot of her sash tighter around her waist and fixed him with a narrowed look. "What are you doing here?"

He smiled faintly, raised his eyebrows. "Did you really think I'd just slink out of here while you were in the shower?"

"Since I told you to, yes."

"Maybe you haven't realized, but I'm not so good with orders."

"I'm not so good with assholes who outstay their welcome," Chelsea snapped.

He raised his eyebrows. "Ouch."

"I mean it, Alex. We're done."

"You really think we're done, Chelsea? You think you've got me out of your system?" Her mouth dropped open and he smiled. Nothing friendly about this one, just a cold curving of his lips. "That's what you wanted, right? Take me to bed and throw me out afterward, with you smugly satisfied that another poor bastard did just as he was told. Well, too bad for you, because I'm not that kind of man."

She leveled him with a look, or tried to. "So I gather."

He rose from the bed and took a step toward her, and then another. He was close enough to touch her but she didn't move, didn't flinch. She stood her ground and eyed him evenly, waited for whatever he'd sling at her next.

"I want to talk about Treffen."

"*Treffen?*" She stared at him in disbelief. "Nice timing."

"It works for me."

"Fine." She folded her arms. "What about him?"

Alex gazed at her for a moment, his expression assessing yet a surprising vulnerability visible in his eyes, quickly hidden. "I want you to take him down on your show."

"Take him down?" Chelsea raised her eyebrows. "What do you think I am, a secret agent?"

"He's evil, and the world needs to know it."

She shook her head, amazed that a man like Alex could use such melodramatic language. "What did he do to you to make you so mad?" A memory suddenly clicked into place. "Wait—didn't he say something against Diaz News, way back when you started? About how biased you really were?"

Alex frowned. "That has nothing to do with this."

"Yeah, right."

"I'm serious, Chelsea."

"So am I. I won't be used for your personal vendetta, Alex. Sorry." She shook her head again. Everything made a sort of horrible sense now. "So that's why you were waiting for me in your limo. Probably why you took me to bed, too. For some ridiculous plan of revenge." And stupidly, that hurt.

"As I recall, you took me to bed."

"Whatever."

"Don't you even want to know what he's done?"

"Not particularly."

"That's shoddy journalism, Chelsea, and you know it. And you think I'm letting personal feelings get in the way?"

"What personal feelings do I have about Treffen?" she scoffed and he smiled, his eyes hard.

"Not about Treffen. About me. You're angry about how much I made you lose control. You're scared about how much I make you feel."

"Who made you such a psychologist?" she snapped, but he had her against the wall and he knew it. Damn the man for seeing so much. Damn her for revealing it.

"I know because I feel the same," he said, his voice even but his gaze glittering into hers. "I'm like you, Chelsea. I enjoy sex, but I leave it in the bedroom. I don't do relationships. Nothing more than a night." He bared his teeth in something like a smile. "No repeats."

"Glad we're on the same page."

"But this was different. For both of us."

Her arms were folded so hard and tight she was hugging herself. Trying to keep the feelings in. "I didn't think you were one for hearts and roses, Alex."

"Do you deny it?"

And no words came, because she couldn't. She just stared at him, wanting to stare him down even though that was impossible. He would always win. "What do you want?" she finally asked, her voice turning ragged.

"I want you to listen. Really listen, and forget about who's calling the shots between us. This is bigger than that, Chelsea."

Her nails dug into her arms as she stared at him, still suspicious and yet also longing to do what he'd just suggested. Stop fighting, if just for a little while. "Fine," she finally said. "So tell me."

Alex stared at Chelsea and wondered what the hell to do next. None of that had been planned. Controlled. Yes, he wanted to talk about Treffen, but he hadn't meant to spout off about feelings. *This was different. For both of us.*

He sounded ridiculous.

And yet he'd meant it. Even so, he couldn't believe he'd admitted as much to himself, much less to Chelsea.

He took a steadying breath. "Treffen's human rights advocacy is a sham, his law firm little more than a front."

She just stared at him, almost seeming amused by what she obviously thought was some personal vendetta. "A front? For what?"

"For a prostitution ring."

Chelsea let out a laugh, one hard bark of disbelief. "Are you telling me Jason Treffen is a *pimp?*"

Alex felt his jaw bunch. "Basically, yes."

She shook her head slowly. "Yeah, right."

"Why don't you believe it?"

"Why should I?"

"Why would I lie?"

She lifted her shoulders in a shrug. "How should I know? Maybe your honest news angle is a front, too, Alex. Maybe you play dirty, and this is how you destroy your enemies, or try to."

"Why should I want to destroy Treffen?"

"He discredited you."

"Ten years ago he tried to discredit me. Because I knew too much."

She still looked amused, which made Alex grit his teeth so hard his jaw ached. "And what did you know, Detective Diaz?"

"Back then I thought it was just a case of sexual harassment, which seemed bad enough. But recently new evidence has come to light." Through Katy and the photo she'd found. Just the thought of that damning picture could bring bile to Alex's throat.

"New evidence that he's a pimp," Chelsea clarified in a disbelieving drawl.

"He runs a prostitution ring, yes. He handpicks the girls from his firm—"

"Lawyers, you mean," Chelsea said, her tone dripping scornful incredulity. It made Alex furious both with her and himself. He'd anticipated resistance, but not disbelief. He should have known better, should have considered this.

It *did* sound crazy. So crazy he'd had a tough time believing it. Believing Austin, believing Katy. *Believing Sarah.* And now Chelsea didn't believe him.

"He chooses young women who are drowning in school loans and desperate to prove themselves."

"Now you sound like a human rights activist yourself."

He took a step toward her, hands balled into fists. "Damn it, this is not a joke, Chelsea."

"I'm not laughing. But I'm not sure where you're going with this, Alex. You want me to buy this sensational story and do what? Confront him on live television?"

"It could make your career."

"If it were true, then maybe. But it would tank my career at AMI, and you know it. Plus I'd be sued six ways to Sunday so thanks, but no thanks. I'm not going to be part of your personal revenge."

"This isn't about me—"

"Then why do you care so much?"

He stared at her, silent and fuming. He wasn't going to tell her about Sarah. That would be too personal. Too painful. "If you knew something like this," he finally said, "wouldn't you care?"

"I still don't understand how you came to know it."

"Treffen's son Austin was my college roommate. And he's still one of my best friends."

Chelsea remained unimpressed. "And his dad let him in on the dirty family secret? 'Hey, son, come pimp with me?'"

"No, of course not. Don't be absurd."

"Then what?"

Alex let out a long, even breath, tried to hold on to his fraying patience. "Austin found out."

"How?"

Katy, Sarah's sister, had confronted him with the terrible truth. But Alex didn't want to bring Katy into it either. "He just did."

"Come on, Alex. Now who's talking about shoddy journalism? If I were going to do this, I'd need facts. Evidence. Preferably a primary source."

"But you've already said you aren't going to do this. Confront him."

"No, I'm not. You have no basis for anything you're saying, and I'd rather not tank my career on your whim, thanks very much."

"It's not," Alex said through gritted teeth, "a whim."

"Then show me some hard evidence."

"Why do you think Treffen announced the separation from his wife?"

"Irreconcilable differences, I thought. Plenty of people separate or get divorced, Alex—"

"He's going to be ousted from his law firm within the month." At least he hoped so, if Hunter was successful.

She just shrugged. "Everyone knows he's been thinking of leaving. He might run for senator."

"No, he *won't*." His voice came out in a savage burst, surprising them both. Alex took a deep breath. This was not going the way he wanted. Expected. *Talk about control.* He needed it back. Thirty seconds tautly ticked by while he stared at her. Finally he let out a low breath. "A woman showed Austin some photographs."

"Photographs?" Her gaze narrowed. "Of what?"

Of Sarah. "One of the—women."

"You mean one of these call girls?" She shook her head, still unimpressed. "And how does one photo of some sexy lawyer prove anything?"

"It was a photograph of a young woman with one of the law firm's clients. Treffen was using it to blackmail the man."

Chelsea's eyebrows arced toward her hairline. "So in addition to pimping his employees, Treffen was blackmailing his clients?"

Alex nodded tersely. "Yes." He knew it sounded incredible. Absurd, even. Could he really blame Chelsea for not believing him?

She was silent for a long moment, her expression clouded. Finally she shook her head. "That's too big a story not to have broken before."

"Treffen's a powerful man."

"Not even a whisper, Alex."

He should tell her about Sarah, he knew. About how Sarah threw herself from the roof of Treffen's office building rather than go on living under the man's sadistic rule. How Katy had come to Austin with so much awful, damning information. Condemning not just Treffen, but all the people who had let Sarah down. Condemning *him*.

The words, the knowledge were there, burning in his chest, a hot lump of fury he couldn't shift. Couldn't admit to. He wanted to avenge Sarah, but he didn't want to drag her name through the mud. The tabloids, the gossip, the endless raking through the media.

Chelsea's expression softened into something intolerably like pity. "I'm sorry. This means something to you, I can see. But this interview isn't about sensationalism for me. It's about respectable journalism."

Alex jerked his head in a nod. "Fine." There was no point continuing the conversation, not now. He reached for his suit jacket. "So I guess we're done here."

Her eyes widened, and she nodded slowly. "I guess we are."

He turned on his heel and left without another word.

In the elevator his phone beeped with a text and Alex jerked it out of his pocket, stared at the message from Hunter. New information. We need to meet.

"Damn it," he said aloud. He should be thrilled that Hunter was keeping up his side of the bargain they'd all made, how each of them would bring down Treffen, but right now his friend's success just brought his own deficiencies and failing into the glaring light. Austin had exposed Treffen to his family. Hunter would oust him from the law firm.

And Alex? What the hell was he going to do?

A few days later Chelsea stood by the doors of one of the opulent ballrooms of the Plaza Hotel that was hosting a charity fund-raiser gala. She didn't attend too many of these dos, but this charity cut close to the bone; it offered support to children who had been abused and removed from their homes, as well as to their current caregivers.

She was particularly interested in the charity's efforts to raise awareness of the different forms of child abuse. Not all abuse looked like abuse. Felt like abuse. And she knew more than anyone how you could think it was your choice and it was still abuse. How you could fool yourself into believing you wanted it.

Still abuse.

She had to believe that, but the trouble was she knew she didn't. Maybe for everyone else, but not for her. The same rules just didn't apply. At least, they didn't feel like they did.

Now she paused on the threshold, took a deep, steadying breath. The crowd mingling in front of her was hardly intimidating, about a hundred well-heeled guests, and she had a passing acquaintance with most of them.

Still she felt her breathing go shallow as her heart rate kicked up and the spots danced before her eyes. Damn it. She pressed one hand against the doorframe and willed it all to recede. *You're stronger than this.*

Then her swimming gaze zeroed in on the one man in the room with whom she had much more than a passing acquaintance.

A man who still felt like a stranger.

Alex Diaz.

And stupidly, inexplicably, she felt better. She had no idea why seeing Alex would calm her, but she'd take it.

And she'd try not to remember how his hands had felt on her body, his eyes burning gold as he evoked a response from her she hadn't given to anyone else, ever.

She'd been trying not to remember that for the past three days. She wasn't making a great job of it.

In any case, it hardly mattered whether she thought of him or not. Whether he made her feel or not. She had a terrible suspicion that he'd only slept with her so he could tell her about Treffen. Maybe he'd thought a little pillow talk would convince her to help him with his revenge plan.

She was glad she'd proved him wrong, even if the realization that he'd been using her made disappointment twist painfully inside her.

Another part of her insisted he hadn't been using her, not like that. Admittedly, they'd been using each other. Pleasurably. But Alex's desire had been real. The intimacy, torturous as it was, had been real.

Hadn't it?

Or had Chelsea lost the ability to judge such things? Her emotional intelligence, admittedly, was pretty low.

Taking yet another deep breath, blinking the spots back, she strode into the ballroom.

She spent the next hour moving around the ballroom, keeping an eye on Alex, partly wanting to go up to him and get that first awkward after-sex encounter over with, partly wanting to stay away. And partly wanting him to come up to her first, which made for a lot of want.

She avoided him.

Even so she was conscious of his presence, knew exactly where he was without even looking.

And then, out of the corner of her eye, she saw the expression on his face change from easy affability to sudden tension, hidden fury. Or not so hidden, at least not to her, because even from fifty feet away she saw how his gaze exuded hatred and his jaw clenched, teeth gritted.

She followed his gaze and saw who he was staring at: Jason Treffen.

Treffen looked distinguished in a crisp tuxedo, the lights from the many chandeliers catching the silver of his hair. He was smiling as a group of sycophants fawned around him, but Chelsea noted that his pale blue eyes were shrewd. Not a surprise, really; the man was a lawyer.

But the look on Alex's face made her reconsider. She'd shut down the talk about Treffen the other night for a lot of reasons, the main one being the thought of working with Alex on anything was far too alarming a possibility. She was too raw, too revealed, to become some kind of partner-in-crime with him.

But that, she knew, really was shoddy journalism.

But neither did she want to believe such horrible things about Jason Treffen. She'd chosen him for her first serious interview subject because she admired his dedication to women's rights in the workplace. Because she believed, passionately, in what he was doing.

He *couldn't* be a pimp and a blackmailer. He just couldn't.

Which was a ridiculous way for her to think, because she knew more than anyone just how low humanity could sink. Including her.

So maybe she should take what Alex said seriously, or at least consider the possibility.

Throwing back her shoulders, she headed for Treffen.

"Ah, Chelsea, my favorite talk show hostess," he said, his voice a confident baritone with the kind of elongated vowels that spoke of a lifetime of entitlement.

They air-kissed, and Jason squeezed her hand.

A few of the sycophants drifted off and Chelsea gave Treffen her sweetest smile. "So I hear you're lawyering up for your interview."

His eyes narrowed a fraction, but his smile didn't slip. "Just a precaution, Chelsea."

"A precaution?" She offered a tiny, pretend pout. "And I thought we were friends."

"I have a reputation to protect." He pitched it just right, regretful but implacable.

"I didn't realize your reputation was in doubt, Jason," Chelsea answered teasingly. "You're a paragon, practically a saint." She arched her eyebrows, curved her lips in a flirty smile. "Unless you're hiding something? Some big, dirty secret?" Her smile widened, inviting him to share the joke.

Treffen stilled for half a second, no more. Then he laughed, that patronizing chuckle of rich, older men that Chelsea couldn't stand. "Very funny, Chelsea." He wagged a finger at her. "Very funny."

Which was absolutely no answer at all. And he was still planning, Chelsea noted, to bring a lawyer to the meeting. Staring into his cold blue eyes, she had a sudden, bone-deep certainty that Treffen really was hiding something.

That Alex might be right.

Smiling as if it were all so amusing, she stepped back. Felt a gaze on her back, knew it was Alex.

She turned, and saw him staring hard at her, eyes like fire.

She let her gaze skip past him and then walked off in the opposite direction. She wasn't about to make Treffen suspicious. And she wasn't sure she could deal with a conversation with Alex.

Get over it, Chelsea. It was just sex. This is your career.

Pushing aside all that damnable emotion, she approached him a few minutes later when she saw him by the bar. "I think you might be onto something, after all," she murmured and she felt Alex tense.

"You mean—"

"You know what I mean," she answered, and moved past him.

Everyone was taking seats for the auction whose proceeds would benefit the charity, and Chelsea sat down in the back, flipped through the pages of the auction catalogue. She'd donated a spa weekend in Arizona and a dinner for two at Le Bernardin, as she did every year.

The bidding started and Chelsea sat back and watched as the first bids batted back and forth between two fleshy corporate types who wanted the VIP box at an NBA game. It went for twenty thousand dollars.

Next item was a dinner for eight catered by a celebrity chef. Chelsea never bid on anything. Who would she invite to a dinner for eight? Who would she take on a girly spa weekend? She didn't have people like that in her life.

She thought briefly of Louise, but knew she wasn't ready to spend that kind of uninterrupted time with her sister. Everything between them still felt too strange, too painful.

She supposed she could ask Michael to something, but their friendship was conducted mainly at work.

And there was no one else, she realized with a funny little pang. No one else at all. She'd never minded before. She'd been glad of her independence, her freedom.

Loneliness wasn't a concept she entertained.

For the better part of ten years she'd told herself she was happy; she had everything anyone could ever want. Money, fame, a beautiful apartment, beautiful clothes, a satisfying—mostly—job.

Yet now, suddenly, she wondered. Wanted…but what? A relationship? Someone in her life who cared, even just a little bit, and more importantly, who knew her—the real her—just a little bit?

Could she really want that? Had Alex opened up that desire in her?

The thought was new and definitely not welcome. Relationships were risky; intimacy meant danger. She had too many secrets to have any kind of honest or real relationship with anyone. She'd accepted that as a price for starting over, but suddenly now she wanted to be real with just one person.

You were real with Alex when he brought you to the most shattering climax you've ever had. You didn't want to be, but you were.

Instinctively her gaze moved through the rows of chairs to find him sitting in the second, legs sprawled out as he lazily raised his program. He was bidding, and Chelsea flipped through the catalogue to find out what it was he'd just committed ten thousand dollars to.

A Family Fun Evening? She read the description in bemusement: a trip around the city in a private double decker bus, VIP tickets to the Big Apple Circus, the works.

What on earth was he going to do with that?

Quickly she realized that while she might have no one to go to the circus with, Alex most assuredly did. Maybe he had siblings with kids, was a doting uncle to his nieces and nephews. Or maybe he'd gift it to someone he knew with children. Maybe he'd go himself with some ditzy bombshell from work. A sharp pang, like a blow to the solar plexus, suddenly made her breathless.

That couldn't be jealousy she was feeling. She never

cared enough about a man even to concern herself with other women, much less be jealous of them.

"Sold to number 17!"

Her gaze jerked back to Alex, and with a ripple of surprise she saw him turn and smile right at her. *Now what was that about?*

She found out as soon as the auction was over. He made straight for her, and Chelsea watched him with a mounting anticipation, even excitement she didn't even try to suppress.

"You know we shouldn't be seen together," she murmured when he stood in front of her, all rangy muscle and restless power. She felt her heart rate kick up a notch just at the sight of him, that golden blaze of intent firing his eyes.

"You mean because of Treffen?"

"I don't want him getting suspicious. And in any case, I'm not sure I believe—"

"He left before the auction ended."

"Oh." She frowned. "Why would he do that?"

"He's limiting his public exposure at the moment. Wants to avoid anything unpleasant." He took a step closer to her. "So what made you change your mind?"

"I haven't actually changed my mind, Alex. Not yet." She eyed him warningly. "But I spoke to him. I could tell he was hiding something. I still need proof."

"I know you do. But I didn't come over here to talk about Treffen."

Surprise warred with pleasure, and even though she knew she shouldn't believe him, she did, because she wanted to. She wanted there to be more than just Treffen between them. "You didn't?"

He shook his head, his mouth quirking up at one corner, a crooked smile that felt like a fist to the heart. "Nope. I came over to ask if you'd go to the circus with me."

She stood still, silent, shock blazing through her. Was he actually asking her out on a *date?* "The circus?" she repeated, her mind spinning. "Why?"

He arched one dark eyebrow. "Because it's fun? Because I have great tickets?" He stepped closer, so she could feel his heat, and it made her dizzy. It made her remember. "Because I want to go with you?"

"Why?" she said again, stupidly, her mind still spinning.

Alex gazed at her for a long moment, his golden gaze trapping her. "I want to see you again, Chelsea," he said in a husky murmur. "Properly."

But she didn't date. Ever. And neither did he. She shook her head, the need to deny instinctive despite the desire already coursing through her. The desire not just for him, although she certainly felt that, but for time with him. For a date. "I don't do dates."

"Always a first time."

"I didn't think you did either."

"Like I said, always a first time."

"And neither of us do repeats."

"Once in a while I'm willing to make an exception." He cocked his head. "But maybe you're afraid to?"

She shook her head fiercely. "I'm not afraid."

"Then prove it by going to the circus with me."

She shook her head, harder now. "No, that tactic might have worked once, Alex, but not this time. I don't need to prove anything to you."

"All right, then tell me the real reason you won't go with me. Are you afraid of clowns?"

Her lips twitched in a smile that felt so good and yet she still tried to suppress it. Why, she wondered, did every emotion feel like weakness?

Because you know where it leads.

"Actually, I do find clowns a little bit creepy," she said lightly. "But I'm not phobic or anything."

"So it's not the clowns. What, then?"

And what could she say? She'd never had a man be so impervious to her put-downs and brush-offs, so deter-mined not just to get her into bed, but to *be* with her.

Did Alex Diaz really want to be with her? At the *circus?*

"Is this about Treffen?" she asked. "A cover so we can talk?"

"No." So flat, so absolute. So wonderful and thrilling and yes, terrifying.

"Why are you making an exception?"

"Because of you." His eyes blazed and his smile was slow. "You're worth it."

This simple statement, so matter-of-fact, made her feel like shivering. Or maybe bursting into tears. What was *wrong* with her? Why did Alex Diaz seem to push every button she had, flip a switch inside her so she turned from ice queen to emotional wreck?

"Were you using me?" she blurted. "I mean, to convince me about Treffen? Did you sleep with me just to gain my trust?" She hated that she'd asked all that, but she needed to know. She just hoped Alex would tell her the truth.

He arched an eyebrow. "You're not radiating trust at the moment, Chelsea, so if that was my ploy it didn't work."

"Even so…"

"This isn't about Treffen. Maybe it once was, but it's not now. It's about—about us." The words didn't come easily, and that made her believe him. *Us.* What a novel concept.

His gaze was steady on her, a golden beam that seared right through her. "Look, I'm not jumping the gun here. I'm not asking for anything but a single date." He held his hands up, his smile crooked. "Trust me."

Relief and disappointment fought within her, and she didn't know which one came out on top. What had she wanted, a declaration of love?

No way.

"One date," he repeated. "Because I'm not done, and neither are you, even if you keep trying to convince yourself that you are."

"How attractive," she retorted because his honesty was stripping her bare and wisecracks were her only defense. "A man who thinks he knows what I want better than I do."

"I think you know what you want. You just don't want to admit it."

She took a deep breath. *Say no,* she told herself. *You don't do dates. Not even one.*

"Please, Chelsea."

I like it when you say please. But this wasn't about control anymore, at least not that kind of control. No scoring points here, just trying to stay safe.

Say no. Save yourself.

"Okay," she said, and she felt as if she'd just taken a swan dive into the utter—and dangerous—unknown.

Chapter Seven

Four days later Chelsea walked into one of AMI's conference rooms, where Jason Treffen and his shark of a lawyer waited. A lawyer needing a lawyer, Chelsea thought cynically, and wondered just how much Treffen had to hide.

She still didn't want to believe he was a pimp and a blackmailer. She half hoped, or more, that Alex was wrong. Mistaken, somehow.

Pretty big mistake.

Jason stood up as she approached, smiling easily as he stretched out one manicured hand. For a man hovering around sixty, he was, Chelsea acknowledged, very attractive, with his full head of silvery-white hair and pale blue eyes in a face whose creases only drew attention to an admirably hard jaw. His lawyer was about what she'd expected. Sharply dressed, pointed face, too much aftershave.

"So nice to see you again, Jason," she said, and returned his handshake with a firmness that made his eyes narrow slightly. Was he suspicious? Or simply used to women like the ones he helped through his charities, women who were weak, who were victims.

Not her.

She sat across the table from him along with Michael, who had murmured his own pleasantries as an assistant fetched coffee and a tray of bagels and pastries none of them would touch.

"So." Chelsea folded her hands on the table and gave Jason Treffen a professional smile. "You have some questions you'd like me to look at."

With a loud snap the lawyer opened his briefcase and took out a sheet of paper that he slid across the table toward Chelsea.

She picked it up, scanned it briefly as annoyance flickered. These questions were the interviewing equivalent of cold porridge. Totally boring. Utterly unappetizing. And they gave all the control to Treffen.

What do you think is the highlight of your career? What made you decide to champion the cause of women?

Nothing controversial or even interesting, just a platform for Treffen to wank off on all his good works. For an hour on prime time.

When she'd first thought of this interview, she'd wanted to explore some of Treffen's more controversial choices, such as offering pro bono counsel to a convicted criminal; in that case, a woman who'd been charged with manslaughter. Digging deeper into the case had shown the woman had been physically abused by her boyfriend for years. Treffen had won the case.

None of the questions on his list touched on any of his controversial cases.

She handed the sheet to Michael as she smiled at Treffen. "This is certainly a starting point."

"It's also an ending point, Miss Maxwell." Chelsea

tensed at the slight sneer in the lawyer's tone. *Nice, choice, Treffen,* she thought cynically. *Great representation.*

She directed her gaze at Treffen. "An interview where we just talk about the highlights of your career won't attract viewers."

"Mr. Treffen isn't interested in being part of your soap opera," the lawyer snapped. "He's not going to sob on your sofa."

"Eric." Treffen spoke gently, but there was steel behind his words. He smiled at Chelsea, and even though it was easy and open, she felt her skin crawl and was surprised by her own response. Was she really starting to believe Alex?

This man, this champion of women's rights, was actually a *pimp?*

She used to think that if Treffen had been her boss ten years ago instead of Brian Taylor, she might not have had to have plastic surgery on her face, or have a huge scar on her left boob.

A scar Alex had seen.

But maybe Treffen would have been worse than Taylor. Maybe she would have ended up pimping herself for many men instead of just one.

"You must appreciate my position, Miss Maxwell," Treffen said, all honeyed sincerity. "I'm a respected lawyer and human rights advocate. I agreed to do an interview with you because I'd like to have a wider platform for the causes I've supported for many years now." His smile widened, inviting her into it. "And of course, it's a wonderful opportunity for you."

Chelsea felt a leap of fury, and she kept her gaze level

with effort. The implication was clear. Agreeing to her interview was another act of charity.

"And I'm sure you can appreciate my position, Jason. I'm not anyone's soapbox."

"Chelsea…" Michael murmured and she took a quick, steadying breath. Never mind what Alex wanted, this was her career she was talking about. Why was she jeopardizing this? The Treffen interview was her chance to finally be seen as something other than Michael's mistress who didn't deserve her own show.

But she still wouldn't be used by any man, even Jason Treffen.

What about Alex?

No, he hadn't used her. He'd taken her, yes, and he'd brought to a shattering climax, but she hadn't actually felt used. Just terribly, painfully exposed.

"Point taken, Miss Maxwell." Treffen was still smiling, but his eyes were cold. "I'd hardly expect anything less from you. But these are the only questions I'm willing to answer if you want me on your show, and I'll need you to sign a legal agreement that you'll stick to the script."

"My interviews are never scripted."

"A poor choice of words," Treffen acknowledged with a graceful nod. "But I'd still like to keep to these questions."

"Part of the appeal of a candid interview is to see where the conversation goes," Chelsea said. She kept her voice mild, managed a smile. No point annoying this man unnecessarily, although she could already tell she was pissing him off. "To engage in a genuine conversation, not just a predetermined question-and-answer."

The lawyer, Eric, leaned forward, his mouth twisted

into a sneer, but Treffen stayed him with one hand, his narrowed gaze on Chelsea.

"Do you think your interview method is really that candid, Miss Maxwell? Because I've watched you and I've admired how you handle your interviewees. How you wrap them around your little finger and they don't even realize it. But then you have a certain charm on camera, don't you? Even when you were a weather girl in Alabama." His voice stayed friendly, even light, but Chelsea felt herself go ice-cold. Her palms tingled, and spots danced before her eyes.

She could not get a panic attack here. Now. Yet the realization that Treffen knew about her, knew her past, made a wave of nausea wash over her.

"It really is an admirable skill," he continued, his voice soft now. "To manipulate people without them even realizing it. But I'm afraid that's not on my agenda."

And what was on his agenda? She wondered sickly. To expose her? Was he actually threatening to reveal her past if she didn't stick to his wretched script?

A man capable of that kind of subtle blackmail could be capable of a whole lot more, Chelsea realized. *Like everything Alex had said.*

"What is on your agenda, Jason?" she asked when she trusted her voice to sound pleasant and relaxed. His eyes sparked anger briefly before he smiled and spread his hands.

"Again, a poor choice of words. I have no agenda, Miss Maxwell. But my reputation is important to me, not to mention the many women I've helped and the charities

I've supported, so if you want me to do this interview, you'll keep to those questions."

And keeping her gaze on his narrowed blue one, she knew he meant it.

"Damn, Chelsea," Michael said when Treffen and his lawyer had left. "Why did you have to piss him off?"

She tossed the sheet of questions in the trash. "It didn't take much."

"I thought you wanted this interview. You've worked hard enough for it."

"I know I have." Chelsea let out her breath in a rush. She still felt shaky, especially when she thought about Treffen knowing where she'd come from. What she'd done. How had he found it out? And why?

Was her own sordid past going to serve as Jason Treffen's insurance policy?

Willing her heart rate to slow, she turned to Michael. "I won't be used, Michael, not by anyone, not even Treffen."

"He's done some research on you," Michael said after a moment. "Don't piss him off too much."

"Or the great human rights activist will take me down?" She tried to sound light, mocking, but everything inside her shuddered.

"He has the power to ruin careers," Michael said mildly, "just as he has the power to make them."

"I know that." And he could do either with hers. And yet it seemed so ludicrous, so impossible. *Jason Treffen.* Champion of women.

Or not.

"What questions do you want to ask him," Michael asked, "that weren't on his list?"

"I just don't want to be controlled." She wasn't about to tell Michael about Alex's suspicions. Not until she had more proof, and maybe not ever. Michael was her friend, but he was also her boss, and she doubted he'd want to put the network in such a vulnerable position.

Which would happen if she did as Alex suggested and confronted Jason Treffen on live television.

Just the thought made her palms sweat. *Madness.* Her career would be wrecked, her show taken away. She could be blacklisted from working on television ever again.

And all for what?

"You are going to sign that thing, though, right?" Michael, asked and Chelsea glanced at the sheet of questions crumpled in the bin.

"I'm not sure."

"He won't do the interview if you don't sign that agreement."

She shrugged, tried to keep it light. "Maybe we can come to an understanding."

"You think?"

Chelsea smiled at the skepticism in Michael's tone even though she still felt queasy inside. "Probably not, but I can try. We still have five weeks."

"If anyone can do it, you can."

Coming from someone else, the words might have been so much hot air, but Chelsea knew Michael meant it. He'd taken a chance on her before. When he'd discovered her she'd been an unpaid intern at AMI, twenty-two years old, working night shifts at a seedy diner in Hell's Kitchen to pay her way. One evening when the regular anchormen of the nightly news had left, she'd sneaked in front of the cameras, practiced her own delivery. And Michael, strolling through the empty studio, had seen her.

He'd watched her for a good while without saying anything, and when he'd finally stepped out of the shadows Chelsea hadn't apologized for her little show. She'd just stared him down, and he'd laughed and offered her a bit piece on the morning news.

It had been her start, and six years later she'd started *Chat with Chelsea;* within a year it had been an outrageous success.

And everyone assumed it was all because she'd slept with Michael. She'd joked with him once that she wasn't that good of a lay, but he'd just shaken his head sadly. Sometimes Michael was too much of a softie; he thought more of her than he should. But then he didn't know her whole story; no one did.

A few people knew bits and pieces. Louise knew about her childhood; Brian Taylor knew about—and had orchestrated—her downfall at the local news station in Huntsville, Alabama, where she'd started as a weather girl at just nineteen years old. Michael knew she'd been desperate and driven and that there had been a man she was trying to forget. The surgeons at the Huntsville Hospital knew how badly broken her nose had been, and how she'd almost died of blood loss from the stab wound that had nearly severed her breast.

But no one, no one but her, knew the whole, sordid story. *Did Treffen?*

Four days after he'd invited Chelsea to the circus, Alex went to meet Austin and Hunter at a bar. Hunter had left him a message, saying he had someone for them to meet. Someone who could help them bring down Treffen, apparently, although Alex had no idea who that could be.

Austin was sitting at a private table, scrolling through messages on his phone, as Alex entered the bar.

"So who exactly does Hunter want us to meet?" Alex asked as he sat across from Austin.

Austin shrugged. "I don't know. Someone important, apparently." He glanced up from his phone. "How are things going with Chelsea Maxwell?"

"Fine."

"Can you give me a little more detail?"

Alex ordered a whisky and tried to keep his voice even. He knew Austin wanted results, just like he did. "She's on board. She just needs evidence."

"What about the photos of Sarah?"

Alex gritted his teeth. He really didn't want to show those photos to Chelsea, or anyone. "I'm talking about a primary source. Someone who can back up what Katy has said—"

"Katy's word isn't enough?"

Alex held up a hand. "Easy, Austin. I know you two are playing happy families now, but we've got to be professional about this. Careful. The last thing any of us need is a lawsuit, and any charges against your father dismissed."

Austin relaxed slightly and nodded. "I know. And we're more than playing, Alex," he added, his mouth quirking in a smile. "I love her."

Alex just about kept from rolling his eyes. "I know. I'm happy for you."

"Here's Hunter."

He turned to see Hunter walk in with an elegant, professional-looking brunette. Her cool, glossy exterior reminded him a bit of Chelsea. She came forward, shaking hands with both of them. "Alex, Austin. I'm Zoe Brook."

"The PR queen of New York," Alex said, and wondered why Hunter was bringing the woman who was meant to rehabilitate his reputation. What did Zoe Brook have to do with Treffen?

Austin seemed to be wondering the same thing. "What are we doing here? If you'll excuse my impatience."

"Zoe," Hunter said, and Alex felt a jolt at the look he saw in Hunter's eyes as he gazed at Zoe. He looked like she could do no wrong. Like he...loved her.

Which made him, absurdly, think of Chelsea. Yet Chelsea was the very last person he'd think about when it came to love. He might have asked her on a date, might want to explore this surprising intensity between them, but it wasn't love. It wasn't even a relationship. It was sex—and the circus.

Alex still couldn't untangle how much of how he acted toward Chelsea was motivated by his plan to get her on his side against Treffen and how much just *was*. She fascinated him. She made him laugh with her hard-ass attitude and whip-smart wisecracks. And she'd quite literally rocked his world when she'd taken him to bed.

But beyond that...

"Your father is a pimp," Zoe told Austin, who stiffened even though they all knew that sordid truth. She turned to encompass both of them with her steely gaze. "Hunter assures me that he was never one of the many johns that

Jason pandered to and then blackmailed." Her eyes narrowed. "What about you two?"

Alex felt a sudden jolt of recognition. Zoe, he could tell, was speaking from experience. *Just like Sarah.* He found it almost incredible to believe this woman had been one of Jason's victims, but he also saw the weary, embittered experience in her eyes. Here was his primary source...the source Chelsea needed.

"You need to tell this story, Zoe," he said, trying to keep the desperation from his voice. "The call girls. The blackmail of all the clients. The world needs to know the truth about him."

"I agree," Zoe answered coolly. "But I can't do that."

Frustration bit deep. "You must know that first-person witness, victim testimony—"

"I was his victim for too long," Zoe answered flatly. "I won't do that again."

So he'd been right. She'd been one of the call girls, just like Sarah. She was exactly what he needed. What Chelsea needed. "I understand where you're coming from," he said carefully.

"Do you think so?" She sounded amused, as if they were at a garden party and he'd just shared an anecdote.

"I wish I could impress upon you—" Alex began, and Hunter slashed his hand through the air.

"Enough." Hunter's voice was implacable, and Alex knew he wouldn't get anywhere with either Hunter or Zoe tonight. But he had a source. If he could convince Zoe...he could convince Chelsea.

He could bring down Treffen.

For now he nodded, pretended to accept Hunter's defense of the woman he clearly cared about.

"Why don't we talk strategy?" Zoe said, sounding as calm and composed as always. Alex nodded again. Fine. They could brainstorm about how to get Treffen out of his law firm, but it didn't solve his problem.

For that, he knew now, he needed Zoe. He just had to wait for the right moment to convince her to cooperate.

He was still thinking about Zoe—and Chelsea—later that night as he let himself into his converted warehouse apartment on the Hudson River. Moonlight streamed through the windows and he stood in front of a series of photographs Sarah had taken over the years; she'd been an amateur photographer with a real, raw talent.

It wasn't until after her death that he'd seen how the subject material had become darker and grimmer. In college she'd snapped photos of children and dogs, cherry blossoms in Boston Common. A few years later the photos had become more contemplative, candids of people alone, hunched over a cup of coffee or wandering through Central Park. And the final photos before her death had caught moments of pain and even anguish: a child crying in the park, a homeless woman huddled on the street, her scarred arms tight around her knees.

Alex hadn't really noticed; the truth was he'd barely looked at her photographs at all, until after her death.

But looking at them now—he'd blown up and framed some of her better photographs and hung them in his apartment—he felt as if she'd been trying to send a message, even a subconscious one.

Just like these people, I'm trapped and lonely and afraid. Help me.

Alex closed his eyes against the rush of emotion he'd never wanted to feel. He could help her now. He could make her death right in the only way left to him: by ruining Treffen.

And Chelsea would help him accomplish that. She had to...no matter what the cost to her, or him...or them.

Chapter Eight

What did she wear to the circus? Her usual safe wardrobe of pencil skirts and crisp blouses was hardly appropriate, but Chelsea didn't do casual, at least not outside the privacy of her own apartment.

With the shades drawn and the door bolted she might put on her one pair of scruffy pajamas, but only if she was feeling particularly low. Even when she was alone she kept herself coiffed; it felt like armor. She had a pair of gray satin men's pajamas that were elegant enough to wear to a cocktail party.

But she couldn't wear them to the circus.

She finally decided on a pair of skinny jeans, a cashmere turtleneck in cherry red and a pair of knee-high chocolate leather boots. It was an outfit a stylist had pulled together for her for an appearance she'd made in Central Park last autumn, for the charity that supported abused kids. She hadn't worn it since.

She swept her hair up into a loose ponytail and kept her makeup low-key: eyeliner, bronzer, a little blush, a little lip gloss. Just the basics.

Hard to believe she'd once used enough face paint to

rival a clown, sprayed her hair to hell and squeezed herself into cheap, too-tight business suits of pink polyester. She'd been a different person then. She hadn't even been a person; she'd been a shell, empty inside, the walking dead.

And you're still empty inside. You just dress it up a little bit better.

She pushed the thought away, but it still lingered there, like a cloud on the horizon of her mind, threatening to darken her whole day and ruin her evening with Alex.

She'd been going back and forth about this date all week. Three times she'd picked up her phone to text Alex and cancel it, the coward's way out. But she hadn't, because in the end she wanted to go too much. Wanted to see him, flirt, have fun.

When had she last had fun *really,* and not just acted like she was?

When had she last been happy?

Forget the penthouse apartment, the high-flying career, the money and the fame and the all-out success. She wasn't happy, and she hadn't been for a long time.

The realization wasn't even a surprise, but it was still aggravating. She'd worked so hard and long, sacrificed so much, for *this?* For this loneliness and emptiness and fear?

Well at least for tonight she'd choose happiness. She'd choose Alex and flirting and clowns and to hell with everything else.

The phone from the lobby rang, and a few minutes later Alex was in her apartment. Dressed in faded jeans and a button-down shirt with a gray T-shirt underneath, his hair a little mussed and his jaw glinting with a sexy five o'clock shadow, he quite literally took her breath away.

Stripped her bare, and he hadn't even touched her. Hadn't even said hello.

"Hello, Chelsea."

And there it was, the husky, knowing murmur that brought a flush to her face and a flare of heat firing her insides.

"Hello." She cleared her throat, hating that she felt nervous. Hating that Alex knew, at least if his slow smile was anything to go by.

She reached for her coat, a bright red Puffa jacket that she'd bought to go with the whole ensemble. *Chelsea Maxwell Does Casual.*

"I like the red," Alex said as she stabbed at the buttons for the elevator. "Makes a change from all the black and white."

She eyed him sideways. "I wear the occasional gray item, thank you very much. And once in a while a very pale pink."

"A soothing palette of colors," Alex assured her. The elevator doors opened and they both stepped inside. "But I prefer the red."

Chelsea didn't answer and they didn't speak until they were out in the street, the air still breath-stealingly cold, and sharp enough to sting her face.

She glanced at the double-decker bus double-parked outside her building. "Seriously?"

"It's totally awesome," Alex answered cheerfully. "You wouldn't believe what it looks like inside."

"A tricked out bus?"

"Come and see."

He put his hand on the small of her back as he led her

toward the bus; it felt weirdly normal. This was what healthy, emotionally well-adjusted people did all the time. They dated. They joked around. They touched each other. She'd never done any of it—it was sex or nothing for her, and she'd been under the impression that Alex was the same.

But tonight was going to be different.

"Goodness," she murmured as she stepped onto the bus. The seats had been taken out and replaced with sofas in screamingly vivid shades of red and purple, and the spiral stairs leading to the top level had been painted in a fluorescent tie–dye pattern.

She watched as Alex poured two glasses of champagne from the bottle chilling in a bucket, and accepted one after only a brief pause. She didn't normally drink, but tonight she felt like relaxing her rigid rules just a little bit, for just a little while.

And then will you go back to the woman you were? Is that what you want? One night of being someone else, of being loose and free and maybe even happy, and then back to icy, in-control Chelsea Maxwell?

She raised her glass. "Cheers," she said, and took a long swallow.

Alex clinked his glass with hers. "To a fantastic, one-of-a-kind evening," he said. "Let's go upstairs."

As she started up the stairs to the open deck, Alex's hand on her lower back once again, Chelsea wondered just what he'd meant by *one-of-a-kind.* Not to be repeated? No promises? She should have felt reassured, not this worrying flicker of disappointment.

Alex had told her he was asking her for a single date,

no more. He'd explained this wasn't his usual MO. *I'm not done.* Which implied, Chelsea realized, that he would be done one day, perhaps one day soon. Perhaps tonight.

Not exactly words to set a girl's heart to fluttering, but then she wasn't looking for fairy-tale flutters, anyway.

Was she?

No, of course not. Just like Alex, she wasn't done, even if she'd told herself she wanted to be. And just like Alex, she would be finished with this—him—one day. One day soon.

As they emerged onto the open top level of the bus, the cold air hit them with a rush. The bus was travelling slowly, but the wind still made Chelsea's cheeks sting.

"Probably better in summer," Alex murmured as he guided her to the railing. "But I couldn't wait."

"Manhattan is beautiful no matter what the season," Chelsea answered lightly, "but we *will* freeze our asses off."

They'd crossed the park and were now driving down Fifth Avenue, the upscale boutiques sparkling with lights. Chelsea leaned her elbows on the railing and took a sip of champagne.

"I've never seen the city from the top of a double-decker bus."

"You never did the tourist thing, hopped on one of those Big Apple buses?"

"Nope."

"I bet you haven't been up the Statue of Liberty or the Empire State Building either," Alex said, and she shook her head. He shook his head right back at her, all mock sorrow that made her want to smile. "Top of the Rock? Ellis Island?"

"No and no."

"Times Square?"

"I try to avoid it."

"I bet you've done the classy stuff. The MoMA, the Met."

"Only for parties." Actually, that wasn't true. When she'd first moved to New York, broke and with her scars still red and raw, she'd spent a lot of time in the Met's Chinese Garden. It had been an oasis of calm order in the seething chaos of the city, of her life. She still went there sometimes, when she needed to steady herself.

"I see I have a mission," Alex said. He leaned his arms on the railing next to her, his shoulder gently nudging hers. "Show you the tourist's version of New York."

"And doesn't that sound appealing." Although funnily enough, it did. Taking in all the silly sights with Alex. Laughing, teasing, joking around. Things she never did, but suddenly wanted to…with him. "Have you done all the touristy things?" she asked. "It seems like most New Yorkers haven't."

"I did a school trip to the Statue of Liberty as a kid."

"That hardly counts."

"Why not? I did it. Climbed all those stairs."

"With all your big talk I thought you were hitting Ellis Island every other weekend."

"Maybe I will, now that I've got a reason." He'd turned to look at her and as Chelsea gazed back the moment felt suspended, separate from the city rushing coldly by, from everything but the magnetic connection of their joined gazes.

She looked away first.

"So," she said, keeping her tone light, ignoring that moment, "have you ever left the city? Lived somewhere else?"

"Four years in Boston for college, but that's it."

"That's right. Harvard."

"Yep."

"With Treffen's son."

"Yes."

"How did Treffen's son find out about him? Assuming, of course, that there was something to find out?"

"You still doubt me?"

"Not exactly." She gazed at him frankly. "I don't know what to think, Alex. It's a lot to take in. To believe. And honestly, I'd rather not believe it."

"I can understand that."

"So? How did he find out?"

Alex straightened, stared out at Fifth Avenue as the Empire State Building loomed over them lit up like a roman candle against a starless city sky. "A sister of one of the victims came forward." His hands tightened on the bus railing briefly. "I know we have to talk about Treffen," he said slowly. "And I get that you need proof. I might even have it for you, shortly. But tonight—let's have tonight just be about this. Let's just enjoy the circus."

Her heart somersaulted in her chest, painful and amazing at the same time. "You really have a thing about the circus, huh?"

He smiled crookedly. "I never went as a kid."

And somehow that admission made her heart ache and yearn. For what, she didn't know. Wasn't ready to consider. "Okay," she said quietly. "No more talk about Treffen tonight."

He smiled and then turned to look back out at the glittering night. "So, you're from Alabama. Did you grow up on one of those big old Southern plantations?"

Not even close, but she wasn't about to admit it. "I had a far more average childhood."

"A happy upbringing in the South," Alex answered, and it took Chelsea a moment to realize he was quoting from her bland and entirely fictitious bio.

"I heard you talk about your dad on one of your shows," Alex said. "I was a little jealous, I have to admit. He sounds like a great guy."

Chelsea froze. Occasionally she referenced her fake past on her show; it was unavoidable when stars asked questions and in any case it was good for ratings. She'd made up a father for herself, a man who had taken her to football games and carried her on her shoulders. She had a mom too who worked part-time as a lawyer but had stayed at home and done the whole baking cookies thing when the kids were little.

Occasionally reporters had tried to dig, to find her fake family, and a couple of times they'd tried to create scandal, running headlines about how she was estranged from her beloved parents. Which, she supposed, was sort of the truth.

"I didn't think you really watched my show," she said after a moment, when her brain finally started functioning again.

Alex shrugged. "I watched a couple of episodes online."

"And why were you jealous?"

"My dad was never in the picture. I don't even know who he was." Alex looked away, and Chelsea had the sense he'd said more than he wished to. Emotion burned in her chest and words clogged in her throat, because she wanted to tell him she knew how he felt, but of course she couldn't.

He thought she'd had a kind, loving dad, when in fact just like him she'd never known her father. Never even known his name. "I'm sorry," she said quietly, and Alex just shrugged again.

"You don't really miss what you've never had, right?"

"I think you do," Chelsea answered. She'd certainly missed the childhood she'd never known growing up. A house. A backyard with a swing. A dad. Safety and happiness, the freedom to worry about little things, like what you got in your lunch box or how hard your homework was.

Not whether you'd have any food at all, or if your mother's boyfriend would wake you up in the middle of the night with his hand under your nightgown.

"Maybe you do," Alex agreed. "I used to imagine my dad surprising us, just appearing one day, like it was all a big mistake that he wasn't around." He shook his head. "That was never going to happen."

"Why not?" Chelsea asked quietly, even though she could guess. Why did any father walk out on his wife and kids? Because he just wasn't interested. Because it—they— weren't enough reason for him to stay.

"He was married to someone else."

Chelsea blinked. "Oh."

"Yeah." Alex gave her a twisted smile, his teeth gleaming in the darkness. "My mother didn't want to tell me. She didn't talk about him at all, but when I was about fourteen and a little too full of myself, I pushed and pushed her and she broke. She told me he was some executive at the office where she cleaned nights. They had a brief fling, and she was deeply ashamed. It wasn't until later..." He stopped then, shaking his head, and even in the dark evening Chelsea could see how his expression was shuttered.

Normally she wouldn't pry. She'd made it her policy not to ask personal questions off the pink sofa, because she didn't want them asked back. But she was curious now, and not just with the idle curiosity of an acquaintance, but with the deep, burning need to understand another person. She wanted to know what had made Alex close in on himself, and how she could open him up again.

What a joke. She did not have the first clue about any of this. Intimacy. Honesty. Understanding. Still, she felt a need, frightening as it was, to try. "What happened later?" she asked quietly. "Did your mother tell you something else?"

"No, not really." The words came slowly, offered up with reluctance, but still offered. "But something about the way she'd talked about him—the disgust—made me wonder if it hadn't been a fling, after all. If she'd been forced."

Chelsea went cold. "How awful," she said softly. "I'm sorry."

"I've never asked her. I visit her every couple of months but we never talk about that." He turned to her with a smile that was both wry and sorrowful. "So you can see how your dad taking you to football games seems like a pretty sweet deal to me. The whole normal childhood thing."

Which she hadn't had, not remotely, yet she could

hardly tell Alex that now. Her whole existence was based on lies, because that was the only way she'd known how to leave the past behind. Now she felt the burden of deception weigh heavily on her. She'd never been fully honest with anyone, never been tempted to try, not even with Michael.

As Alex held her gaze, his smile still a little wry and somehow sad, she *was* tempted. She wanted to tell him that her mother had never spoken about her father, but she and Louise had found a photo in their mother's underwear drawer of a man with sandy hair and the same gray-green eyes that they had. He'd looked so friendly, with an easy, open smile, and it had made her wonder what she'd done to make him leave.

She forced the words, as well as the impulse, down. There was no point in being honest with Alex, because this wasn't going anywhere. It was one date, maybe some sex.

Alex hadn't offered anything else, and she wasn't looking, not really, not even if in these unguarded moments she felt everything in her yearn for something more. Something deeper.

"I suppose it's easy to take what seems normal for granted," she said, although this was pure conjecture. She'd never known normal. "It's freezing out here. Maybe we should go back down."

"Wait."

Chelsea stilled as Alex put his arm around her in a gesture that, in its casual spontaneity, felt weirdly more intimate than some of the other things they'd done. "Look."

He pointed into the darkness, and Chelsea turned to see the Statue of Liberty illuminated in the harbor, her torch-bearing arm held proudly aloft.

"I *will* take you there," Alex said, and for a second, no more, Chelsea let her head rest against his shoulder, enjoying the weight of his arm around her, the shelter of his embrace.

"I consider myself warned."

Laughing softly, he led her back downstairs.

They drank another glass of champagne as the bus headed back uptown to the circus at Lincoln Center, and Chelsea started to feel pleasantly relaxed and a little dizzy. She normally abstained from alcohol, and two glasses of champagne pretty much went to her head.

Which made this evening feel a little more reckless with possibility.

"I could get used to this kind of travel," she said as she stretched out on the purple sofa. Alex grinned.

"Makes for a change from pink, doesn't it."

She crossed her arms above her head and her feet at the ankles in an affected pose of nonchalance. "It certainly does. Why did you bid on a Family Fun Evening, anyway?"

Alex came to sit beside her, lifting her stretched-out legs and plopping them back on his lap. "Because like I said, I never got to go to the circus as a kid."

"I've never gone either, actually," Chelsea said, and Alex arched an eyebrow.

"That surprises me, just a little. Based on your bio, I would have assumed you'd had every classic childhood experience."

Chelsea just shrugged. So she might have overdone it a bit with the false bio, cramming in every wished-for detail of her lonely childhood.

Alex stroked one hand up her jean-clad leg, letting his fingers curl under her knee. He didn't even seem aware he was doing it, his brow furrowed and his mind clearly on something else, but something about the way he touched her, with such thoughtless ease, made Chelsea yearn all the more.

"When were you in that car accident?" he asked, jolting Chelsea right out of her moment of quiet pleasure.

She almost asked *what car accident* before she remembered that particular lie. No one ever saw her scar, so it hadn't tripped quite as easily from her tongue in the telling, and maintaining it was just as hard now.

"Umm…ten years ago."

"It must have been a pretty serious accident."

"It was." Accident was one way of looking at it, she supposed. Assault would be another. And utterly idiotic on her part for letting it get to that point still a third.

Alex lifted his head to meet her gaze, his own liquid and dark. "You don't like to talk about it."

She arched her eyebrows. "It shows?"

"A little bit," he acknowledged wryly. "Sorry. I'm not trying to pry."

Yes, you are, Chelsea thought. *You've been prying your way into my life and even into my heart since the moment I met you.*

She didn't say anything though, and a moment later the bus came to a halt in front of Lincoln Center and the driver turned back to them with a smile.

"End of the line, I'm afraid."

"Time to see some clowns," Alex said with a grin, and he reached for her hand.

It felt entirely natural for Chelsea to take it, to let

his strong brown fingers encase hers as he pulled her to her feet.

She was still enveloped in that fragile little bubble of happiness as Alex led her into the big top erected on Lincoln Center's plaza. Crowds milled and pressed around her, and she saw half a dozen sharp, curious glances, and knew she'd been recognized.

She was a celebrity, far more recognizable than Alex, whose work was almost always behind the scenes. She was used to being stared at, but usually it was from behind the tinted window of her own limo, or at least the protection of her usual business or evening wear ensemble, so she looked and felt distant, untouchable. *Safe.*

Now, even with Alex's hand threaded through hers, his presence steady and sure right beside her, she felt that terrible yet familiar lurch of panic. Her heart started beating hard and spots danced before her eyes. Perfect, an oncoming anxiety attack and she knew from experience how hard it was to suppress it. Her palms went to pins and needles and she had to remind herself to breathe. *In. Out.*

Even so she felt her vision start to tunnel, her head go light. She could *not* faint. Not here, not in the middle of everything, with Alex by her side. Another breath, but suddenly it was so hard to breathe, like taking treacle into her lungs. Her head felt like a balloon floating on a string and her heart still pounded so hard it hurt.

"Chelsea?" Alex tugged on her hand, his voice rich with amusement. "Come on, slowpoke. I really don't want to miss the clowns." He turned to face her for she'd stopped moving; she felt as if she couldn't move, as if her feet were glued to the floor. "Chelsea," he said again, quietly, because it must have been obvious that something was wrong.

She tried to open her mouth to speak, but nothing came out. She wasn't even sure if she managed to get her mouth open.

Then she felt Alex's arm around her waist, warm and strong, and gently he pulled her to his side. "Come on, Chelsea," he murmured and with his arm still around her he guided her to their seats in the front row, the circus ring just meters away.

She sat down jerkily, and he slid in next to her, his warm thigh nudging hers. The simple touch brought her a much-needed comfort and she dragged a deep breath into her lungs, felt her vision return and with relief she knew the attack was receding.

But it was still too late to pretend it hadn't happened.

Alex didn't speak for a moment, and Chelsea stared blindly at the program someone had placed in her lap. Finally he spoke.

"You told me you weren't afraid of clowns," he said, all mock accusation, and relief rushed through her, cold and sweet, that he was going to make light of it. She couldn't have handled anything else, and maybe he couldn't have either.

"Do you think I'd ever actually admit it?" she joked back, and her voice thankfully sounded normal.

"Have you considered therapy?"

"I thought coming face-to-face with my fear might help."

Alex's eyes glinted amusement, and maybe something more. Something like admiration. "Clearly it hasn't. But considering your condition, it was brave of you to agree to come with me to the circus."

There was, Chelsea thought, just a little too much truth to this silly conversation, and it had nothing to do with clowns.

"It's called coulrophobia, you know," Alex said, and his voice was quiet now, thoughtful. "The official term for a fear of clowns."

"I didn't know there was an official term."

"Quite a few people legitimately suffer from it," he answered, and then turned to face her directly, his gaze holding no amusement at all. "But not you."

No, not her. She was afraid of a lot of things—too many—but clowns wasn't one of them. She took a deep breath and opened her mouth to say something—but what? What could she say, how could she begin? There was so much he didn't know. So much she didn't want him to know, wasn't ready to admit even if part of her craved the release of all those secrets, the true and total revealing of herself.

Alex was silent for a long moment, and Chelsea stared at her program again, the lurid colors of the clowns and costumes on the cover blurring. "You know," he finally said, his voice quiet and yet conversational, "I could find out whatever secrets you're hiding. Probably in a matter of minutes."

Chelsea's insides iced. "I'm sure you could, considering you have your own news network," she answered after a moment, when she trusted herself to speak and sound normal. She turned to him, her eyebrows raised. "Is that a threat?"

His gaze felt like a searchlight moving over her face, seeing into her soul. "No, it's a promise. Because I won't go digging, Chelsea. I don't want to find out about you that way. I'll wait until you trust me enough to tell me."

That quiet promise reverberated right through her. She hadn't known he'd even wanted her trust, her secrets. And the fact that he did still scared her near senseless. She swallowed, looked away. "I thought this was just a date, Alex. Sex and the circus." She turned to look back at him, raised her eyebrows again, this time in challenge. "Right?"

Alex frowned, a sudden confusion shadowing those golden eyes. "Yes," he answered slowly. "Right."

The lights dimmed then and the show started. Alex stared straight ahead as the ringmaster came into the circus ring with a flourish and a thundering of applause.

He barely noticed. His brain reeled and raced. Why on earth had he said that? Meant it?

This whole evening had been an aberration. A date. Flirting. Talking about his mother. His dad. He didn't do any of it, ever, and yet ever since he'd asked Chelsea to go out with him he'd been breaking all his rules. Acting on instinct, out of a need he didn't even want to name.

Because it felt so good to be real with someone, to *say* things. Because Chelsea was like him in so many ways: tough, strong, independent, isolated.

And yet she also had panic attacks. Secrets. Did he really want to deal with all that?

He blinked the circus back into focus and then turned to Chelsea, half expecting her to be rolling her eyes at all the over-the-top antics of the performers. He'd bid on the tickets because he'd always wanted to go to the circus as a kid, and he'd wanted to share that experience with Chelsea even if it was ridiculous and corny.

What he hadn't expected was for her to be enthralled. There was no other word for her expression as she leaned forward in her seat, her hands clasped to her face, her eyes like silver stars as she watched two acrobats perform a half dozen backflips in a row. He almost laughed aloud when she gasped and put her hands to her throat when a trapeze artist did a death-defying twirl through the air. And she laughed aloud, a crystal peal, when the clowns started running dizzy circles around the mat, making Alex's heart swell.

Hell, he wasn't even paying attention to the clowns or the acrobats. The far more interesting show was the play of honest emotions across Chelsea's face. So much of her was artifice, he realized, and when he got glimpses of the real woman beneath the talk show hostess mask, it made him want to know her even more.

It also made him want to touch her. To draw her onto his lap and lose himself in her softness—for a woman who was bent on making the world think she was hard, Chelsea Maxwell could be almost unbearably soft.

"So," he said when the lights finally came on and she rose, blinking, from her seat. "You like the circus."

It was a statement, because her enjoyment had been so wonderfully obvious, and for a moment the magic still had her. Everything about her was flushed and soft and pretty; her hair fell in curling tendrils about her face, her rosy lips were slightly parted and her eyes still sparkled.

"I loved it," she admitted it with a little laugh. "Who knew?"

"I certainly didn't," Alex answered as he slid his arm around her waist. "But then there are a lot of things I don't know about you."

She shook her head, and just like that the doors swung shut and the walls came down and Chelsea Maxwell was back to doing what Alex was fast realizing she did best.

Hiding.

The more time he spent with her, the more Alex believed a real and warm heart beat beneath the layers of ice, a warm and even generous woman hid underneath the bad-ass attitude.

But just what did he intend to do with that information?

A limo was waiting for them outside Lincoln Center. Chelsea turned to him with an arched eyebrow. "No more double-decker bus?"

"One way only, I'm afraid. But in any case I can't make love to you on a bus, with the driver right there. I do have my limits."

Heat flared in her eyes as she slid into the luxurious leather interior. "And who says you're going to make love to me in a limo?"

Alex sat next to her, his denim-clad thigh nudging hers, and the driver closed the door. "Is that a challenge?"

Color touched her cheekbones, which just made him ache all the more to touch her. Hold her. Bury himself so deep inside her he forgot his own name. "Merely a question."

"Then I'll answer it," Alex answered softly. "*I* say." He wrapped one hand around the back of her neck, his fingers curling around warm, delectable skin, and drew her slowly toward him. He felt her resistance leach out of her as he brushed his lips against hers in a soft hello of a kiss. Heard her give the tiniest and most telling of sighs as her body relaxed and she leaned a little bit into that kiss, lips parting under his in this small surrender.

In response he merely brushed his lips against hers again, once, twice, even though his libido was begging him to go deep and hard and fast. Last time their kisses had been about control, about losing it or having it or forgetting it altogether. There was no balance of power in this kiss; there was only sweetness.

And sweetness must have been what Chelsea wanted because he felt her hands come up to his shoulders, drawing him closer as she steadied herself on the seat, lips touching his, her breath coming just a little bit faster. But he still set the pace and she let him as he continued to kiss her softly, taking his time, savoring the feel and taste of her. Delicious.

He brought his hand up to cradle her face, his thumb grazing the corner of the mouth he still kissed. His fingers slid up the softness of her cheek and he paused because his fingertip touched dampness. When he drew away he saw a single tear sparkling on her eyelash like a dew drop.

What the hell?

Chelsea quickly averted her face, bringing her hands up to her face and flicking at the corners of her eyes as if she could deny that one treacherous little tear.

And Alex didn't say anything, didn't make light of it or mention it at all, because her tear terrified him. What the hell was he doing, trying to reach this woman? Trying to *affect* her?

"I thought we were going to get it on," Chelsea said, her voice just a little bit clogged. "Wasn't that the idea, Alex?" Sharper now, a demand. "Because we're halfway back to my place."

"Then we'd better not waste another minute," Alex answered and he pulled her onto his lap. He kissed her deeply then, and she responded, their tongues tangling as he felt a moan rise in his throat. He slid a hand down the front of her jeans and pressed against her. She pressed back in response, causing heat to rise in his groin.

"This isn't going to be easy," he murmured, and she pulled back, arched an eyebrow, all haughty challenge.

"I don't do easy."

He flicked open the button of her jeans and tugged at the zip. "And I wouldn't have it any other way."

It wasn't easy. But it was fast and hard and hot, and most of all it was mindless. After that tear, Alex knew he needed that now. He was pretty sure Chelsea did, too.

There was safety in wildness, a comfort in going hot and deep. You didn't need to think then. You didn't have the brain space to wonder or care.

You just felt, and it felt good.

Afterward Chelsea rested her damp forehead against his shoulder, let out a shuddering breath. Her jeans were caught around her hips, as were Alex's. The limo pulled up to her building and Alex quickly reached over to press the lock button. Chelsea laughed; he could feel it reverberate through her as well as him, pressed as she was against him.

"Quick thinking."

"I'm good like that."

"Yes, you are. Condom in the back pocket, I noticed. Very prepared."

"I'm a regular Boy Scout."

"Thanks for that," she said, and suddenly, stupidly, he felt cheap. He, the master of the one-night stand, felt like a gigolo. She'd cheapened something that had already been cheap, or so they'd both believed. Sex and the circus.

Right.

Chelsea hit the unlock button and Alex knew he should say something. Ask her to stay. Pull her back toward him. But the memory of that single tear kept him silent, because he didn't know what to do with a Chelsea who cried when he kissed her. Who had secrets that must hurt, secrets that would make her someone other than the strong woman with the bad-ass attitude. Secrets that made this complicated and emotional and intimate, and he didn't play that way.

And so he stayed silent as she opened the door and slid out of the limo, shooting him one fleeting glance over her shoulder.

"Goodbye, Alex," she said, and he heard the finality in her tone, saw it in her face. Felt it in himself.

Time to pull back. Time to focus on Treffen, and not on this pseudo-relationship they'd both been flirting with.

A sad little smile twisted her lips as she closed the door and Alex just watched. Chelsea might have wanted to leave, but he'd let her go.

Chapter Nine

She never cried. She didn't *do* tears, and certainly not all because of a kiss.

She hadn't cried when she'd had her first awful, slobbery kiss at all of six years old. Her mother's boyfriend, Bo Fielding, had become a bit too friendly. She hadn't cried for a whole lot of dispiriting kisses throughout her teens, when she'd kept trying to prove to forgettable boys that she was worth loving. And she hadn't cried when Brian Taylor had kissed her and bit her lip so hard she'd needed stitches.

She wasn't going to cry now, not because Alex had kissed her so softly and tenderly it had reminded her she had a heart and it *ached*.

She'd never, not once, been kissed like that before.

Blinking hard, Chelsea stepped into the elevator and took several steadying breaths as it soared toward her penthouse. She kept telling herself to be careful, to stay hidden, but then Alex started stripping away her layers without even realizing it. And she had a feeling he didn't even want to; he hadn't exactly been thrilled or even touched by her tears.

No, Alex wanted simple, just like she did. The trouble was she didn't seem capable of simple anymore. Something had opened up inside her and she didn't know how to stuff it back down again, pretend it didn't exist.

So here she was again, running back to her bolt-hole in the sky, knowing that Alex had managed to peel away another layer, touch her soul a little more deeply.

And she didn't think she would ever run far or fast enough to escape that.

But she'd try.

She spent the night working on her laptop, sketching out new interview questions and ideas, because sleep at the best of times was a passing acquaintance, and tonight she knew it would be a stranger.

She worked hard and long to keep from thinking about Alex, from reliving that kiss again and remembering how it had felt as if a hand was being plunged right down inside her, grabbing her heart and squeezing it hard.

It wasn't a comfortable feeling, that. But it sure as hell woke you up. Made you feel alive.

And she hadn't, Chelsea acknowledged, felt that alive, or alive at all, in a very long time.

Around 3 a.m. when her eyes became gritty and she'd bolted her third cup of black coffee she typed *Jason Treffen* into the internet search box on her web browser.

The usual websites and accolades came up: his ground-breaking work with women's rights through his law firm and charity; photos of him looking debonair and dignified, another shot with his family, a sulky-looking son and a too-pretty daughter, a wife whose smile seemed just a little bit fixed.

Was that just a random moment caught on camera, or something deeper, darker? Did she know about Treffen's side activities?

Chelsea peered closer, zoomed in on Treffen's face and gazed into those blue eyes that were creased in a smile and looked as clear as a summer sky.

Even now she had trouble believing what Alex had said. All right, Treffen had some secrets. Clearly. She hadn't imagined the coldness in his eyes, the implicit threat of revealing her past. She wasn't that paranoid. But plenty of people, even paragons, had secrets. Treffen might have dodged a tax bill, not pimped his employees.

Yet she knew what men were capable of. With so much bad experience behind her she tended to judge most men harshly, and too often she'd been right. Why should Treffen be any different? Michael might have slipped beneath her defenses, just a little, and as for Alex…

It always came back to Alex. Her fingers stilled on the mouse and she stared into space, willing everything in her not just to stop thinking about him, but to forget him.

Forget the touch of his hands on her body, the slide of his lips over hers. And far more difficult, forget how he made her laugh even when she didn't so much as crack a smile. She felt it inside, all the lightening and loosening of her tightly-held self…and if he kept at it, if she let him, she might fall apart completely. She might come apart like so many loose bolts and screws, the Chelsea Maxwell machine, never to come together again.

Why was Alex so determined to wreak his revenge on Treffen, Chelsea wondered. Plenty of terrible things happened in the world, God knew, but Alex seemed to take Treffen personally.

Which made her wonder just what he might have at stake.

She frowned, not liking that Alex had secrets but knowing that he must have them, just like she did. And whether or not it was shoddy journalism, she didn't feel like digging. Didn't want Alex to dig either.

This was about Treffen, and Treffen only.

Three days later she finished filming a show and hurried back to her office to check her mobile yet again for messages. Alex hadn't called. Of course, he hadn't said he would call. She might be expecting some contact over Treffen; after all, they had to work together on this.

She was waiting for that, she told herself. A professional call, not a personal one.

Yeah, right.

Her phone buzzed and Chelsea practically leaped across her office to answer it. It was her sister, and she let out an involuntary sigh as she greeted her.

"Hi, Louise."

Her sister huffed a laugh. "Don't sound so excited."

"Sorry, I was expecting someone else to call."

"Oh? Someone interesting?"

Her sister sounded so hopeful on her account. "Just a work thing," she answered, and Louise let out a little sigh. Chelsea gave a rather brittle laugh. "Sorry to disappoint you."

"I just want you to be happy, Aurora," Louise said quietly, "even if you don't think you deserve to be."

There was so much about that statement that hurt. Chelsea took a deep breath. "My name is Chelsea now."

"I know." Louise was silent for a moment, and Chelsea had a feeling she wanted to say something else. Something she didn't think she could handle.

"So why did you call? We're not meant to have our monthly dinner for another week."

"I thought maybe we could do lunch."

"Lunch? But—"

"I know, it's not part of this routine we've fallen into. A very comfortable routine, for both of us. But I know how I operate, Aur—Chelsea, and I think you're the same way. Another fifteen years could go by and we'd still be meeting for dinner once a month."

And she was fine with that. "So why the change?"

"Because you're my sister, my only living relative that I know about, and I want to be closer to you."

Chelsea didn't think she could handle two people in her life trying to get closer to her. But then, maybe Alex was done with closeness. With her. Maybe he didn't even want her help with Treffen anymore. "Okay," she said after a moment. "I'm free for lunch today. Twelve-thirty okay?"

"Perfect." Louise cleared her throat. "Thanks, Chelsea," she said quietly, and Chelsea thought she heard the ragged note of tears in her sister's voice.

Louise was waiting by the iconic statue of Atlas as Chelsea emerged from AMI's building onto Rockefeller Plaza. The sky was a hard, bright blue and there was just a hint of spring thaw in the air.

"Hello, Louise."

Louise smiled and then to Chelsea's surprise, gave her a

hug. Her arms closed around her sister automatically, even though neither of them were huggy people. At least Chelsea wasn't. She'd assumed Louise was the same.

"What's all this about?" she asked as she stepped away. "Lunch, hugs…I thought you liked comfortable routines."

"I do. Usually. But maybe life's too short to stay comfortable."

"Maybe it's too short not to," Chelsea answered lightly.

"That's how I usually think. But…" Louise stopped, a certain vulnerability shadowing her eyes. "You're my sister, Chelsea. I've spent the last ten years wondering about you, wishing—" She shook her head, her hair flying. "Let's eat."

Wishing what? Chelsea wondered. Wishing things had been different, that they'd been closer? Sometimes she'd wished that, when she'd let herself. Most of the time she didn't give in to the impulse, to the cold sweep of loneliness it caused.

"Let's eat," she agreed.

A short while later they were seated in a deep leather booth at one of the upscale bistros that populated midtown and catered to corporate types.

"So, tell me something exciting that is going on in your life," Louise said. "Since nothing exciting is going on in mine."

"Nothing?" Chelsea sipped her water. "Those women's studies lectures must be pretty high octane, Louise."

Louise rolled her eyes. "Totally. They're almost too much, sometimes."

Chelsea smiled, enjoying this unusual banter with her

sister—at least until Louise dropped the smile and leveled her with a look.

"So tell me what's going on."

"Nothing's going on."

"You seem different."

"Different?" Chelsea raised her eyebrows. "How?" *Why* had she asked that? She interviewed people for a living, for heaven's sake. She knew how to shut down a line of conversation. And yet somehow she was curious about what her sister had noticed.

"I'm not sure. Edgier, somehow, and yet more relaxed at the same time. If that makes sense."

And it sort of did. "I didn't think you knew me that well."

"I knew you growing up, Chelsea," Louise said quietly. "You might have changed quite a bit on the outside, but—"

"Don't." *On the inside you're still the same.* Chelsea shook her head. She so did not need to hear that. "Enough emo," she said and reached for the menu. "Let's order."

She tried to steer the conversation away from her personal life during their meal, on to slightly safer subjects.

"You know, I don't even know where you went to college," Chelsea said as they dug into huge salads.

"There's a lot you don't know about me, or I know about you."

Chelsea speared a tomato. "Well, let's start with where you went to college," she said lightly, her tone faintly repressive. *That, and no more.*

"NYU, here in the city."

"So you've been living in New York a long time?"

"About eight years."

And she'd been here for ten. Amazing to think they'd both left Alabama for the Big Apple, had lived within a few miles of each other without ever knowing it.

"I looked for you, you know," Louise said abruptly. She bit her lip, her gaze sliding away from her.

"And you found me." *Keep it light.*

"No, I mean before."

Chelsea tensed. "When?"

"A couple of years ago. Six, seven? After…well, when I was in a good place."

And what did that mean, Chelsea wondered. She wasn't going to ask. "I'd already changed my name by then," she said and Louise nodded.

"You never told me why you did change your name."

"I told you there was someone in Alabama I'd rather avoid."

"A man."

"Yes—why are you asking all this, Louise?" Her skin prickled and she felt a sudden, terrible lump in her throat. "I thought we agreed to let the past just lie."

"Did we?"

"Maybe not in so many words, but you don't seem all that keen to rake it up. Your personal history. You haven't told me a damn thing about the last fifteen years. All I know is that you went from trailer park trash to tenured professor."

"And you to talk show host and celebrity."

"Thank God we both managed to move on."

Louise nodded slowly, then raised her dark gaze to Chelsea's. "Except sometimes I don't think we really have."

Chelsea shook her head. "Is there something in the water that is making people go all emo and personal lately?"

"So there is something going on in your life," Louise shot back. "Something personal. Some man."

"No—"

"I can tell, Chelsea. I might not know you now, but I knew you when you were six. Ten. Sixteen."

"And I don't want to remember any of that."

"I know."

Chelsea opened her mouth to tell her sister to stop with the interrogation when suddenly she thought, *screw it.* She was so tired of putting people off. Pushing them away. And what did it matter if her sister knew what had happened? Chelsea didn't think she'd condemn or judge her; she certainly wouldn't blab to the tabloids.

And it would feel so good to tell someone a little bit about her life, like lancing a wound.

"Okay, you want the truth?" she said and Louise's gaze widened in surprise even as she nodded.

"Absolutely."

"I met this guy. His name is Alex. He originally sought me out for a—a work thing, but…" She trailed off, not knowing how to explain. How much to say.

"But?"

"It became kind of personal. More personal than I ever expected, or even wanted." Except part of her did want it. A big part. She swallowed hard.

"And?" Louise asked quietly.

"And that's it, really. I think it got too intense for him—I got too intense for him, and he backed off." She swallowed again. "Quickly."

"Have you talked to him about it? About what happened, whatever it was?"

"No."

"Then—"

"It's just as well," Chelsea said abruptly. "I'm not interested in a relationship."

"Why not?"

She just shook her head. Too much water under the bridge.

"What about Michael Agnello?" Louise asked and Chelsea stared.

"What about him?"

"You're close to him." Louise shrugged. "So I'm asking."

"I've never slept with him." Louise nodded, and Chelsea suddenly asked, "Do you believe me?"

Her sister's eyes turned dark with sorrow. "Yes."

"I'm capable of it," Chelsea blurted. Now, *why* had she said that? "Sleeping with someone for a job. I did it before."

"Fifteen years ago we were both desperate," Louise answered calmly. "Desperate people are capable of a lot of things."

"What were you capable of, Lou?" Chelsea asked softly, using the childhood nickname that hadn't crossed her lips in well over a decade.

For a second, no more, Chelsea thought Louise might tell her. Her mouth twisted and her eyes darkened even more and then she shook her head. "We're talking about you. And this guy."

"I want to know about you," Chelsea said, and realized she meant it. Louise shook her head again.

"Another time. Tell me about Alex."

And so she did. She told her about the night in her apartment, leaving out a few salient details, and their one date. She even told her about the tear.

"I never cry," she said, although in that moment she actually felt close to tears yet again. "But when he kissed me like he knew me...almost like he...like he..."

"Loved you?" Louise filled in softly. Chelsea's jaw dropped.

"Don't be ridiculous. We barely know each other. He doesn't know me at all, never mind *love*."

"You're not making sense, Chelsea."

"I don't need to make sense," she snapped. "This has nothing to do with love and all to do with—with—"

Louise raised her eyebrows. "Yes?"

"Oh, just stop." Chelsea sagged back in her seat. "I can't take anymore. I don't talk like this to anyone and there's a reason. It's completely draining."

"I know." She straightened, thankfully brisk now. "So what are you going to do?"

"About what?"

"About Alex. Are you going to call him? See him again?"

"He hasn't called since—"

"What are you, thirteen? Do you have to wait for the boy to call? I don't think so." Chelsea just shook her head and Louise leaned forward, touched her hand. "Look, Chelsea, I get it. This stuff is scary. Putting yourself out there. Letting yourself be rejected."

"I don't see you doing it," Chelsea muttered.

"No, but I wish—I wish I could." She sighed. "We've

both got enough emotional baggage to sink a ship, I know. No dad. Mother one step up from a hooker."

"Louise—"

"And other things." She bit her lip, suddenly looking near tears. Chelsea felt that painful lump of emotion burn in her chest. "Look, life is short, Chelsea. Really short. Do you want to live all alone in your ivory tower of an apartment until you die and no one finds you until your rotting corpse starts to smell?"

"What a lovely image—"

"Seriously, that's what you're looking at." Louise took a breath. "What I'm looking at, if neither of us tries to let someone in."

"And if he doesn't want to be let in?" Chelsea asked, her voice coming out in a tremble although she'd been trying for a snappy comeback.

"You won't know that until you ask him," Louise said simply. "You can't risk your heart and stay safe. It just doesn't work that way."

Chelsea's phone buzzed and she grabbed her bag from the floor by her seat, reached for it, her heart starting to thump. It wasn't Alex. It was a text from Michael, reminding her to sign the form Treffen's lawyer had sent over.

She hadn't even thought about Treffen today. Maybe she should seek Alex out about that. She still needed that evidence; it would at least get her in the same room with Alex. Seeing him again, touching him…

Or maybe she'd just keep it professional. If she could.

"Call him, Chelsea," Louise said, and there was a hint of laughter in her voice now. Chelsea realized she was still staring blankly at her phone. "See him again. You don't have to make a big declaration but give it a chance."

"Chelsea Maxwell is here to see you, Alex."

Alex stilled, his hand resting on the mouse trackpad of his laptop, as his assistant's voice came through his phone's intercom.

Chelsea was here?

His pulse kicked up and anticipation as well as a wary sort of trepidation fired through him. He hadn't called her since she'd left his limo over a week ago now. He'd wanted to, and on several occasions he'd gone so far as to pick up the phone. But then he'd stopped, because he hadn't known what to say. What he felt.

That tear had freaked him out. He'd wanted to shatter Chelsea's icy composure, but not melt it. He hadn't wanted her to *cry*.

Except part of him had wanted to put his lips to that tear and kiss it away. To ask what had caused it and to make her smile again, this time from the heart.

And didn't that freak him out even more.

"Alex?"

Belatedly he realized he hadn't answered his assistant. "Send her in, please."

A few seconds later Chelsea opened the double doors to his penthouse office, closing them behind her with a neat click. She was dressed in classic Chelsea Maxwell style: a narrow black skirt skimming her knees and cinched tight at the waist with a thin patent leather belt and a crisp, pale pink blouse with gray pin stripes. Her hair was pulled back into an elegant coil, her makeup understated yet sexy. Everything about her was sophisticated, polished, cool.

It made Alex want to rise from his desk and take her in his arms. Pop those little pearly buttons on her blouse one by one and yank down the zip of her skirt. It also made him hard, and he remained seated behind his desk.

"Chelsea." He nodded toward her, knowing he was behaving like an ass. They'd had sex. Twice. And more than that, more intimately, they'd actually talked. Shared things. And he'd felt the damp warmth of her single tear on the tip of his thumb.

"So I thought you were going to show me some evidence."

Treffen. She was here because of Treffen. He felt a stupid mix of disappointment and relief, as well as a healthy dose of guilt. He'd texted Hunter several times in an attempt to get closer to Zoe, and left messages with her business asking her to talk. Pretty pathetic attempts to reach her, really. But he'd been focused on Chelsea and what was happening between them.

And that was your mistake.

He might not be able to make Zoe talk, he knew. But he still needed some evidence for Chelsea, and he knew what that had to be. "I do have evidence," he said, his voice as cool as Chelsea's.

"So let's see it." She raised her eyebrows, waiting, everything about her brittle and hard and so different from the woman she'd last been with him. But that was a good thing, Alex reminded himself. This was how they both needed to play it.

"Fine." He took a key from his inside pocket and unlocked the bottom drawer of his desk, withdrew a slim manila folder. He took a deep breath, then flipped it open and handed Chelsea a single photo of Sarah.

Chelsea took it, and Alex watched her face as she gazed down at the photograph. Her face went completely, utterly blank, as if she'd power-washed all the emotion away.

It was a strange reaction, because Alex had stared at the photo too many times and it still made his mouth twist, his bile rise. Sarah, naked, spread-eagled on a bed, her body beautiful and pale, and her eyes full of misery. He looked at the photo and he felt like punching something. Hurting someone.

"Who is this?" she asked after a moment and Alex cleared his throat.

"One of his call girls—"

"Obviously. I mean, who is she? Is she around? Can she tell her story?"

Alex felt his hand clench involuntarily into a fist. "I'm afraid not. But her sister has come forward. She's the one who first approached Austin with information."

Chelsea's eyes narrowed. "And she's willing to speak?"

Alex thought briefly of Katy. "She's angry and determined to find justice."

"But she's still a secondary witness. Is there anyone else?"

"There might be."

Chelsea stared at him hard before shaking her head. "That's all you've got, Alex? Really?"

"Austin confronted his father and he didn't even deny it—"

"Was their conversation recorded?" He shook his head.

"Would Austin be willing to go on live television and confront his father there?"

A pause. "I don't know."

"Then what do you know?" Chelsea demanded and suddenly furious and far too raw, Alex rose from the desk.

"I know that Treffen is a monster who has to be stopped. That he's turned promising young lawyers into women with wrecked lives. All right, yes, I have one photo. One victim who isn't willing to speak—yet. But I know what he's done, Chelsea. I *know*."

She stared at him, and all her icy polish seemed to dissolve right in front of his eyes. Her lips trembled and she pressed them together. "I believe you," she said softly.

That was all it took. All he needed for his own resolve to break. He pushed back his chair, strode around his desk, papers fluttering to the ground. He reached for her, crashed his mouth onto hers. He wanted her too much to be gentle or slow, and in any case that took them both into dangerous territory. She must have felt the same because she met his kiss with a passionate fury of her own, driving her fingers into his hair, pushing against him.

Buttons popped, scattered and bounced across the parquet floor. He swept aside her blouse, cupped her breasts through the thin silk of her camisole. She mewled in the back of her throat and tugged down the zip of his trousers.

The door wasn't even locked, Alex realized hazily as he hoisted her onto his desk. Papers went flying and his laptop was skirting precariously with the edge of the desk, but none of it mattered. Nothing mattered but this. Her. *Them*.

He slid his hands up under her skirt, felt the elastic of her garter and groaned.

"Are you *trying* to drive me crazy?" he muttered against her mouth and in answer she locked her legs around his hips and brought him even closer to her heat and softness. Her skirt tore up the back, the sound like a screech in the room where the only noise had been their own ragged breathing.

He pushed the material up higher so it bunched around her hips. "Chelsea…" he groaned against her mouth, trying to press every part of his body against hers, and then he realized he didn't have a condom.

She felt his hesitation and shifted restlessly under him, arching her hips to bring him into exquisite, aching contact again.

"I don't have a condom," he said, and she let out a groan of her own.

"I thought you were a Boy Scout."

He let out a ragged laugh, everything in him pulsing. "I've never actually had sex in my office before."

"And at this rate you won't ever." She pulled away from him, clambered off the desk. Alex adjusted his own clothes, watching as she took a few steps away from him, her back to him, clearly trying to repair some of the damage they'd both done to her clothes and hair, and realizing within seconds how useless a task that was.

"This skirt was new, you know," she said, her back, now straight and so very taut, still to him.

"I'll buy you another."

"Not much help now." She did the one remaining button on her blouse and turned around to stare at him. He couldn't tell at all what she was feeling, and he shouldn't even care. "I can't go out like this."

"Did you have a coat?"

She rolled her eyes. "In the *foyer*."

"I'll get it."

When he returned Chelsea was standing by the floor-to-ceiling windows overlooking the Statue of Liberty, one hand clutching her ruined blouse together.

Alex's heart turned right over. Or maybe it squeezed, or expanded, or broke. Something happened, and it hurt, because the sight of her standing there, looking so lonely and proud, just about leveled him.

And he was about to hand her her *coat?*

"Chelsea." She turned, and he saw that her face was pale, her expression veiled. "Don't go."

She arched an eyebrow, still proud, still defiant. "And what am I supposed to do? Sit here in these rags while you get on with work?"

"No." He offered a smile, small, tentative. This was all so new. "I can't see you doing that."

"Neither can I."

"Come home with me."

She didn't speak, but he saw her surprise. It flared in her eyes and tensed her body, and still she just looked at him. So he kept speaking, because after he'd said it he realized how much he wanted her to come home with him. Stay with him.

And it had nothing to do with Treffen or revenge.

"Come home with me," he said again. "Back to my place. Right now. I'll leave work."

"Alex..."

"Stay the night."

She stared at him, her face bloodless now, eyes like wide pools, the gray-green of a forest lake.

"Chelsea," he said, and it was a plea. A promise...except he didn't know just what he was promising. How much.

"Okay," she said softly, and Alex's heart did that painful thing again. Squeeze or lurch, leap or soar, it *hurt*.

This was new for both of them. New and strange and completely terrifying. But they were doing it. God help them both, they were doing it.

Chapter Ten

She was breaking another of her rules. In the past ten years she'd never gone back to a man's place. Never put herself in so vulnerable a position. The interactions she'd had were always on her terms, at her place. And she kept a can of pepper spray in her bedside drawer.

Although if she was honest, Chelsea acknowledged as she headed out of the Diaz building onto Hudson Street with Alex, there hadn't been that many men. Certainly not as many as people thought. Just a few forgettable men who had given her a little pleasure and had not got within spitting distance of her heart.

Men who had eased that endless ache of loneliness only a little, not nearly enough.

But she hadn't wanted any more than that.

And now? Now there was Alex.

Her body still ached from his touch, and she felt the dull throb of remembered and still unsatisfied desire. She couldn't believe how reckless she'd been, how *rough*. She didn't do that. Frantic sex on an office desk…*not* a turn-on. Not at all, considering her history.

And yet with Alex it had been different. Strong and sexy

and somehow empowering. They'd come at it as equals, and even as he'd been tearing her blouse off she'd felt safe. Maybe she needed that. Maybe she needed to reclaim all those years of subjugation, just in a totally different way than she'd thought.

A limo was waiting at the curb as they emerged from the building. "Do you keep a condom in the car?" Chelsea murmured, only half joking, as the driver leaped out to open the door for her; Alex had got there first.

"You must think I lead a far more exciting life than I do," he answered as he slid onto the seat next to her.

"Come on, Alex, you've got a bit of a reputation," she answered. She pulled her coat more tightly around her. Her blouse was practically in shreds and the slit in the back of her skirt was a good six inches longer than it had been or should be. As for her hair, her makeup…she didn't even want to know.

But she still wanted Alex.

"You look beautiful," Alex said quietly.

She turned to him. "How did you know what I was thinking?"

"You started trying to fix your hair."

Belatedly she dropped her hands and glanced out the window at rows of disused warehouses and old factory buildings that lined the waterfront. "Nice neighborhood."

"I like my privacy."

The limo had pulled up in front of what looked to Chelsea like an abandoned warehouse, three stories of weathered brick.

The driver opened the door and Alex stepped out, drawing Chelsea by the hand toward the door of the warehouse, a slab of solid steel with a huge padlock. "Seriously?" she said, nodding at the padlock.

Alex grinned at her in the descending twilight. "Seriously," he answered, and she felt a thrill of something—fear or wonder—because suddenly she wasn't sure whether he was talking about the door.

Alex took a key card out of his pocket and swiped it against a panel affixed to the warehouse; the huge door swung open on silent hinges and Chelsea shook her head.

"Now you're just showing off."

He chuckled softly. "Maybe a little." He led her into a dark hallway; motion-sensitive lights switched on as they stepped inside.

Chelsea glanced at the large, old-fashioned elevator, its iron grille open to the stripped girders and beams. "Do you own this whole place?"

"I have the top floor. But Diaz News owns the building—the other floors are guest accommodation, offices and storage."

"Diaz News, huh?" She stepped into the elevator, Alex's hand at her back. "That's still you."

He acknowledged her point with a nod. "Still me."

He pressed a button and the elevator moved upward through the exposed building, then stopped and the doors opened onto the top floor, one huge open space.

The apartment was completely open plan, with bookcases or counters used as dividers. Chelsea stepped in, Alex's hand still on her back. "What do you think?" he asked, and she could tell by his tone, light as it was, that he cared at least a little about the answer.

"Give me a minute," she said, and began to stroll

through a space that had been marked in every way by the man who lived there. Oak bookshelves with tattered paperbacks, a mixture of philosophy, nonfiction and a few well-thumbed thrillers. An acoustic guitar on its stand in the corner. Blown-up black-and-white photographs that captured the poignant minutiae of life: an elderly man on a park bench, his gnarled hands resting on a walking stick; a young child at a playground, with a scraped knee and a single tear sliding down his cheek; a woman strolling in Central Park, her face tilted toward the sun.

Chelsea could feel Alex's eyes on her as she wandered through the apartment, taking everything in. It felt like far more of a home than her luxurious, sterile penthouse did. His personality was stamped on everything while she'd intentionally erased hers. She finished her silent, self-guided tour in his bedroom area, separated from the rest of the apartment by tall bookcases, and stood in front of his king-size bed. Already images danced through her mind, the two of them twined together amid the navy silk sheets, hands and legs and lips...

Desire arrowed inside her and she turned to him, wondering if he could guess the nature of her thoughts. From the glint in his eye, she thought he probably did.

"I like it. It feels like a home."

"I think I've always wanted a space of my own."

"There's plenty of that." She glanced down at herself. "I think I need to borrow some clothes."

"Not a problem, if you don't mind them hanging off you a bit." The grin he gave her was teasingly wolfish. "I certainly don't."

He took a pair of sweatpants and a gray T-shirt faded

to buttery softness from a drawer, and handed them to her. Chelsea resisted the urge to press the clothes to her face and breathe in the scent of him. "The bathroom isn't open plan, is it?"

"Nope, in the corner."

He pointed her to a door in the corner and she went to change.

Five minutes later she returned, the waist of the sweatpants rolled over so they didn't fall off her hips, the shirt nearly sliding off her shoulder. She felt self-conscious and yet also surprisingly comfortable in Alex's clothes, clothes she'd never, ever wear, and just about as far as possible from her usual crisply tailored outfits. Her armor.

She walked toward Alex who was stretched out on one of the leather sofas in the living area, his feet propped up on a solid, scarred coffee table of dark wood.

He glanced up as she approached, his gaze sweeping over her. "I like it. The new Chelsea Maxwell look."

She laughed softly. "A T-shirt and sweatpants? I don't think so."

"A very sexy look," he told her, all seriousness even though his eyes sparkled with humor. "They look very easy to take off."

"Is that a promise?"

"Absolutely."

She sat down on the sofa next to him, glanced around at the comfortable space. "No TV?"

"I get enough of that at work. This is my escape." He slid his arm around her waist and drew her against him in a move that wasn't seductive so much as gentle. He took a deep breath, let it out slowly. "I've never brought a woman back here, Chelsea."

"Never?"

"Never."

She nodded and then, even though it went against every self-protective instinct she had, she leaned her head against his shoulder and closed her eyes. Spoke the truth of her heart. "This is scary, Alex."

"I know."

"I've lived my life the way I have for a reason."

His arm tightened around her waist, fingers splayed against her belly. "So have I."

And neither of them asked what the reason was. That was as emotional or honest as they could go right now, Chelsea suspected.

Alex rose from the sofa, tugging her by the hand toward the corner of the apartment where a wrought-iron spiral staircase led, Chelsea assumed, to the roof.

"Time to show you the pièce de résistance of this place."

"Which is?"

"Just wait and see."

She followed him up the twisting steps and through a door onto the roof. Stopped and stared at the glassed-in pool, Manhattan in all of its sparkling glory visible on one side, the inky darkness of the Hudson River on the other.

"Very nice. Your own private rooftop pool, and for a man who doesn't even like to swim."

He laughed softly. "But no one can ever push me in and watch me drown."

She walked slowly around the pool, gazing out at the lights of the city. "You don't need water to drown," she said quietly, and then wished she hadn't. Too much information. Too much vulnerability.

But Alex didn't respond, just watched her, and while she felt relieved that he wasn't going to pry, she also wondered if he just didn't want to know. Maybe that would be easier all around. Just skim the surface of all that intensity, all that emotion, but don't actually dive into the damn pool.

A thought which should have brought reassurance, but instead she felt only a restless disappointment.

"Time for dinner," Alex said, and they walked back downstairs.

"Are you going to cook for me?" She asked as she slid onto a high bar stool in the kitchen area and propped her elbows on the black granite countertop while he went around to the other side.

"You wouldn't wish that on your worst enemy, I'm afraid. How do you feel about takeout?"

"I feel fine. That's my usual MO, anyway."

"How about pizza?"

"How about Thai?"

He shook his head, amusement glinting in his eyes. "Nothing's easy with you, is it?"

"Nothing," she agreed solemnly, and suddenly the air felt charged between them, expectant, as they both remembered and wanted still.

Alex cleared his throat. "So, Thai. I think I have a menu somewhere."

A few minutes later he'd put an order in and they wandered over to the living area once more. Chelsea perched on the edge of one of the huge sofas. She felt ill at ease, awkward in a way she never allowed herself to feel. Everything about this felt weird and yet somehow normal, too. Just an evening at home with her lover, eating takeout. So normal, and yet so alien to her sterile, isolated existence.

Alex sat down next to her and put his arm around her shoulder, drawing her against him again, and it felt that same weird mix of normal and bizarre to put her head on his shoulder, relax into his body. It felt so unbearably good to be so close to someone, to touch.

He kneaded the muscles in her neck with his strong fingers, laughing softly as he did so. "You are as taut as a bow."

"I'm not used to this."

"To what? Sitting on a sofa?"

"Basically." She straightened to look at him. "I haven't had any kind of meaningful relationship in ten years, Alex." As soon as she said the words she wished she could snatch them back. They made her sound so lonely, so pathetic. Hadn't she just told herself they wouldn't go deep? Yet here she was, practically telling him the opposite.

Because the opposite, despite every self-protective instinct screaming otherwise, was what she wanted.

Alex regarded her thoughtfully. There was, thankfully, no pity in his gaze, just consideration. "I haven't either."

"Just a lot of one-night stands."

"Basically. That's what drew me to you at first, you know. I thought you were the same."

"I was. Am."

His mouth quirked in a small smile. "Which one, Chelsea?"

She shook her head, her confusion making her honest. "I don't know."

"Me neither. So at least we're on the same page here, right?"

But what page was that?

Alex leaned forward and brushed her lips with his own. Ah, this page, she thought with relief. This page, she liked. And these kisses just about undid her. They were so sweet, so tender, so *much*. He would kill her with these kindnesses. He'd melt icy Chelsea Maxwell, and what— who—would be left?

The intercom buzzed with their meal and reluctantly Alex eased away from her. "We're not done," he warned her with a smile and Chelsea smiled back, although she was starting to hate that expression. *We're not done.* But they would be…when? Which one of them would decide?

As Alex paid the delivery man Chelsea rose and went into the kitchen to search for cutlery and plates. She wouldn't think about when this would end, she told herself. She was going to stop wondering and worrying and being afraid and just enjoy this time with Alex…for however long it lasted.

They spent the rest of the evening lounging around, eating far too much Thai food and chatting about everything and nothing.

Chelsea told him how Michael had discovered her practicing her delivery in the newsroom after hours, how she'd felt ridiculous and yet he'd actually given her a chance. How the idea behind *Chat with Chelsea* came when Michael overheard her talking to a washed-up celebrity at a cocktail party, and was impressed with how she'd been able to draw her out.

"I wasn't even trying, then," she said with a little laugh. "She was just drunk and wanted to talk."

"And you were in the right place at the right time?"

"I suppose." Although she didn't like to attribute all of her success to dumb luck.

"It's not just luck," Alex said softly, and she looked at him in surprise.

"You're doing it again. How did you know what I was thinking?"

"I don't know. I just do."

He *knew* her, Chelsea thought. She'd fought against it, still kept so many secrets, and yet he knew her. And she liked being known.

"Come on," Alex said softly, and reached for her hand. He drew her up from the sofa and across the open apartment, moonlight streaming in through the long sash windows and sending slanting beams across the oak plank floor.

Chelsea followed him, her hand linked with his, to the bedroom area, and then to the bed. He turned to her with a smile and then tugging gently on her hand he drew her right up to him, so her hips bumped his and she felt the powerful evidence of his arousal.

"Hello," he said softly and she closed her eyes as he whispered a kiss across her mouth.

"Hello."

He slid his hands behind her neck, plucking the pins from her hair and sending it streaming down her back in a dark river. "I've never actually seen you with your hair down," he murmured, with another whisper of a kiss across her jaw.

Chelsea shuddered in response. "Is that a euphemism?" she joked feebly, for her brain was starting to short-circuit as Alex moved his mouth from her jaw to her throat and then to the shadowy vee between her breasts, his mouth inches from her scar.

She tensed, because in ten years she'd never let a man kiss her breasts. Never even taken her top off. And yet she remained still and silent as Alex slid her T-shirt up over her breasts. She still wore her camisole and bra, but it didn't feel like enough. His hands slid over the silk to cup her breasts.

He gazed up at him, his eyes dark and liquid. "May I?" he asked, and his fingers tugged gently on the edge of her camisole.

She swallowed and nodded jerkily, her heart starting to thump. Alex began to slip the camisole off and she grabbed his hand.

"Wait…" She wasn't ready to be that naked. She knew he'd seen her scar before, but then she'd been hiding behind her anger and pride. This was different. Now she had nothing to hide behind but this scrap of silk, and Alex seemed to understand that for he smiled and dropped his hands.

"Okay," he said, and kissed her again, and Chelsea sagged against him in relief. She wanted to say she was sorry for not trusting him that much yet, but the words tangled on her tongue and then he kissed them away, and they didn't speak for a long time after that.

It was as far from the raw urgency of their previous encounters as possible. This was sweet and tender and slow, and it melted everything inside her so she felt like there was nothing left.

As Alex moved inside her she wrapped her legs around him and drew him in even deeper, his gaze fastened on hers. And when she came, crying out in a sob of both joy and surrender, he kissed her lips.

Afterward they lay tangled among the bed sheets just as she'd envisioned, limbs and fingers laced together, the only sound the ragged draw and tear of their breathing as their heart rates slowed and the moonbeams slid silently across the floor.

Chelsea had no words for what just happened, no way to express the truth of her soul. She wanted to tell Alex how he'd broken her right open, how everything in her felt exposed and that wasn't necessarily a bad feeling. She wanted to tell him so many things, from the ugly episodes of her childhood to the lost years of her late teens, drifting through a series of broken relationships, to the three years of hell with Brian Taylor.

She wanted to tell him, but she wouldn't. It was too much to share, too much for him to take in. She still wasn't sure he wanted to hear it. In fact, she was pretty sure he didn't.

Eventually Alex fell asleep, and Chelsea watched him for a while. Asleep he looked so relaxed, almost boyish. His dark, lush lashes feathered onto his cheeks and his lips were slightly parted on a sigh. She could see the dark hint of stubble on his jaw and she brushed her lips against it. He stirred, tangling one hand in her hair and drawing her against him. She curled into him for a moment, savoring his solid warmth, and then as he settled back into sleep she rose from the bed and slipped on the T-shirt and sweat-pants he'd stripped from her just hours before.

She wouldn't sleep tonight, she knew. As much as she craved the comfort of another body close to hers all night long, she knew she wouldn't be able to relax into it. Let go of all the tightly-held anxiety and fear.

She slipped from the bedroom area and went up the spiral steps to the pool. The door squeaked as it opened but Alex didn't stir.

Chelsea slipped out into the night. The city stretched around her on every side, the buildings lit like jewels against a dark and fathomless sky. She walked slowly around the pool, fighting an inexplicable sorrow. She'd had the sweetest, most wonderful time in Alex's arms tonight. She felt as if she were teetering on the edge of a whole new world, vibrant and frightening, and yet...

She didn't know if she could jump into it, as much as she wanted to.

And more importantly, she didn't know if Alex could catch her if she fell.

Alex woke to darkness and an empty bed. He tensed, hating that smooth expanse of sheet for even though he almost always slept alone, in a single night he'd got used to Chelsea lying next to him. He missed her.

He lay there for a moment, processing that, resisting it. Things had changed so suddenly and intensely between them, and even though he'd enjoyed this evening, hell, yes, he didn't know how much further down this road he was willing to go. How much he *could*.

A glance at the floor told him she'd put his clothes back on, so at least she hadn't left.

He rolled off the bed and reached for his boxers.

Another quick glance told him she wasn't anywhere in the apartment; the bathroom door was open, the room dark and empty. He headed upstairs, paused when he saw her at the far side of the pool, her back to him as she stared out into the night.

Her hair was loose about her shoulders and she'd wrapped her arms around herself; she looked lonely and sad and beautiful, and Alex felt a lurch of panic deep inside.

Too much.

"Couldn't sleep?" he asked and she didn't turn around.

"No. I'm an insomniac, I'm afraid."

He took a step toward her, but the pool remained between them, a chasm of water. "What are you thinking about?" he asked after a moment's pause, and then wished he hadn't.

"Nothing much, really." She pressed one palm against the glass, her fingers spreading out, long and slender. "Just how amazing your apartment is, really."

Somehow he didn't think she was just admiring the architecture, but he didn't want to press. Maybe he should be ashamed of that, but frankly there had been enough emotional firsts today for both of them. He just wanted her back in bed, with his arms around her and her body fitted to his.

"You've come such a long way…" she said quietly. "Do you think you have?"

"In one way, yes. But in another…" He shrugged. "I'll always be that poor boy from the Bronx."

"Yes. You can never escape the past, can you?"

Alex's whole body twitched with the need to stop this conversation. Take her downstairs. "You can learn from it," he said, and it was meant to be a stopping point.

"Yes. Yes, you can. Learn not to make the same mistakes twice."

What the hell, Alex wondered, was she talking about? Whatever it was, he knew he didn't want to know. "Come back to bed, Chelsea," he said, and finally she turned around, gave him a sweet, sad smile that just about broke his heart. And silently she walked around the pool and then taking his hand, led him back to bed.

Chapter Eleven

Alex gazed moodily out the window of his office and then back at the text Hunter had sent him that morning.

Back off. Zoe's not speaking.

So Zoe could help Hunter but not Alex. Confront Treffen in his place of his business, with all his partners there as she and Hunter had done last week, but not on live television.

A few days ago Treffen had made the public announcement that he was leaving his law firm. He'd made a crap excuse, of course, but he was out. And while Alex, along with Hunter and Austin, had known it was coming, he'd still felt fiercely satisfied.

And *dis*satisfied at the same time, because he was still no closer to getting Chelsea the source she needed.

And if he was honest, he hadn't even tried too hard. He'd barely *thought* about Treffen since Chelsea had seen the photo. Somehow it had all got lost in the rush of their relationship.

Relationship. Where the hell had that word come from?

They didn't have a damn relationship. They'd had sex. Three times.

This morning she'd left his bed, gathered her torn clothes and buttoned up her trench coat to her chin. With every button Alex had felt as if she were hiding herself from him, her expression back to chilly Chelsea rather than the warm, open woman he'd loved half the night long. And he told himself that was a good thing.

He knew he didn't want to hear about Chelsea's sadness and secrets, and he was pretty sure she knew it, too. Keep it light, or at least lighter. Hadn't they gone deep enough already? This shit wasn't easy. It hurt. And even as he craved more of Chelsea he was still debating the merits of walking away. Walking away as much as he could, anyway, because he still needed her to bring down Treffen.

Blowing out an impatient breath, Alex thumbed a text back to Hunter.

Chelsea won't confront Treffen without a primary source. We need Zoe.

Or if Zoe still refused, maybe he could find someone else. Maybe she would name another victim. In any case he needed to stop all this ridiculous navel-gazing about what he did or didn't feel for Chelsea and just start *doing*. He'd find another one of Jason's victims. Someone who was willing to speak.

You need to tell Chelsea about Sarah.

There was so much he'd omitted. He hadn't told her that Sarah was his friend, or that she'd killed herself. He hadn't told her how he'd let her down. And he didn't want to. Couldn't admit to any of those things, to the pain inside him he'd refused ever to acknowledge or feel.

Find someone else. Another woman whose life had been destroyed by Jason Treffen. That was the easier, if less honest, solution, and he was going to take it.

Several hours later he headed uptown for his weekly squash game with Jaiven. He hadn't seen his friend since they'd had a beer at a bar in the Bronx and he'd had Chelsea Maxwell on his mind.

Still did.

He hadn't called her, although he'd thought about picking up the phone all day. They'd left things so abruptly and undecided that morning; looking back Alex realized Chelsea had basically hightailed it from his apartment without so much as a backward glance. And he'd let her. Maybe it was better that way, he told himself. Easier, at least.

Then again, maybe it wasn't.

"So did you end up getting it on with whatever chick was driving you crazy?" Jaiven asked as he hit the ball hard against the wall.

Alex hit it right back at him. "Good memory."

"So I'm guessing you didn't."

"How do you reckon that?"

"Otherwise you would have just said yes."

"Maybe I want to keep my personal life private."

"Personal life?" Jaiven smashed the ball against the wall. "I thought we were talking about sex."

"Whatever," Alex growled, and missed his shot.

An hour and three vicious games later, Alex had won but only just. They showered up and retired to the health club's juice bar on the top floor.

"So who is she?" Jaiven asked as he downed a protein shake.

Alex shook his head. "No one you would know." Not personally, anyway.

"Because you've got it bad, my friend." Jaiven shook his head, pretended to shudder. Or maybe it wasn't pretend. "Better you than me."

He did have it bad, Alex realized with a start. He wanted—needed—to see Chelsea again, and soon. Not just for sex, although he was certainly looking forward to that. But he wanted more than simple—or not so simple—sex. He wanted to eat takeaway—he'd insist on pizza this time—and sit on a sofa with her legs on his lap. He wanted to tell her about his day and the anchorman who was being a complete pain in the ass about his contract. He just wanted to *be* with her.

What the hell was happening to him?

An hour later Alex was back in his office, dialing Chelsea's mobile. She answered on the second ring.

"Yes?" She sounded guarded.

"What are you doing tonight?"

"I have to catch up on some work, Alex."

She was, Alex decided, in careful retreat mode. Well, he was on the attack. "Fine, I do, too. Let me come over. I'll bring dinner."

Her breath came out in a sharp hiss. Such a simple suggestion, and yet so much more than either of them were used to. "Chelsea," he said softly, and it was enough.

"Okay," she said, "but I really do have to work."

He showed up at her apartment at ten minutes past seven with a pile of paperwork and a huge pepperoni pizza.

Chelsea answered the door still dressed in her work clothes, an ivory silk blouse and a narrow black skirt. She shook her head at the pizza. "You've got to be kidding me."

"You know you love it."

"I haven't eaten a piece of pizza for years."

"That's sad."

Her lips twitched. "Maybe so. I suppose one piece won't kill me. I'm not filming tomorrow."

Alex brought the pizza over to the glass-and-chrome coffee table in the middle of her living room. He glanced around at the white leather sofas, the expensive-looking rug of white faux fur. "This place is begging for a grease stain. How do you eat in here?"

She shrugged, sitting on the edge of one of the sofas. "I don't. I eat in the kitchen or out."

He handed her a piece of pizza, and she took it, sitting on the sofa opposite him as if they were having a business meeting over dinner. Alex didn't know whether to laugh or groan. Or get the hell out of there.

What was he playing at, really? And yet still he spoke. "Which part of this freaks you out, Chelsea?"

Her eyes flared surprise and she looked away. "What do you mean?"

"You know what I mean." Alex could hardly believe he was saying this stuff, and yet the words kept coming out of his mouth. "Last night was intense and it scared me a little, or even a lot, but I still want more. Want you."

"Do you really?" He heard the jagged note of cynicism in her voice and frowned.

"Yes—"

"I think you want a little of me, Alex," she answered. "I think you want some fun times and some hot sex and a little bit of casual sharing about our lives. But the whole package? The real deal?" She gazed at him steadily. "I don't think you're prepared for that."   •

He felt exposed under her stare, revealed in a way he really didn't like because he knew she was right. And he didn't know what to do about it. "Maybe I'm not," he said after a long, taut moment. Chelsea just shrugged, and he forced himself to ask, "What *is* the real deal, Chelsea?"

She shook her head, gave him a bleak smile. "Like I said, you don't want that, Alex."

And damn it, he felt relieved. "Fine," he said after a moment. "Let's eat pizza for now."

And eating pizza was good. They recovered their banter, a little light flirting. Kept it easy and safe. Chelsea ate three slices before she groaned and sank against the sofa, her hands pressed against her still-flat stomach. "I'm going to split my skirt."

"I kind of liked that look."

She laughed and shook her head before her expression grew serious again. "You know we need to talk about Treffen. I read in the news that he's out of his law firm. Who managed that?"

"Hunter."

She nodded slowly. "Have you found someone else to come forward?"

Everything in him tensed. "Not yet."

She was silent for a moment. "Treffen's asked me to sign something."

"Restricting the interview to certain questions?"

"Yes."

Alex nodded. "I expected as much."

"And you know what will happen if I violate it?" she asked, her voice sharpening a little.

"He'll sue you," Alex answered. "And you'll probably get sacked."

Her eyes sparked. "Oh, well, as long as you *know.*"

"As long as *you* know, Chelsea." He pushed his pizza away. "I know what I'm asking you."

"I don't think you do."

"This interview might end your time at AMI, but it could make your career. And Treffen can't sue you for defamation if the charges are true. He'll be in prison."

"You hope."

"Yes. I do."

She sighed and shook her head. "I need more, Alex. I can't go on live television with nothing but a single photo and a pissed-off sister. You know that. You mentioned a witness, didn't you? What about her?"

"She's not willing to speak."

"Will she to me?"

He hadn't considered that. Would Zoe speak to Chelsea, even if she wouldn't go on television? "Maybe."

"And you haven't got anything else?"

He was silent, because he knew he had more to tell her. The words didn't come, yet she must have felt the weight of them unspoken for she sat up, stared at him hard.

"You haven't told me everything, have you?" She pressed the heel of her hand against her eyes. "I'm so stupid. So blind. Of course you haven't. You wouldn't go after Treffen like this, you wouldn't hate him so much, if it wasn't personal. I should have realized that before."

Alex's throat dried. His face and mind both blanked. Chelsea dropped her hand. "Who was she?"

"I don't know—"

"Bullshit, Alex. I thought we were trying to be honest here. If not about—about us, then at least about Treffen."

He opened his mouth, and that was as far as he got.

"Who was she? The woman who has made you so determined, so desperate to bring Treffen down? Was she a girlfriend? A lover?"

He tried to form a word, but somehow his lips wouldn't move. He could feel his heart thudding, the blood draining from his head. *Why was this so hard?*

"It was her, wasn't it," Chelsea said softly. "The girl in the photo. You loved her."

Somehow he managed to nod. Speak. "Sarah. Her name was Sarah."

"What happened to her?"

"Wasn't it obvious—" His voice came out ragged, savage.

"I mean after. Because you told me she wasn't available to speak."

"She's dead."

Chelsea's mouth dropped open and she shook her head, her eyes dark with sorrow. "Oh, Alex."

"She killed herself. Threw herself off the roof of Treffen's building."

"I'm so sorry."

He nodded jerkily. Now that he'd started telling her about it, he wanted to get it all out. Purge himself, even though he didn't think he'd feel better with the truth all out there. Most likely he'd feel worse. "We were friends all through college. Best friends, really. It was never romantic. She was dating one of my roommates, Hunter Grant."

"The ex-NFL quarterback."

"But I was friends with her first. Not that it matters, but we both came from tough backgrounds. No family picnics and holidays to Florida like you had."

He glanced up, saw something like regret or maybe even guilt twist her features before she nodded back and said, "Go on."

"She was like a sister to me, a little sister. I looked out for her, teased her, even punched Hunter once when I thought he was being a douche."

Chelsea gave a small, wobbly smile. "Knowing his reputation, I'm sure he was."

"But in the end…" He stopped, not wanting to admit the rest. Just how terribly he'd let Sarah down. "She got in over her head," he said, the words coming out stiltedly. "I don't know how it happened, how I—how I didn't see. She got herself sucked into Treffen's hellhole and I didn't even notice. I didn't…" *Listen when she tried to tell me.* He couldn't say it. Couldn't exonerate or explain himself. And he didn't want to admit such shaming weakness to Chelsea.

"How could you ever imagine such a thing?" she asked sadly, and he shook his head.

"I should have realized. Should have suspected." Should have listened to what Sarah was trying to say, even if she hadn't had all the words.

"It's easy in hindsight," Chelsea said, and Alex averted his face. He didn't want her to see the guilt in his eyes, the knowledge that he wasn't saying everything. That he didn't need hindsight because he'd had enough information back then. Enough to wonder, to press, to comfort. *To save Sarah.*

But he wasn't going to say that now. He couldn't. He didn't like talking or even thinking of Sarah. Not in the privacy of his own mind, and certainly not to Chelsea. It was why he hadn't talked about Sarah before now. Why he'd stared at that damned photo for far too long even as he longed to rip it up and make sure no one ever saw it again.

She'd said he wasn't ready to hear her secrets; neither was he ready for her to hear his.

"Alex." Chelsea's voice was so soft, so aching with regret and sorrow and compassion, that Alex felt tears sting his eyes. He blinked them furiously back. He didn't deserve her understanding or pity. He didn't want it. "It wasn't your fault," she said and he didn't answer. Felt everything in him freeze, because damn it, it was his fault, but he wasn't about to say that to Chelsea.

"Alex," she said again, and closed the space between them, putting her arms around him and drawing his head down to her shoulder. Alex didn't resist but he didn't relax into the embrace. He didn't deserve her comfort, even if he craved it. Craved the absolution that wasn't Chelsea's to give. Only Sarah could give it, and she was dead.

Chelsea eased back and gazed at him steadily, thoughtfully, her gray-green eyes searching his face, and finding—what? Could she see the guilt he was trying so hard to hide? He opened his mouth, scrambled for something to say.

This isn't going to work, Chelsea. Leave me alone, damn it. I can't take any more of this.

But Chelsea didn't give him the chance to protect himself. She simply took him by the hand and led him to her bedroom. With her face grave and yet determined, she lifted her top over her head.

Alex watched as she slid off her camisole, unsnapped her bra. Stood bare before him, nothing hiding her scar from him, a scar he knew she felt incredibly self-conscious about, a scar with a terrible story behind it.

She shrugged out of the rest of her clothes and when she was naked before him she undressed him. Gently, almost reverently, her fingers whispering against his skin. And then she kissed him, softly, but he needed her too much and he pulled her to him, kissed her back with a desperate urgency that rose like a howl inside him.

And she returned it, kiss for kiss, touch for touch, until she pulled away suddenly, leaving him feeling so bereft he nearly cried out, and then she sank to her knees in front of him.

"Chelsea—" he began, because he knew this was a kind of vulnerability for her. She glanced up and said softly, "Let me." And then she took him into her mouth.

Alex shuddered as he felt her lips close over his sensitive skin and his hands tangled in her hair. "Chelsea," he managed, his voice hoarse with longing and pleasure, because the sensation was exquisite but he also knew how much this was costing her. Going down on her knees before him, as he had with her. Subjugating herself, exposing her scar.

She was giving him everything, and he gave it back, shuddering and crying out her name as he came.

Later, as they lay in bed, having made love with slow,

sweet gentleness, he traced her scar with his fingers, brushed his thumb over the ridged, puckered flesh.

She rolled into him, curling her body around his like a question mark, his fingers still on her scar. "It wasn't a car accident," she whispered, and he didn't ask any questions. He just held her, because he knew that was what she needed. He needed it, too.

Chapter Twelve

Chelsea lay next to Alex, his arm heavy across her as he slept, and she stared up at the ceiling wondering when she'd last given so much to a man. Memories she'd suppressed for so long played through her brain in a painful yet necessary montage.

Brian Taylor's considering gaze as she'd gone into the open auditions for weather girl. *And just what would you do for this job, Miss Jensen?*

Why I'd do just about anything, sir.

She'd batted her eyelashes. Smiled coyly. Left no doubt as to just what she was talking about.

And he'd taken her at her word—or rather her implication—and risen from his chair. Called for a private meeting with her and practically dragged her from the room, all in front of two executives, a secretary and a messenger boy. She'd gone with him, her face burning but her chin still held high, and as soon as the door had closed behind them he'd pulled her into a cupboard and yanked her skirt up, had her over a mop and pail. Fast. Dirty. And potentially soul-destroying, if she'd had a soul left to lose.

But she hadn't.

Other memories, just as bitter. The smirks and innu-endoes from all the staff. The leers and come-ons from every male employee of the news station. And Brian, al-ways Brian, taking her whenever he wanted. Treating her however he liked.

She'd faced up to it all, had held her head high. She'd been unabashed, unapologetic, about her choices. A girl did what a girl had to do, she'd quip to friends. She'd stared down rivals. She'd stayed strong, until that self-confident swagger had been taken from her along with two teeth and 20/20 vision.

When she'd emerged from the hospital she'd been an-other person, a person she hated to remember. Desperate, paranoid, with severe anxiety attacks and three differ-ent prescriptions to help keep her sane. Thank God she'd risen above all that. Thank God she'd had the strength to start over.

And now she wanted to start over again, and this time for real. With Alex. She wanted a relationship, a healthy, positive, loving relationship. She was tired of her cold, iso-lated existence, armoring herself with a glamorous image and a lot of attitude.

She wanted to be real, just as Alex had been real with her.

Sort of.

Had he told her everything? She'd sensed something in him, a darkness he'd been trying to hide, and God knew she understood about that. About hiding. About darkness.

And just the thought of being honest about her own se-crets had everything inside her curling up, an emotional armadillo. *Protect yourself at all costs.*

Besides, even if she actually worked up the courage to tell Alex about her past, he still might not want to hear it. He'd admitted as much last night. Things might have changed for her; seeing Alex even just a little bit vulnerable had opened up a desire, even a need, to be vulnerable herself.

A little. Baby steps, right? Maybe they'd still get there, wherever it was they were going. It might just take a long time.

Gently she cupped Alex's cheek, rested a thumb on his lips. Then she leaned over and kissed him softly, too softly for him to wake, and wondered what would happen now.

She must have slept, even though she hadn't expected to, because Alex kissed her awake sometime after dawn. They made slow, sweet love and Chelsea lay there, sated and as happy as she'd ever been, before she glanced at the clock.

"It's after *six*—" She rose from the bed in a flurry of panic.

"Is that late to rise in Chelsea World?"

She threw him a dirty look. "Don't pretend you're not a workaholic."

"I won't, but I don't feel like one now. Come back to bed." He reached one appealing arm out to her. "Call in sick."

"I can't."

Ruefully Alex smiled and dropped his hand. "I suppose I can't either. How about this weekend?"

"This weekend?"

"Let's go away."

A wary and surprised pleasure rippled through her. "Where?"

"How about Miami? An easy flight and it will be warm this time of year."

"Okay," she said, and felt that wary pleasure bloom into something lovely and precious. A weekend away. So normal, and yet so wonderful.

Smiling, he threw off the covers. "Now in actuality I am running late. I don't suppose you have a men's razor in your medicine cabinet?"

A smile tugged at her mouth. "Sorry, no."

"I didn't think so."

"I've never had a man stay the night before."

"I've never stayed over before."

He gave her a long look, one that told her clearly just how new this territory was—for both of them. Amazing how quickly they could go from banter to emotion. To honesty.

And yet still keep so much back.

She went into the bathroom, a hymn to luxury with a sunken tub and two-person shower. "Definitely no razor," she quipped as she opened the medicine cabinet and took out her facial cleanser.

"Whoa, what's with the Band-Aids?"

Chelsea paused, one hand still clutching the cleanser. "What...?"

Alex flipped the door once more. "Were they on sale?" he asked, his eyes glinting amusement even as Chelsea started to flush.

Okay, so she had way too many of them. Boxes and boxes of all different sizes, from ones for your little toe to huge sticking plasters. She could see how it might seem a bit...neurotic.

She closed the bathroom door firmly. "I like to be pre-pared."

"I'll say." She felt Alex's considering gaze on her and knew he was wondering. Also knew she wasn't ready to explain. That happy childhood? Not so happy. And when-ever, as a child, she'd needed a bandage, there never had been one around. No one to care about her stupid skinned knees. Her mom hadn't run to kiss her boo-boos.

Such a small thing, and yet its power over her psyche was evident in the stockpile of sticking plasters in her cabi-net. She hadn't even realized she'd been collecting them; only that whenever she went to the shops she stuck a box in with whatever else she was buying. Just in case. Just to be safe.

Even though she'd never actually *felt* safe. She hadn't felt really safe until she'd been with Alex.

It was only when she was at work and a list of the same old preapproved questions had been faxed over that she felt that lurch of panic. Three weeks until her big, prime-time interview. Could she really think about sabotaging it? Confronting Treffen?

Just the thought made her palms tingle, spots dance. She willed the panic away. Alex *had* to find someone else to come forward. They'd both acknowledged that; until then, she couldn't do anything.

Even if the look in Sarah's eyes as she'd lain naked and supine on that bed haunted her, because she'd recognized it. She'd seen it in herself, in every photo of her that had been taken during her three-year tenure in Huntsville.

She hadn't wanted Alex to know that, hadn't shown any emotion on seeing the photo at all. But she'd felt it. She'd felt the despair right down to her soul, as if Sarah had been crying out to her. *Learn from my mistakes.*

She hoped she had.

Two days later she boarded a plane to Miami and settled into a sumptuous seat in first class next to Alex.

She watched him peruse the newspaper he'd been offered, one hand casually resting on her thigh, and was amazed they'd both arrived at this place. On the outside they looked like any other normal couple, and yet in its normalcy this moment seemed so precious, because for once things felt easy. Right.

Alex made her feel this way. Alex, this powerful, complex, compassionate man...whom she loved.

She was helpless to keep herself from feeling it, or even from wanting to feel it. It had simply gone too far for that. Forget staying safe, sane or self-protected. She loved him, wanted to love him even though she knew the risk.

Alex might decide she was too difficult or damaged and say he'd had enough. He was done. Would she even blame him? She knew she was a mess. She just didn't know how long she could hide it.

Three hours later they checked into a luxurious resort right on Miami Beach. Alex stepped out onto the wraparound balcony and breathed in the balmy air. Amazing how happy he felt. Amazing how good it had felt to tell Chelsea everything.

Well, almost everything. His hands tensed on the balcony railing as realization rushed through him, along with a scorching shame.

You haven't told her everything, asshole. You haven't told her anything.

And she hadn't told him…stuff. Stuff he still wasn't sure he wanted to hear. He sighed restlessly, hating how much he knew they were still hiding, and yet knowing neither of them was ready for more.

This, he decided resolutely, would have to be enough. A warm, sunny day. A beautiful hotel room. A gorgeous woman.

He heard the snick of the sliding glass door and Chelsea joined him on the balcony. "Enjoying the view?" she asked and he nodded and smiled, felt the tightness inside him ease.

This was enough. It had to be.

"So what shall we do this evening?" Chelsea asked lightly, her shoulder brushing his as they gazed out at the ocean. "Dinner on the beach, or downtown or in Coconut Grove?" She turned to slide him a flirty smile. "Or we can just order in."

"That last option is definitely the most tempting," Alex answered, "but I'm taking you to Allapattah."

"Alla-where?"

"A Latino neighborhood in western Miami."

She eyed him thoughtfully and then nodded. "Okay."

What he didn't tell her, because he didn't want to freak her out, was that he was taking her to his mother's.

Although in reality it was freaking *him* out. It had seemed natural two days ago, when he'd called his mother. She lived in Miami now; why shouldn't they all meet up? But now it felt like he was assigning an importance and a depth to Chelsea's place in his life that alarmed him more than a little.

But hell, maybe he was. Alex swallowed and gave Chelsea a quick smile. She smiled back, her face softening, everything about her relaxed and open and appealing.

Maybe he was.

He'd told her to dress casually for dinner, forgetting that she didn't do casual. She'd packed a pair of crisply tailored capris, another of trousers, an LBD and a few classic tops but nothing really casual. Nothing she felt like wearing now.

So while Alex was in the shower she nipped down to one of the boutiques in the lobby of the hotel and bought a sundress. A floaty, silky number in sunshine yellow. It had skinny straps and the top was cut so you could see the top of her scar, just a tiny bit of puckered flesh. She'd never worn anything like it in the ten years since Brian Taylor had beaten her senseless before taking a knife to her.

But she'd wear it now.

She wore only a little lip gloss and left her hair loose around her shoulders. She'd bought a pair of strappy sandals, too, that were a far cry from her usual stilettos.

As she stepped out into the main room of their suite Alex gave her a long look.

"You look," he said as he came toward and kissed her, "amazing."

And she felt amazing.

But how long it would last? How long before one of them decided that this was all a bit too much, a bit too intense and emotional, and it was time to back off?

Out on the balcony Alex had seemed preoccupied, and she'd wondered what he was thinking. She hadn't dared to ask.

Some relationship.

Baby steps, she reminded herself just a little bit desperately. Baby steps, even if some of them were going backward.

They drove in the rental car, a convertible in cherry red, through Miami as the sun sank over the ocean and the city night came to life.

"So where exactly are we going?" she asked as he left Miami's downtown for a residential neighborhood. "Do you know some super secret restaurant?"

"You could say that," Alex said as he pulled up in front of a small bungalow with a neat garden. "My mother is a great cook."

Shock turned her rigid. "Your mother?" she finally repeated in disbelief and no small amount of panic. "You're taking me to your mother's?"

"Yes—"

"But I thought you grew up in the Bronx!"

"I did. But she moved to Miami when I went to college to be closer to her sister, my aunt Patricia."

Chelsea shook her head, her hands pressed to her cheeks. "You should have told me, Alex. I'm not ready for this—"

She didn't think he was ready for this either. He'd just rocket-launched their relationship, frail little fledgling that it was, into the stratosphere. *She was meeting the parents.*

"I didn't tell you because I knew you'd freak out," Alex answered calmly. "My mother is a very loving, very accepting person. And she'll accept you." He drew a breath, let it out slowly. "This isn't some test or goal post, Chelsea. It just is. She lives in Miami, and I wanted to see her. That's it. I promise."

Was that a promise or a warning? *Don't read something into this, Chelsea.*

Fine, she wouldn't. But she still had to go meet his mom.

"Okay," she said, and her voice sounded calm. Thankfully. Alex gave her a quick smile.

"Now let's go. My mother makes a mean empanada."

Chelsea followed him toward the bungalow, her heart starting to thud and her palms going damp. Was she having an anxiety attack, she wondered with a lurch of panic, then realized she wasn't. No, she was just experiencing the normal nerves at meeting her boyfriend's mother.

Her boyfriend. Could she really call Alex that?

She swallowed past the dryness in her throat and tried to pin a bright smile on his face. Alex, she knew, still thought she'd had a happy childhood, would be familiar with family gatherings, when in fact nothing was further from the truth. She'd never met her mother's relatives, and Thanksgiving, Christmas and birthdays had usually passed unremarked. This was new territory in so many ways.

"Alex!" A woman opened the door of the bungalow and held out her arms. Alex stepped into them with a sheepish smile, and she spoke in rapid Spanish for several seconds before she turned to Chelsea.

"Welcome. My name is Beatriz," she said in English. "I am so happy to meet you."

"And I'm happy to meet you," Chelsea murmured. She liked the look of Alex's mother; she was tall and proud-looking, with dark hair streaked with gray and the same golden-brown eyes as Alex had. "Come inside," Beatriz urged, and reached for Chelsea's hand. "Everyone wants to meet you."

Chelsea felt herself go rigid once more. "Everyone?" She shot a panicked look at Alex, who was looking surprised and not a little discomfited.

"Who did you invite, Mama?" he asked and Beatriz clucked.

"Just Patricia and her girls, their husbands and children. You know."

That sounded like a lot of people, Chelsea thought, and she felt her vision start to swim. Okay, *now* she was having an anxiety attack.

"Just a sec, Mama." Alex tugged Chelsea by the hand, kept her outside while Beatriz went into the bungalow. "Shit. I should have known she would do something like this." He glanced at her, and she was touched to see concern shadowing his eyes. "If you're not okay with this, we can leave."

"Are you okay with this?" she asked, heard that sharp note of cynicism enter her voice. Alex frowned.

"It isn't ideal, but that's hardly the point right now, Chelsea. You're not okay in crowds, and I don't want to make things worse for you."

Or worse for him. Chelsea had a feeling Alex was seriously regretting this little dinner, and whatever impulse that had made him arrange it.

Well, too bad. She wasn't going to turn tail and run. Not because of a panic attack, at any rate.

"Just give me a minute," she said, and he nodded. She

bent over, taking several deep breaths as she willed her heart rate to slow, her breathing to even. She felt Alex's hand low on her back, rubbing in slow circles, and just that little touch gave her the courage to straighten, smile.

"Okay," she murmured, and standing tall and proud, she entered his mother's house.

It was crazy. Loud, vibrant, with people crowding the small rooms, laughing and shouting, sharing food and drink. Chelsea felt instantly overwhelmed, but also accepted. No one looked at her askance or wondered why she was here. No one even glanced at the scar peeking over the top of her dress.

Beatriz's sister Patricia grabbed her by both hands, kissed her on both cheeks, and gushed about her show. Alex's cousins asked for her autograph, shyly, but then they also asked about her, not Chelsea Maxwell the celebrity, so she felt like a real person and not just a talk show host.

She felt great...until she glanced over at Alex and saw him frowning. He wasn't enjoying this evening quite as much as she was, and she was afraid to know why.

They stayed until after midnight, and finally Alex stated, rather tersely, that they needed to get back to the resort. Chelsea's insides lurched a little at his tone; he almost sounded angry.

She helped clear the picnic table where they'd eaten delicious *sancocho* and black rice with shellfish, followed by the empanadas he'd promised his mother would make.

She was stacking plates by the sink in Beatriz's small kitchen when the older woman came in, stood in the doorway.

"Please don't hurt him."

Chelsea tensed, everything in her icing over. She turned slowly to Beatriz who was gazing at her with the same steady certainty she'd seen so often in Alex's eyes. "Why do you think I would?"

"You have been hurt before, yes?" Surprise made Chelsea speechless. "I can tell, because I have been hurt, too," Beatriz said quietly. "By a man."

Chelsea remembered what Alex had suspected about his father and tried to find her voice. "Yes," she confessed quietly, "I have. But that's…that's what makes me so grateful for Alex."

"He is a good man," Beatriz acknowledged. "And I want him to be happy."

Chelsea flinched. "You think he can't be happy with me?" she asked, knowing it was what she was afraid of herself. That her secrets, her pain, would be too much for him. They'd drive him away.

"I think when you have been hurt once, you think you will be hurt again. It can be hard to trust. To love."

"I know," Chelsea whispered. She blinked back tears and Beatriz smiled in sympathy.

"I know how it hurts. You have scars—and I am not talking about that." She gestured to the inch of ridged flesh above Chelsea's dress. "Scars on your heart, on your soul. They go deep." Chelsea just nodded. "I only say this because Alex cannot heal those scars," Beatriz said quietly. "Not truly. No man can heal you. Only you can do that."

Again Chelsea simply nodded. She understood what Beatriz was saying, even if she wasn't sure she believed it. She didn't know if she could be healed, by Alex or anyone. She wanted to believe she could, but…

She wasn't sure she did.

She was quiet during the ride back to the resort, and so was Alex. On the surface the evening had been a success, but underneath?

Maybe it had been too much for both of them.

Don't hurt him.

She didn't want to hurt him, but she also didn't know if she could help it. She'd made so many bad choices in her life, choices that haunted and hunted her to this day. Choices that would hurt Alex because she still didn't know how to trust, to love. A relationship still felt like a minefield, and inching through it was exhausting. Overwhelming.

Too much.

And yet these past few days had been wonderful. Hard, utterly draining in some ways, but still wonderful. And she knew she wasn't going to let it all go that easily. She'd been burned in the past, yes, but she still wanted to try. She wanted, she realized with a lurch of pure panic, to tell Alex the truth.

It was up to him just what he did with it.

Chapter Thirteen

So he was a complete idiot for taking Chelsea to his mother's house for dinner. What the hell had that been about, anyway? He should have known his mother would go crazy; he'd never brought a woman to meet her before. *Never.*

And he knew he'd done it because part of him wanted to go the distance with Chelsea, and part of him wanted to run the hell away. Get off this train while he still could.

And he had a feeling Chelsea knew it. Maybe she felt as conflicted as he did. They both still held secrets, and nobody was pressing anybody else for more truth-telling. Soul-baring.

Not a tempting proposition in the least. *I'll keep my secrets neatly tucked away, thanks very much.*

Except they weren't tucked away so neatly anymore, and neither were Chelsea's. He'd shown her the photo. He'd told her about Sarah. She'd spoken about her scar. She'd admitted to her panic attacks.

It seemed like those secrets were going to spill out, whether they liked it or not.

Unless he ended it.

Why did that thought seem like hell on earth? How could he make this thing *work?*

As soon as they were back in their suite of rooms he took her in his arms. He didn't want the messy complications of words. Just this. This was simple. Easy. And she must have understood what he was doing because she wrapped her arms around his neck and clung to him with an urgency that made his heart ache.

They made love without speaking. Not one word, because even that would shatter the fragility of this intimacy, the safety of sex. Afterward they held each other as closely as they could, arms and legs twined, hearts beating against each other.

And still they didn't speak.

When morning came Chelsea woke him with a kiss that stole his heart right along with his breath. Kissed her way down his body, tasting him, teasing him, before she shook her hair back in a move of feminine power as old as time and straddled him.

He remembered the first time they'd had sex—and that's what it had been, just sex—and she'd done the same. Now, whether either of them wanted to or not, it felt completely different. She rose above him, naked and unashamed, a smile curving her lips as she rode them both to pleasure in what felt, damn it, like an act of love.

Afterward they showered together and made love again, and eventually they managed to get out of the hotel and hit the beach, do the kind of touristy things Alex had promised they'd do in New York.

He didn't know why everything felt so poignant, so bittersweet. He was enjoying himself, walking along the beach hand in hand with Chelsea, tasting shrimp in the outdoor market and having lunch in Little Havana. He was having the time of his life, and yet it also felt... fleeting. Almost like an ending. Almost as if they'd both come to a wordless agreement last night that this was all they were going to have.

That night a limo picked them up at JFK and they drove in yet more silence back to Alex's place.

Up in his apartment Chelsea walked quietly around the open space. She stopped in front of the blown-up black-and-white photographs that adorned one exposed brick wall.

"Did Sarah do these?"

Surprise—and panic—flashed through him. "How did you know?"

"I don't know. They just seem so...sad."

"The subjects became sadder closer to her death," Alex admitted. "Looking back, I feel like I should have known." *Because she as good as told me.* He swallowed the words, looked away.

"You always do," Chelsea agreed, "looking back."

There was too much quiet sorrow and regret in her voice for Alex not to say something. Trouble was, he had no idea what to say, and even if he did know he still wasn't sure he wanted to say it. "Chelsea—" He stopped, helplessly, and she turned to him.

"I want to tell you some things."

Shit. What could he do now? Her expression was both remote and determined, and unease crept along his spine, soured his gut. "Okay," he finally said, and he heard how reluctant he sounded. Knew Chelsea heard it, too, saw the hard glitter enter her eyes as she lifted her chin, threw her shoulders back, every inch the icy and elegant Chelsea Maxwell.

"I slept my way into my first job."

It wasn't what he'd expected. He felt a mild surprise, a twinge of censure, but overall an acceptance, almost a relief. *That's it?* "Okay."

"I walked into the interview and offered, point-blank, to sleep with the boss to get what I wanted. He took me up on my offer, and I got the job as weather girl for a local news station in Huntsville."

"I guess you knew what you wanted." The words felt like marbles in his mouth, unfamiliar, uncomfortable. He didn't know what to say. He didn't know what she wanted or needed to hear, and frankly he just wanted this to be over.

Something flashed across her face, too quickly for him to know what it was. "I guess I did. Look me up if you want, on the internet. Aurora Dawn Jensen. That's who I was. Who I am."

A different name? He was surprised, but still not really *affected*. It just didn't seem like that big a deal. "I don't need to trawl the internet, Chelsea—"

"I didn't grow up the way I let you believe," she cut across him, her voice hardening, sharpening. "I lied about that. I don't know who my father was, and my mother was useless. Her string of boyfriends were even worse. I was your classic trailer park trash."

She waited, and Alex shrugged, still not sure where she was going with this. "Why did you lie?" he asked, and she flinched.

"Because I wanted to believe it. I wanted to be some-one different."

Well, he could understand that. Hadn't he wanted to be different at Walkerton Prep? Not the poor kid from the Bronx in the secondhand uniform who came to school on a bus rather than a limo or helicopter. And yet somehow he couldn't find the words to tell her that he understood, that whatever she was telling him was okay, he could take it.

Maybe he couldn't take it. Maybe he didn't really want to know all this, because it would throw all his deficien-cies into the light. *This* was why he didn't do relation-ships. Because he had no idea how to handle someone else's pain. Because he couldn't stand the thought of that person seeing his own.

"I lied about everything, Alex." Her words came faster now, too fast for Alex to process. To know how he felt, much less how he should respond. "Chelsea Maxwell— the woman you think you know—doesn't exist. I made her up when I moved to New York, to have a new start. But she isn't real."

"You're real, Chelsea," he finally managed, but his voice sounded feeble to his own ears and she just shook her head.

"You think so? Well, I think I'm still the stupid girl who thought the only way she could get a job was if she got on her back. Or on her knees, as it happened. Or in a broom closet, on a desk, in the elevator, in a parking lot—"

Alex flinched, held up a hand. He did *not* want those images in his head. "Chelsea. Stop."

"Why?" Her eyes glittered, although with tears or defi-ance he couldn't tell. "This is the real deal, Alex. Are you ready for it?" She didn't wait for an answer. "I had an affair with Brian Taylor for three years. A sick, sordid little affair that I chose, because I wanted to be on TV that much."

He could hear the loathing in her voice, but he didn't understand it. She'd never apologized for her choices, and he accepted that about her. But now he didn't know what she wanted from him.

"And then what happened?" he finally asked.

"Things got a little out of hand. Brian always liked to inflict a little pain, but he got carried away and I ended up in ER with a smashed-in face and this." She gestured to the scar on her breast. "He'd caught some guy looking at my chest and flipped out." She drew another breath. "Dragged me out of an office party by the hair. He took me into his office and no one intervened. No one called the cops or so much as knocked on the door while he beat me to a pulp and then went at me with a knife. So I know how it feels to be pushed into the pool, in a matter of speaking. I know what it feels like to have everyone watch you drown."

He stared at her, his mind spinning with all this new knowledge, this terrible, new understanding. Now he got why she chose one-night stands. Why crowds gave her anxiety attacks. Why she acted hard and cold and in control because she knew what it was like not to be.

And yet he didn't say anything. He couldn't.

"No one knows all that," she said quietly. Her face was still shuttered, blank, and she wouldn't look at him. "No one knows the whole story except for you."

She waited then, waited for his words, for *something,* and he came up empty. What the hell was he supposed to say?

That it was okay? It obviously wasn't. That he didn't care about her past? But he did, because it mattered.

Maybe he should just hold her, but he couldn't move. And he knew why.

Because he hadn't wanted to know this. Didn't want to go this deep. Hell, if Chelsea said all this, he'd have to say his shit, too. He'd have to admit to his weakness, and he knew where that led. Nowhere good.

"Say something," she said, and her voice broke. Alex just stared.

"I'm sorry—"

"Oh, Alex." She shook her head, wiping at her eyes before the tears spilled. "You know, your mother was afraid I'd hurt you. She saw through me that night in Miami. She saw how much I was hiding. And I was afraid of hurting you, of not being good enough for you. Not strong or whole enough. But in the end maybe it's you who will hurt me."

"I don't want to hurt you," he said quietly, and meant it. But *don't want* was different from *won't*.

"I know you don't. But I can see on your face you don't want to deal with all this." She gestured to the space between them, but he knew what she really meant. With her. "It's more than you bargained for. I get that. And the truth is…the truth is…" Her voice wobbled. "I need someone who does want to. Who's willing to take the risk." She drew herself up, threw her shoulders back like the woman he'd first seen striding out of her apartment building, the world served before her on a silver platter. "I want someone to think I'm worth it," she finished quietly, and before he could form a response she turned from him, opened the elevator's grilled door, and was gone.

Alex stared unseeingly at the latest headlines scrolling across the top of his computer. The world could be going to hell and he wouldn't know. Didn't care.

His world was shot.

It had been fourteen endless hours since Chelsea had left his apartment. Since he'd listened to her pour her heart out without a single word of sympathy in response.

What the hell was wrong with him?

It wasn't until she was gone that his mind had kicked into gear and he'd sprung from the sofa, ran down the stairs and wrenched open the steel door to the freezing February night. She must have run like hell to get out of there so fast.

He took a cab to her apartment and asked the doorman to ring up. No answer. He called her mobile, texted her a dozen times, nothing.

Too little, too late. He knew that, felt it in the emptiness that whistled through him. He remembered staring down at Sarah's broken body, confusion replaced by a dawning horror.

A growing realization that this was all his fault. Just as it was...again.

"Alex?" His assistant's voice through the intercom interrupted his nonperusal of the news headlines. "Hunter Grant and Zoe Brook for you."

Alex frowned. Hunter had never visited him at his office before, but he could guess the reason why he was here now. He wanted to talk about Treffen.

And maybe he needed to focus on that, because at least he could redeem one broken situation.

He pressed the button on the intercom. "Send them in."

They entered together a minute later, holding hands. Alex eyed the way Zoe clung to Hunter, how every finger of his was threaded through hers, and decided Hunter must have figured out that love thing. They both looked rather grimly determined now, but there could be no denying that they cared about each other. Loved each other.

Too bad it didn't seem like he was capable of something like that. But maybe it was for the best. He didn't deserve Chelsea; at this point, she'd be better off without him.

Alex greeted them both before settling back in his chair. "This is a pleasant surprise," he said, "but I sense this isn't a social call."

Zoe spoke first, her voice low and firm. "No, it isn't." She gazed steadily at Alex, her hand still encased by Hunter's. "I want to come forward with my story. I'll speak to Chelsea, on TV if need be."

Alex knew he should feel triumphant but instead he only felt weary. He nodded slowly. "I'll put you in touch with her. You're sure you want to do this?"

She nodded grimly. "I need to set the record straight about Treffen. About myself." She took a deep breath. "It started out so innocently, or so I thought. I didn't think anything of it when he asked me to go to dinner with a client, and suggested I wear a cocktail dress because he was an old guy who liked to flirt. Harmless, he said." Her voice choked. *"Harmless."*

A look of anguished concern crossed Hunter's usually sardonic features. "Zoe, you don't—"

"No, Hunter, I do. You know I do. I've lived with this for what feels like forever, because I've felt so ashamed at being so stupid, so easily manipulated." She shook her head. "Treffen is a monster. He'd threaten us all—his girls, he called us—and he loved to see us flinch. Cringe. Beg."

He thought of Sarah, and then, suddenly, with an understanding that was painful in its clarity, he thought of Chelsea.

He thought of all the things she'd said, as well as the things she hadn't said. The things she'd implied.

I know I'm still the stupid girl who thought the only way she could get a job was if she got on her back. She didn't believe in herself, because no one else ever had.

Brian liked to inflict a little pain. She'd suffered abuse of the worst sort for three years.

I don't know who my father was, and my mother was useless. Her string of boyfriends were even worse. And maybe even abuse as a child.

God, why hadn't he seen it? Heard what she was really saying? He'd been so consumed with his response that once again he'd failed to really see and hear what was going on. What someone was trying, quite desperately, to tell him.

He should have leaped up from that damn sofa and taken her into his arms. Kissed away the tears she still stubbornly refused to shed.

Instead she'd walked out on him, before he could push her away, which was what she'd assumed he would do, what he had done in his silence.

Somehow he managed to bring his focus back to Zoe

and Hunter. "I'm sorry for what you endured, Zoe. I know Chelsea Maxwell will want to talk to you."

Zoe's face was pale but she nodded resolutely. "Just tell me when and where."

Somehow she'd made it through another day. Three days since she'd left Alex's apartment and every hope of happiness she'd ever had. Three days since she'd looked into his eyes and seen the shock and fear, felt his silence as the rejection it surely was.

Three endless days.

She'd get over it, Chelsea knew, just as she had before. How many sorry relationships had she had, after all? The string of no-hope boyfriends as she'd drifted through Alabama looking for someone to love her. Brian Taylor, whom she'd convinced herself she loved even as he humiliated and hurt her over and over again.

And now Alex. But Alex was different from every other man she'd known. Completely different, and so was she, because she actually did love him. She loved Alex with every fiber of her being, every shard of her broken heart. She loved how safe and special he made her feel, how beloved and desired. She loved his ambition and his sensitivity, his kindness and his humor.

Too bad he didn't love her in quite the same way. Too bad she'd seen in his face that he wasn't ready for the real deal, the messed-up, no-holds-barred version of herself. And the good thing, she told herself, was that she'd figured that out—and knew she needed more.

Avoiding him now was her only option, because the

thought of seeing him made her feel as if she were being flayed, every nerve ending exposed to air and pain.

She knew he might want to apologize. Then again, maybe he didn't. Maybe he was thanking his lucky stars that she'd walked away before he had to. But if he did want to explain, she knew she'd be too weak not to take what little he'd offer. She'd forget that she'd seen the truth in his eyes, heard it in his silence.

And the simple fact was she was afraid. If this felt like agony, what would it feel like a week, a month, a year down the road, when Alex decided he'd had enough of her crazy? He might not turn on her like Brian had, but it would hurt even more. He wouldn't stab her in the chest; he'd shatter her heart.

So she deleted his messages and texts without even reading them. Gave instructions to security at work and the doormen at her building. Cut him off completely.

Eventually he'd give up.

Three days after she last saw him she left work and was about to step into the private town car waiting by the curb at the back of Rockefeller Plaza when a shadow disengaged itself from the wall, and suddenly he was there, right next to her, arms folded, face set, yet looking so wonderful she wanted to rush right into his arms.

She didn't move.

"Hello, Chelsea."

His husky murmur of a voice still had the power to make her want. Yearn. She shook her head. "Why are you here?"

"I had to figure out some way to get you to see me. Hear me. Because you didn't give me much of a chance last time, Chelsea, but I admit the chance you did give me I blew. Big-time."

"It doesn't matter."

"Can you really say that? Mean it?" He took a step closer. "Or are you just afraid?"

"You keep asking me that."

"And you keep telling me that you're not."

Frustration boiled over. "Fine, I'll tell you now that I am. I'm afraid, Alex. I'm afraid of a relationship with you because I've been burned before and it hurts. And I don't have the strength to go through it again."

Even in the darkness she could see the anger blazing in his eyes. "Are you comparing me to that scumbag of a boss? Brian Taylor?"

"No, I'm not. You're totally different. It's me who's the same." Her voice wobbled and then thankfully hardened. "I'm still messed up, Alex. I've tried to act like I have it all together but I don't. Not remotely."

He let out a huff of laughter. "You think I do?"

She shook her head, wanting to be clear. Needing him to know. "I get panic attacks. I stockpile Band-Aids. I haven't been honest or real with a single person in my life in ten years."

His voice lowered and he took a step closer. "You were real with me."

"And look where it got me. You didn't want my *real*, Alex."

"I admit I didn't respond as I should've," he answered steadily. "I failed you. I was—I was scared, Chelsea. I don't like to admit it, but there it is. You were trusting me with all this truth, just like…" He took a deep breath, let it out. "Like Sarah did."

Chelsea frowned, shook her head. "What do you mean?"

"She told me, Chelsea. Sarah told me about Jason. She didn't spell it out, but it was enough. It should have been enough. Except I didn't listen."

She stared at him, opened a mouth to say something, but didn't know what.

"I was consumed with my career," Alex continued, his voice now ragged with pain. "With proving myself. That last night, the night she died, she tried." His voice nearly broke. "I was the last person she saw, Chelsea. The very last. And she tried to tell me what Treffen was doing to her, but I just wanted a fucking *news* story. I asked her…" He stopped, swallowed, and started again. "I asked her to give me a quotation for a story on sexual harassment. A *quotation*. And about ten minutes later she left me and went up to the roof of her building and threw herself off."

Chelsea felt everything in her soften in sympathy. "Oh, Alex—"

"I didn't want to tell you that before. I didn't want to admit to it, to being that kind of man. But you trusted me with your truth, Chelsea, and I pretty much acted the same way as I did with Sarah. I'm sorry, God, I'm *so* sorry, that I didn't handle it right. That I didn't know how, and that I didn't even want to, because if you told me your secrets, I'd have to tell you mine." He held his hands out, palms up. "So here they are, Chelsea. You can choose what to do with them."

Chelsea stared at him, wanting to believe him. Wanting this to be enough. But it wasn't, because she knew Alex.

Knew he was trying to make amends, but did he really feel it? Want her? She didn't see it in his eyes. Didn't hear it in his voice.

"You know what I saw when I looked at that photograph?" she asked. Alex shook his head.

"I saw myself. That expression in Sarah's eyes…as if she were dead inside, but nobody knew but her. Nobody saw it. That's how I've been, Alex. That's how I've felt for so *long*—" She took a quick, steadying breath. "You woke me up," she said when she trusted herself to speak evenly. "You brought me back to life, but it's not enough. Not for the kind of relationship I want now."

"I know it isn't." Those were not the words she wanted him to say, and yet she wasn't surprised. "I'm sorry," he added, and she didn't like those ones either.

"I know you are," she managed.

Alex stared at her for a long moment. "I checked the hospital report, Chelsea. You had a broken nose and jaw, a severed artery in your chest, and three fractured fingers. *My God.*" He shook his head as if to clear it. "Do you know what I wish I'd done when you told me about it all? I wish I'd held you, the way you held me. I wish I'd kissed your tears. I wish I'd been as strong as I know you are."

She felt one cold, lone tear slip from her eye. "I wish you had, too."

He nodded slowly, accepting, and she felt like grabbing him by the lapels of his coat and shaking him. Telling him it wasn't too late, that they could still forgive and try and love again.

Except he didn't love her enough. She knew that; he knew that. Because if he did, he wouldn't be telling her what he'd wished he'd done. He'd be doing it. He'd be fighting for her, and God knew she needed a fighter.

Alex stared off for a moment, his expression hidden, and then he said abruptly, "Zoe Brook came to me yesterday."

Startled, Chelsea blinked. Swallowed past the tightness in her throat and tried for businesslike. "The PR specialist?"

"Yes. She's the source I mentioned before. She was one of Treffen's victims."

"Will she talk?"

"She wants to talk to you."

Hope bloomed in Chelsea's soul, even amidst all the wreckage. "I want to talk to her."

"Good. She'll contact you." He stepped back, and it felt like a farewell.

So that was it, Chelsea thought bleakly. She loved him, but he didn't love her, at least not as hard and as much as she did. And what had started as a desperate attempt at reconciliation had turned into a business meeting.

She nodded jerkily, her own farewell. They stared, didn't speak. But something in Chelsea yearned so hard and deep she reached out and touched his cheek. Didn't say anything, because her throat ached too much. But he must have understood because he turned his head so his lips brushed her palm. Another farewell. And then he stepped away and opened the door to her car.

He let her go, just as she'd known he would.

Chapter Fourteeen

It had been her choice to go, but Chelsea still felt unbearably lonely as she headed uptown to her apartment and another night alone. Back in her living room she powered up her laptop and went to work. She had three weeks to research Jason Treffen, to find out everything she could and orchestrate the man's complete ruin—as well as her own.

Six hours later she leaned back against the sofa and gazed around her apartment with gritty eyes. The stark black and white had soothed her once, but it just felt sterile now, as empty and icy as her Chelsea Maxwell persona.

Her gaze fell on the white canvas with its jagged black lines that Alex had made fun of. The thing *was* ugly, she thought. And stupid. She could sell it for a hundred thousand dollars and give the money to charity.

She could *start* a charity…something for women who had been in abusive relationships. Smart, accomplished, successful women who still had been debased and demoralized by the men they thought they loved.

A slight smile formed on her lips and she turned back to her laptop.

A week later she called Louise. The ache of missing

Alex still bit into her hard, but she told herself in time it would lessen. Heal, even. Hopefully.

But she needed to start dealing with things. With all that emotional baggage Louise had talked about, before the ship sank.

They met this time up by Columbia, and headed for a diner near the university's main buildings. Cracked vinyl booths and peeling tables, and the best waffles in New York, or so Louise had assured her.

"But you don't eat waffles, do you?" she said as she leafed through the huge, plastic-covered menu.

"Maybe I do now," Chelsea answered, "if they're as good as you say."

Louise looked up from the menu. "You seem different, Chelsea."

"You told me that last time we met."

"I know, but then you were all nervy. High-strung. Now you seem…calmer."

Chelsea gave a brief smile. "I don't know about that. Trying to be, more like."

"How?" Louise cocked her head. "And why?"

"Do you really need to ask why?" Chelsea took a sip of her water. She wanted to change, wanted to deal with things and put them to rest, but that didn't mean it was easy. "Did I ever seem happy to you, Louise?"

"No," her sister answered quietly, "but you seemed determined for everyone to think you were."

"Yes, I was. Desperately determined to have finally made a success of my life."

"And you've changed your mind about that?"

"I've decided it's not worth it. Faking it all the time.

Living my life so no one gets close, no one knows who I really am."

Louise leaned forward, a small, sad smile playing about her lips. "And who are you really, Chelsea?"

"I'm Aurora Dawn Jensen," Chelsea answered quietly.

"This isn't just about a name."

"No," she agreed, "it isn't. Although you know why I picked the name Chelsea?" She let out a soft huff of laughter. "Because I'd read a book as a kid about a girl who had her own horse. Some pony club type book, and the girl's name was Chelsea." She paused, her throat tightening. "When we were growing up, I always wanted to be that girl." She glanced at Louise, shocked to see tears coursing down her sister's face. "Louise—"

Louise shook her head, the tears falling unchecked. "I should have protected you, Chelsea. From Mom's boyfriends. I should have been a better sister—"

"It wasn't your fault."

"But I saw how they looked at you and sometimes— sometimes how they touched you." She let out a hiccuppy sob, dashing the tears from her face as she angled her head away from the few other diners who were, thankfully, oblivious to this sorrowful drama unfolding right here amidst the waffles and coffee. "I didn't do anything."

"You did, Lou," Chelsea said quietly. "I remember how you'd yank me out of bed and have me sleep with you instead."

"But not often enough."

Chelsea shrugged. "You were only eighteen months older than me, Louise. You did the best you could."

"No, I didn't." Louise dabbed her still-streaming eyes

with a napkin. "I really didn't, Chelsea. Because I was—I was jealous."

Chelsea's jaw dropped. *"Jealous?"*

"I know how stupid it sounds. How stupid it is. Jealous of some disgusting drunken men pawing you? I *know*." She let out a ragged sound, something between a sob and a laugh. "But I was. They didn't look twice at me. Momma didn't look twice at me. You were her little star, parading about in those child beauty pageants."

"I hated those beauty pageants."

"I know you did. And I did, too. I told you over and over again how stupid they were, but the truth was I would have done anything to be in one. For our mother to think I could be in one, that I wasn't ugly and stupid and forget-table." Louise buried her face in her hands, her shoulders shaking, and Chelsea left her side of the booth to slide next to Louise and put her arms around her as she cried. To hell with the other diners and what they thought. This was more important.

"It's not your fault, Louise. It really isn't. You were eight, nine years old. A child. You've got to remember that."

"I knew what I was doing."

And hadn't she said that about herself? Hadn't she made it a point of pride? But maybe nineteen wasn't, in some ways, that different from nine. Maybe she'd still been a child inside, desperate to be loved, thinking the only way someone could love her was if she gave him everything she had.

Louise snuffled against her shoulder and Chelsea stroked her hair. "You know, you've got to forgive yourself for the

things you didn't do as much as the things you've done."
She thought of Alex, and she felt an ache deep inside.

How long would he beat himself up for failing Sarah?
Failing her? It shouldn't matter, because she knew it was
over between them. Knew he didn't have enough to give
her.

And at least, she told herself, she knew that. At least she
knew she wanted, and maybe even deserved, more.

After a moment Louise eased back and gazed at her
with reddened eyes. "What do you have to forgive yourself for, Chelsea?"

Chelsea smiled wryly. Her sister didn't miss a trick. "For
being stupid, mainly. And desperate. And just…sad."

"Is this about sleeping your way into a job?"

She nodded. "Not just that, though. I could almost excuse that, because I was desperate for work." She sighed
and leaned back against the booth. "Desperate for love,
too. I stayed with this guy for three years, Louise. Three
years of being humiliated and used." Her throat thick-
ened and she blinked hard, the memories assailing her like
knives, sharp and painful. "Of letting a man treat me like
absolute shit. Like I was worth nothing, less than nothing.
I can't forgive myself for that. Not easily. And it's kept me
from trying with anybody else, even a man who—" Her
voice caught. "Who's worth trying for."

Even if he didn't want to try.

That afternoon Michael came over to her dressing room
as she got ready to film. Hair and makeup perfect, her
outfit crisply tailored, the stylist was putting the finish-
ing touches on her face.

"I just heard from Treffen. He wants you to sign off on those questions by the end of today."

I bet he does, Chelsea thought. Yet still she hesitated, because she knew once she signed that piece of paper all bets were off. Her career at AMI would essentially be over.

"Chelsea?"

"I'll sign and fax it over after the show."

"You don't want to negotiate?"

She gave him a wintry smile. "You don't negotiate with terrorists."

Michael raised his eyebrows. "You really don't like this guy, huh?"

"I don't like being told what to do." Michael, of course, didn't know the truth about Treffen. And Chelsea wouldn't tell him, because it would compromise him and threaten his own career. She'd be the only one to go out in a blaze of glory, even if the prospect still made a thrill of terror run coldly through her.

"You could say no to the interview," Michael suggested quietly.

"And miss out on prime time?"

"There'll be other opportunities."

No, there wouldn't. Not like this. She'd never have another chance to confront a man like Treffen. A man like Brian Taylor.

She turned to smile at Michael. "I'll do the interview, Michael, and I'll sign the paper. Don't worry about me."

"Five minutes till air."

Chelsea nodded at the production assistant and turned to Michael. "I'm trying to change," she said quietly. "It might not seem like it, but I am."

She reached over and kissed his cheek, and Michael squeezed her hand. And then she walked onto the studio set.

Her guest today was a feminist journalist who'd had some racy and unfortunately naked photos taken years ago, and then recently discovered and plastered all over the internet and newspapers.

She sat across from Chelsea now, her face composed but her eyes dark, full of a despair Chelsea understood all too well. And for the first time since she'd started *Chat with Chelsea,* she felt not just an empathy for the guest on her show, but an admiration. They'd made mistakes and they were willing to acknowledge them. They wanted to move on and they had the courage to try.

Did she? Did Alex?

"Two minutes, Chelsea."

She nodded, took a breath, and then gave her guest a genuine smile.

The show went well. There were tears, and heartfelt confessions, and at the end Chelsea did something she didn't normally do. She stood up and crossed the set and hugged the woman, whose arms closed around her in surprise and gratitude.

"That was fantastic," Miles, the producer, gushed as Chelsea came off the set. "The hug—what a perfect touch, Chelsea! How did you think of it?"

She eyed him coolly, knowing that in another lifetime—a few short weeks ago—that hug would have been nothing more than the art of manipulation. Today it had been real.

"I didn't think of it, Miles," she said. "I just did it."

A week passed, and then she met with Zoe Brook,

heard her sad, sordid story. She spoke with Katy Michaels, Sarah's sister, and they drew up interview questions, discussed tactics.

She tried to focus on the things that mattered now. Healing herself. Preparing for her interview with Treffen. Trying not to think about Alex.

But she still thought about him. All the time, she thought of him. Sleepless night after sleepless night she lay in bed and remembered the feel of his body against hers, the taste and smell and sight of him. She thought about going to see him, about giving him the second chance he hadn't even asked for, but she didn't. Couldn't. She was still too fragile, too afraid. And Alex hadn't so much as sent her a text since he'd let her walk away.

But she couldn't avoid him forever, and three days before the interview with Treffen, she showed up at Diaz Network's offices. Alex's assistant, a slender young woman with straw-blond hair and huge green eyes, blinked nervously at her. "Ms. Maxwell? Alex is off-site at a meeting, but he told me to text him immediately if you ever came here."

She felt a ripple of surprise, a wary thrill of hope. "Did he?"

"Do you mind waiting a few minutes?"

"Not at all."

She sat in the elegant lobby and ran through all the things she needed to tell Alex…about Treffen. She wasn't going to touch the emotional stuff, not today. Not when so much was already on the line. And ten minutes later he burst through the door, out of breath and his hair ruffled.

"Chelsea—" So much feeling in that one word, but she

didn't know what it was. She smiled, and it felt as if that smile could slide right off her face.

"Hello, Alex."

"Come into my office."

She followed him into the huge penthouse office, the floor-to-ceiling windows showing Manhattan in all of its sparkling glory.

Chelsea closed the door behind her and Alex stared at her, his gaze roving over her. She gazed back, her heart starting to thud just from looking at him. Wanting him.

"I've missed you," he said quietly and that dangerous hope ballooned inside her, set her soul soaring. *Hope.* So dangerous. So wonderful.

"I've missed you, too," she managed, and Alex regarded her with dark, sorrowful eyes.

"Have you?"

She nodded, then swallowed. They couldn't go there, not now. "I came here to talk about Treffen."

He inclined his head, that sadness still in his eyes. "Okay. So tell me about Treffen."

"I spoke to Zoe Brook. And Katy."

"Good."

"Zoe's going to appear on the show."

Alex nodded. "Treffen won't go for that."

"He won't know."

"He'll be pissed as hell."

"Well, that's the idea. If I can't make him lose his shit completely, there's no point."

A smile flickered across Alex's face and then was gone. "Are you sure you want to do this?" he asked, and she stared at him for a moment, trying to understand what was going behind that inscrutable golden-brown gaze.

"Don't you want me to? Don't you want to see Treffen humiliated, make him pay?"

"Yes. I do." He paused, flicking his gaze away from her to stare out the window for a moment, but Chelsea knew his mind was on other things. Other memories. "But I don't want to be blinded by a need for revenge. I was blinded before, by ambition. And there's not much difference, really. Blindness is blindness, whatever the cause."

"But what he's done—"

"He's been ousted from his law firm, estranged from his family. He'll be prosecuted even if it doesn't all go down on live TV."

"I know that. But he's a lawyer, Alex, and a millionaire. He'll be able to cover it up, just like he has everything else, and I want the world to know what he's done." She took a breath, let it out slowly. "I'm doing this for me as much as you or anyone else, Alex. Because I know what it's like to live in fear. In terror. And shame." She swallowed hard. "So much shame."

"Chelsea—"

"You've helped me to move past it, Alex, even if you don't realize it. Knowing you, being with you…" *Loving you…* She swallowed back the words. "It opened me up again. Made me realize it's okay to want more. To be happy."

He didn't speak for a long moment, and she could see his throat working, a torment in his eyes, one she didn't really understand. Was he regretting his actions, or lack of, before? Or was he just cringing under her sudden onslaught of honesty now?

"I'm glad," he finally said, and she nodded.

Neither of them spoke for a few moments, and Chelsea longed for Alex to say something real. Hell, maybe she should. *I miss you* didn't begin to cover it. *I love you* was terrifying.

"You know if you confront Treffen on live TV," Alex said suddenly, "he'll feel cornered. Trapped. He might go for you."

"Someone's gone for me before," Chelsea answered. "This time I'll handle it."

His mouth quirked up in a tiny smile but his eyes were still sad. "I don't want you to be hurt."

But I already am. "I told you, I want to do this. I don't want men like Treffen getting away with it anymore. Too many men do."

"Brian Taylor did," Alex said softly and Chelsea gave him a bleak smile.

"He got eighteen months for assault."

"And now he's hosting his own cable show."

"Seriously low-budget," Chelsea told him with a tiny smile. "Local access only. Pathetic."

Alex smiled, his eyes and teeth gleaming in the darkness. "If anyone can bring Treffen down, it's you, Chelsea. Whatever else you think about me, please know I believe in you."

She nodded, and her heart, shattered as she'd thought it was, broke all over again. She loved this man. But it wasn't enough. He had to love her back just as much, just as hard, and she knew he didn't.

★ ★ ★

Alex stared at Chelsea, at the grief he saw in her eyes, felt in his soul. It wasn't enough. *I believe in you* wasn't *I love you*. It wasn't tearing down the barriers he'd erected around his heart, opening the floodgates to his soul.

He'd tried the other night, but he knew he was still holding back. He had to jump into that damn pool, not hover at the edge, dipping in a toe. But just like back at Walkerton Prep, he was afraid. He knew what happened when you told people your secrets. They let you drown.

And even though Chelsea hadn't done that—yet—he still couldn't force himself into the water. And he knew that's what Chelsea wanted. Total truth. Complete commitment. Unconditional love. The real deal.

He didn't know if he was capable of any of it, or even if he deserved those things, after Sarah. How many times did you fail someone before you decided not to try? Not to risk someone else's heart, never mind your own?

Because he'd meant what he said. He didn't want Chelsea to be hurt, and yet he knew he'd already hurt her.

"I'm glad you're doing the interview," he said. If he couldn't give her everything, he'd at least give her this. "For your sake. Forget revenge, forget ratings. I'm glad you're doing it because Treffen has done to dozens of women what Taylor did to you."

Chelsea drew in a ragged breath, and he saw the denial in her eyes. Impulsively he reached for her hand; it was ice-cold in his.

"I know you don't want to believe it. You can't. You're still clinging to the idea that it was all your choice. Maybe that makes you feel stronger somehow, more in control.

And maybe it was your choice to offer yourself to Brian at that interview. But three years, Chelsea? With your past, your pain? It was abuse, pure and simple. It wasn't your fault, or your stupidity, or whatever you convinced yourself it was." He smiled sadly. "I wish I'd told you all this before."

"I wouldn't have believed it."

"And now?"

"I—I don't know."

Alex squeezed her hand. "*I* know."

She squeezed back, gave him a trembling smile. "You keep making me cry."

"I want to make you smile. To laugh. I—I want you to be happy, Chelsea." *Say it, damn it. Just tell her you love her. Tell her everything you're keeping back. How afraid you are of all of this. She probably knows, anyway.* "I'm so proud of you, Chelsea."

Coward.

She smiled, that confident, glittering Chelsea Maxwell smile, but this time there was heart and humor behind it. A real, live, wonderful woman, not just a perfect, polished persona. "Wait until you watch me kick Treffen's ass."

The Treffen Session, as it was being billed by the network, was being filmed on a closed set with high security, as Treffen had requested. There was no pink sofa, just two club chairs and a coffee table, a few tasteful prints and bookshelves with leather-backed books behind them, so it looked like the library of a stately home.

Chelsea sat in her dressing room as the makeup artist touched up her face. The hair on the nape of her neck prickled and nerves jumped and plunged in her belly.

"You look a little pale today," Sonya said as she swept a bit more blusher across Chelsea's cheekbones. "Are you feeling okay?"

"I'm fine." Ten minutes ago she'd left her letter of resignation, admitting full culpability, on Michael's desk. She knew he wouldn't see it until the interview was finished.

She'd also met Treffen briefly before he'd been taken away to be prepped by stylists. He'd shaken her hand and looked at her with those cold, shrewd eyes and it had taken nearly all of her strength to shake his hand back with a professional yet friendly firmness, give him a brisk smile as if everything was going according to plan—to his plan.

I think this is going to be a very good show, he'd said, and Chelsea had heard the arrogance in that statement. He thought he was untouchable. She'd realized a while back that the only likely reason Treffen had agreed to be interviewed was because he needed to do some damage control. Polish that spotless reputation.

Not a chance.

Absolutely, she'd told him, smiling in the flirty way she knew he liked. *I think it's going to be fabulous.*

"Ten minutes until air, Chelsea."

She nodded, everything inside her buzzing with both adrenaline and anxiety. No panic attacks now. She couldn't mess this up. She had Zoe Brook styled and made up, ready to go. It had taken some doing, bringing both Zoe and Katy Michaels onto the set without alerting anyone. She'd cleared them as personal friends and she and Katy had helped Zoe with her hair and makeup. Now Zoe and

Katy were hiding out in an unused dressing room, trying to avoid seeing Treffen.

Chelsea only hoped it all went to plan, that Zoe would be able to walk onto the set when she called her. If security prevented it, or her producer Miles or even Michael himself got wind of what was going down and pulled the plug...

Well, she'd just have to go for it, for as long as she could. She just hoped it was long enough.

"I think you're ready," Sonya said, and Chelsea gave her a quick smile.

"Thank you," she said, "for everything."

Sonya looked a little startled and Chelsea knew better than to say anything more. After ten years this would be her last day at AMI, but she couldn't alert anyone to that fact. She couldn't make anyone suspicious.

Taking a deep breath, she walked out onto the set and took her place in one of the club chairs.

Sound and light technicians were still running around, running checks and calling out to each other. Treffen was nowhere to be seen; it was five minutes until air.

She'd miss all of this, she thought as she looked around. She'd miss the buzz of live TV and the excitement of conducting interviews. She'd miss the way she engaged with people on her show, because sometimes it had felt like the most human connection she had in her life.

But that would change, because she was changing—or trying to. Maybe it wouldn't be with Alex, but she'd find happiness with someone, someday.

Why did that thought hurt so much?

Just then Treffen walked onto the stage, looking as

coiffed and charming as always. Chelsea rose from her seat to shake his hand and he smiled back, all easy charm, but his eyes still looked cold and shrewd. The eyes of a snake. She couldn't believe she'd never seen it before, not until Alex had told her. Alex had opened her up to so much, so much pain and beauty and joy and love.

"Two minutes."

Chelsea sat back down, glanced down at the cards with Treffen's printed questions. *Tell me about your humanitarian works.*

As if.

"One minute."

Treffen sat completely still as one of the sound technician fiddled with his mike, and they ran a last sound check before they went live. Chelsea's heart was thundering so hard she could barely hear her own voice; it hurt her chest.

Then as the seconds counted down and the light that indicated filming was imminent started flashing, Chelsea felt herself go very still, very cold with purpose. She felt the eyes of all the assistants and technicians on her, Treffen's eyes on her, and knew there were three men standing in the wings who desperately wanted this to work. Alex, Austin, and Hunter all wanted to be there when Treffen went down.

If he went down. If she could actually make it happen.

She adjusted her mike, glanced offstage and saw Alex standing in the shadows. Panic lurched through her because if Treffen saw him…

But then he smiled at her and there was so much confidence and trust in his eyes that she nearly choked up. She'd tell him she loved him, she decided suddenly. She'd say the words, even if he couldn't say them back. It was important, to her at least, that he know.

She smiled faintly back, and then the intro music started and the light went to green.

Chelsea Maxwell and Jason Treffen were on the air.

Chapter Fifteen

Alex's nails dug into his palms as the intro music faded and Chelsea began the interview. He'd met up with Hunter and Austin at the front of the building, saw how tight their faces looked, how terse their greetings.

Everything rode on the next hour.

He might have told Chelsea it didn't matter, that he didn't care about having his revenge, and for her sake he was trying to make that true. But damn if he didn't want to see Treffen go down in a big ball of flames. And he wanted Chelsea to be the one to light the match.

"Do you really think she can do this, Alex?" Austin had asked in a low voice as they made their way to the recording studio. Alex had, by pulling a dozen different strings, arranged for VIP passes.

"I know she can."

"She won't chicken out?"

"No." And he believed that. He believed, a hundred percent, heart and soul, in Chelsea. Too bad he was too much of a chicken shit to tell her that he loved her. That he wanted the real deal, too, even if it scared him senseless.

Now he focused on the interview taking place in front of him.

"Jason, I'm so delighted to have the opportunity to interview you tonight," Chelsea said. Her voice was as warm and rich as melted chocolate, her smile engaging, her manner relaxed. Alex knew how tightly wound she must be, and his heart swelled with pride.

"It's a pleasure to be here, Chelsea."

"I doubt there's a person in all of the United States who doesn't know of the work you've done, and the causes you've supported. You've been championing the causes of the oppressed for over two decades."

Jason preened a little bit, and next to him Alex felt Austin tense. Hunter's fists clenched. "It's been my life's work, Chelsea."

"Let's talk a little bit about what first drew you to it," Chelsea said, and Alex caught Hunter's penetrating stare. So far Chelsea was going by the book, but Alex knew that's what she did. She eased her guests into a sense of security and intimacy, so they'd share all the more.

And Jason was going to share, whether he wanted to or not.

"When I first started practicing law," Treffen began, obviously settling in to talk about himself for a while, "women didn't have nearly as many opportunities as they do now. There were no female partners in my law firm, and very few women lawyers. It just didn't happen." He made a face of regret that Alex thought looked ridiculous but people always seemed to buy.

Chelsea nodded slowly, seeming to drink it all in. "And how did you change that, Jason?"

"I set about recruiting promising young women to work in my firm. To give them the opportunities they deserved and had earned."

Next to him Austin looked ready to explode. Alex felt his own latent rage start a familiar surge. The arrogant deception Jason had been enacting for so long was diabolical.

"If they deserved these opportunities," Chelsea said with a faint, puzzled frown, "and were qualified to work as lawyers, I'm not sure I see how magnanimous that is. After all, you're just not showing prejudice." She smiled sweetly as Jason's eyes narrowed. That astute observation was clearly not part of the script. "I know you've done so much more, Jason. No need to be modest now." She threw the cameras a smile, inviting every viewer in with that knowing look. "The world wants to hear about you."

Jason relaxed slightly. "Well, I suppose you're right, Chelsea, although I never looked at it that way before. Giving these women opportunities they deserved—even though no one else would—might not seem like much of a humanitarian effort." He gave a rather smug smile. "But I've also set up scholarship funds for girls from disadvantaged areas—"

"I think," Chelsea interjected sweetly, "you mean young women."

The air seemed to crackle. "Is that what we call someone who is seventeen years old?" Jason joked, but Alex could tell he was furious. "Sorry. This old man's not always up on the PC terms."

"Understandable," Chelsea murmured. "But it's really about how you view someone, isn't it?" Jason stared at her, nonplussed, and Chelsea leaned forward as if inviting a confidence. "Why don't we talk about Sarah Michaels?"

Jason froze, if only for a second. Alex had to admire the man's control. If the camera hadn't cut to him just then, no one would have noticed that moment's pause, the quick blink.

"Sarah Michaels," he repeated neutrally.

"You do recall the young woman who worked for you ten years ago?" Chelsea's voice was soft with sorrow. "She killed herself by throwing herself from the roof of your building."

A whisper ran backstage like wildfire. Alex imagined it running through the whole world, millions of people now glued to their televisions. And he knew how wrong he'd been to want to suppress Sarah's part in this, to hide it because he was hiding himself. She deserved this vindication.

Jason had gone utterly still, his body still deliberately relaxed, his expression inscrutable. "Of course I remember Sarah." He shook his head. "Such a tragedy."

"Yes, it was," Chelsea agreed. She shook her head, looking down, seeming lost in sorrow for a moment before she glanced up and nailed Treffen with a look as hard as granite, as cold as ice. "And entirely preventable."

Jason gave her a tight-lipped smile. "Suicide is always preventable, I believe."

Chelsea inclined her head. "Not the most compassionate of views, but I do see what you mean."

"I felt very sorry for Sarah," Jason said, seeming to realize how cold his comment had sounded. "Very sorry for her family. She was, in fact, a close friend of my son's. We all grieved." He stared straight at Chelsea as he said it, and even Alex could see the warning in the older man's eyes.

Don't go there, his gaze was telling Chelsea. *Don't go there, or I will take you down.*

"And the reason for her suicide?"

Treffen didn't blink as he continued to stare steadily at Chelsea. "Obviously she was a troubled young woman. She was dating Hunter Grant, the former NFL quarterback?" He lifted his eyebrows, inviting Chelsea and everyone watching into his implication. "I don't imagine that was a happy relationship."

Hunter half started forward and Austin checked him with his arm. A growl emerged low from his throat.

"Bastard."

"Just wait," Austin murmured.

"I don't know about the complexities of her relationship with Hunter," Chelsea said with a thoughtful nod. "But I did speak to Katy Michaels, Sarah's sister, and she seemed to think *you* were involved in her sister's suicide, Jason."

Behind him Alex could hear production assistants whispering furiously to each other.

"What the *hell*—"

"Cut to commercial?"

He tensed, and then saw someone senior hold up a warning hand. *Wait.*

They were going to see what Chelsea would do with this. It made good television, after all. Good ratings.

"I really have no idea what you're talking about, Chelsea," Jason said. His voice was pitched just right, between perplexity and sorrow. "As I said, I felt very sorry for Sarah. And suicide is always so painful for those left behind. I imagine Katy feels the need to blame someone, and I can see how I'm the likely target."

"Why would you be the likely target, Jason?" Chelsea asked, her voice all honeyed sympathy.

"My law firm demanded a great deal of young people. Long hours, an intense work ethic, demanding cases. It might be that Sarah cracked under the pressure." He spread his hands, all wry regret. "It happens."

"It does happen," Chelsea agreed. "But I'm afraid that's not what Katy told me."

Jason's eyes narrowed slightly. "She's a troubled young woman, Chelsea. I wouldn't pay attention to what she says." His voice was pleasant, his words so obviously a warning.

"It's hard not to take an allegation like hers seriously," Chelsea answered. "Do you want to know what she's accusing you of?" She spoke just as pleasantly as he did, and her words were just as clearly a challenge.

Jason held her gaze for a moment, and Alex knew he was debating whether to suppress it entirely or ride it out. Which would be the better tactic? Finally he let out a little laugh. "I'm not sure I do. Whatever it is, it's completely unfounded and most likely quite nasty."

She had him on the run, that was for sure, Alex thought, and his heart swelled with pride.

"It is nasty, Jason. But I'd like to hear from you how unfounded it is. And of course you can't answer any allegations, when you're not aware of what they are." Chelsea held his gaze, and Alex saw how stony Jason looked now, his jaw tight.

"As I'm sure you know, Chelsea, malicious gossip always swirls about famous people. People like me—or you."

Alex could hear the implied threat in Jason's voice, and he knew Chelsea heard it, too. Damn, what did that bastard know about her?

"Oh, trust me, I know that, Jason," Chelsea assured him. "Which is why I'd like to get this cleared up tonight."

"I don't think there's anything to clear up. In my case, Chelsea, the gossip is malicious and completely false. But that's not true for your case, is it?" He smiled, the smile of a predator sensing victory, and everything in Alex tensed.

"I assume," Chelsea answered, unruffled, "that you're referencing the abuse I suffered from Brian Taylor when I worked at Alabama Broadcasting Communications ten years ago."

Jason opened his mouth but no words came out. He looked, strangely, at a loss. "Yes," he finally said, "although I don't know if I call sleeping your way into a job abuse."

Chelsea leaned forward, her eyes glittering. "Let me tell you what I call abuse," she said, her voice quiet and cold and so very certain. "Luring—what were your words?— promising young women into working for your firm and then blackmailing them into prostitution. You've run a prostitution ring for high-end clients for nearly twenty years, Jason, sourced by your own employees."

The stunned reaction backstage was a tide of whispered, frantic discussions about whether to cut the cameras. Jason just stared at Chelsea, his expression utterly even.

"That's disgusting, and utterly untrue."

"So you didn't encourage young women in your employ to sleep with clients?" Chelsea asked. Nothing sweet or honeyed about her now; she was hard and perfect. "You didn't blackmail these same clients over it? You didn't coerce women into performing these sordid acts by paying off their scholarships and giving them fully-paid internships?"

"No." Jason bit out the single word.

"You can't explain this photograph?" Chelsea asked, and slid the photo of Sarah from a folder beneath her chair.

Jason's eyes widened as he glanced at it, and his jaw bunched harder still. "No."

"Can you explain why Zoe Brook, a celebrated PR specialist, is ready to come forward with her story?"

"Zoe Brook? She has a personal axe to grind, I'm afraid." He shook his head sorrowfully. "It happens."

"She worked for you for several years, Jason," Chelsea reminded him coolly. "And you blackmailed her into prostituting herself with your clients."

Jason leaned forward, his eyes glittering. "Chelsea, I know you like for the guests on your talk show to sob and spill secrets, but this is a little much. I'm a respected professional, and I can't have these kinds of accusations thrown at me, especially when there is absolutely no basis except for a couple of crazy women—" He stopped suddenly, and Chelsea smiled.

"I have one of those crazy women in the wings, Jason. Zoe Brook is here and she wants to talk to you."

Jason sat back, a stony look on his face. "This is a ridiculous attempt to discredit me."

"Why would anyone want to discredit you, Jason?" Chelsea asked, her voice both steely and sweet. "Everyone loves you. You're a champion of women's rights, although

I admit you're not sounding like much of one at the moment. I didn't want to believe this of you, and I have to say, it took some convincing. I had to see photos, and I spoke with both Katy Michaels and Zoe Brook. Now I want the world to hear Zoe's story. I want you to hear it, Jason."

Zoe Brook appeared on the side of the set, pale and yet full of purpose. "Hello, Jason."

Jason eyed her coolly. "You're just angry because I let you go from the firm, Zoe. Your work was shoddy and this is clearly all part of your revenge. As I said earlier, I believe in granting opportunities to women—but they have to deserve them. They have to be qualified."

"The only thing you cared about your female employees being qualified for," Zoe answered, "was servicing your clients. But I won't be silent any longer, Jason. I won't be your victim."

Once again Alex heard a furious buzz of whispers, like someone had poked a wasp's nest, from the production assistants. The cameras continued to roll.

"This is outrageous," Jason stated. "And I refuse to listen to any more of these accusations." He stood up, preparing to leave the set. "I can assure you," he finished icily, skewering Chelsea with a look, "you'll be hearing from my lawyers."

Alex knew it was probably only a matter of minutes, or even of seconds, before they cut the show. The network would not want a lawsuit.

Chelsea stood up as well, facing Treffen. "You can't bluff your way through this one, Jason," she said, her eyes and voice hard. "You've been managing that for twenty years, but the act is paper-thin now, and you know it. Your career is ruined. Your family knows the truth about you. And now the whole world does, too. It's over. You know it's over, even if you're pretending otherwise. You *know*."

Jason stared at her for a long moment, his stony features slackening into a look of bleak hopelessness. "You stupid bitch," he said quietly. "You have no idea what you're doing. What you're opening up with this. It's not just—" He stopped suddenly, his face now twisting into an ugly sneer. "You haven't learned anything since you spread your legs for that two-bit producer in Alabama, have you?" Then he raised his hand and slapped her across the face.

Chelsea's head whipped round and Alex started forward, checked by Hunter.

"Damn it, let me—"

"You can't punch Treffen on live TV," Hunter told him calmly. "Trust me, I know how these things go. It'll just turn him into a victim."

Fury still surged through him, but Alex stepped back.

He could see Treffen's handprint on Chelsea's face, and she was grinning in triumph. The cameras had stopped rolling, and two security guards were now flanking Treffen, whose face had gone blank and shuttered.

Chelsea had done it. She'd broken Treffen.

And she'd broken him, too, he realized. Broken him in all sorts of ways, shattered all his attitude, all his armor. And he had to tell her.

He strode forward, and she turned to him, still grinning. "I did it—"

"I love you." It was amazingly easy to say. To feel. "I love you," he said again, because she looked shell-shocked, and hell, he just wanted to keep saying it. "Not just for this," he added, gesturing to the set, "but for everything. For you, Chelsea. I love you for you."

Her grin widened, a silly, sloppy thing. "You could maybe say it one more time."

"I love you. I love you." He snatched her into his arms, buried his face in her hair. "I love you and I can't believe I've been so afraid to say it, to admit it, for so long."

"It's okay," she said as her arms came around him. "Because you said it now. I believe it now."

Security guards were taking Treffen off the set, and Hunter, Austin and Katy were there, jubilant but also determined to make sure Treffen wasn't let off with just a few questions or a warning. Reluctantly Alex released Chelsea. There would be time later to say everything in his heart, he knew. And time, he hoped, to hear it from her. Those three little words.

It was thanks to Michael, Chelsea knew, that she wasn't escorted from the building by security. Jason Treffen might be arrested, might pay for his crimes, but she'd pay for hers, too. She wouldn't work for AMI again, and amazingly, that was okay.

Hunter and Austin had gone out with Zoe and Katy, to celebrate but also to go over the events of the evening, to process it all and to decide what the next steps would be. Chelsea had told Alex to go with them; she needed to finish up, quite literally, at AMI.

Still she wished she'd asked him to stay as she went to clear out her office, the building quiet now after the chaos of the interview. Michael was probably meeting with AMI's team of lawyers, and figuring out the damage control. She'd talk to him later, try to explain. She thought he'd understand.

She walked out of AMI and ten years of her life without a flicker of regret. A little bittersweet sorrow, yes, and a lot of memories. But for once in her life, no regret.

Alex had texted her that they were all in a private room at the Plaza Hotel, with a magnum of champagne at hand.

Please join us, he'd texted. Join me.

She stood on the threshold of the room she'd been directed to, her gaze taking in Zoe snugged against Hunter, Katy and Austin holding hands.

And Alex. Alex sat alone, a flute of champagne dangling from his fingers, a thoughtful look on his face as he listened to everyone else's excited chatter. Then he turned his head slowly and met Chelsea's gaze with a blazing one of his own.

Chelsea felt her heart swell and fill. She was walking into a crowded room and she didn't feel remotely anxious or afraid.

She felt sure.

I love you, she mouthed, and Alex kept his gaze on hers as he smiled and held out his arms.

She walked straight into them, and when they closed around her she felt as if she'd finally found a safe place. The only place.

"I love you," she said, her voice muffled against his shoulder, and his arms went around her more tightly.

I love you. Such sweet, simple words, yet words that held so much power, Alex thought as he hugged Chelsea. So much joy. He would never tire of saying them now. Of meaning them and feeling them.

Hunter glanced over at them, his arm around Zoe, his expression amused. "Come and join the party, you two," he said, one eyebrow arched. "Unless you want to get a room?"

"Maybe later," Alex said, and with his arm snugged around Chelsea's waist, he drew her toward his friends.

They were all talking about Treffen and what would happen next, and for the first time when he thought of Jason and Sarah and all the rest, Alex didn't feel that flash of rage, that surge of guilt. He felt...he felt at peace.

And blessed, because he had Chelsea in his life. Because he'd been given a second chance, they both had, and not everyone got one of those.

"Okay?" Chelsea asked softly, looking at him, her dark eyes searching his face.

"More than okay," Alex answered. There would be time later to talk, to share, to admit everything he'd felt and held back and wanted still. Lots of time, because they had the rest of their lives. "More than okay," he said again, his voice rough with emotion, and Chelsea smiled in both understanding and agreement, and then softly kissed him.

★ ★ ★ ★ ★

KATY let out a long breath and started walking back down the empty corridor, back to the party.

Back toward Jason Treffen.

Talking to him had just about made her lose her mind. It had taken everything in her not to grab his glass from his hand and pour it over his head. Then break the glass on his face.

She considered the man as good as her sister's murderer, so she was short on charitable feelings where he was concerned.

The door to the ballroom opened, and she froze.

Oh. Her breath left her in a rush, a current of electricity washing over her skin.

It was him.

The man whose eyes were like an endless black hole, drawing her in, a force she couldn't deny or control. When he had looked at her, she'd felt as if she were grounded to the spot. She'd felt like he had looked and *seen* her.

Seen everything. More than that, she'd looked back and she'd seen him.

Had seen a grief in him. An anger.

It had been, in some ways, like looking into a mirror.

"It's you," he said, his voice deep, smooth. Like really good chocolate. "I was hoping to run into you."

"Wh-why were you hoping to run into me?" she asked.

"Because you're the most beautiful woman here. Why wouldn't I want to see you?"

"You're a flirt."

"That's the thing, I'm not really." He put his hands in his pockets, a wicked half smile curling that sinful mouth.

"I have to get back."

She started to walk past him and he took her arm, stopped her progress. She looked up and met cold, dark eyes.

"To who?" he asked, his voice gentle, an opposing force to the hold he had on her.

There was something about that grip. Commanding. It spoke to every secret fantasy that lived in the dark shadows inside her. The parts of herself that had looked at every man she'd even tried to date and found them lacking.

But not him. He wouldn't be lacking. Something shivered inside her, a whisper.

He would know what you wanted.

* * *

The first step to revenge in the **Fifth Avenue** *trilogy*
Austin has the plan…
June 2014

HARLEQUIN®
Presents®

Revenge and seduction intertwine...

Behind the Scenes of *Fifth Avenue*:
Read on for an exclusive interview with Maisey Yates!

It's such an exciting world to create. Did you discuss it with the other writers?
There was a lot of discussion! Thankfully we live in a world of Skype and FaceTime and we were able to spend time not just emailing, but having face-to-face discussions, in spite of the fact that we're in different states and countries. I love technology.

How does writing a trilogy with other authors differ from when you are writing your own stories?
Kate and Caitlin are not just fantastic writers, but they're friends as well, which made collaboration and communication so much easier. There's a fine balance to constructing a series that will have different elements executed by different authors. I'm used to focusing on an individual book, but in this case a broader awareness was required.

What was the biggest challenge? And what did you most enjoy about it?
I think the biggest challenge was pinpointing which series elements needed to happen in which book. There has to be excitement and new revelations in every installment of the series, and making those decisions was tricky! I think what I most enjoyed was brainstorming as a group. Watching this germ of an idea expand and grow. We each brought a unique perspective to the overall series, which created something I'm not sure would have been possible if we'd simply tackled it as individuals.

As you wrote your hero and heroine was there anything about them that surprised you?
I think Austin surprised me the most. He has such a huge amount of decency, and so many ideas about what it means to be a good man. Which is why he's so conflicted by what he sees as "dark desires." They don't mesh with who he thinks he should be. But even I was surprised by the full intensity that he had hidden beneath his suit!

What was your favourite part of creating the world of *Fifth Avenue*?
I love the idea that such a beautiful world, insulated by money and power, could be hiding something so dark. I think digging in and exposing all the ugliness beneath the glitter, and really going for the scandal, was so much fun!

If you could have given your heroine one piece of advice before the opening pages of the book, what would it be?
Probably DON'T sleep with your mortal enemy's son. (Katy says: But he's superhot and good with a tie. Me: I retract my advice.)

What was your hero's biggest secret?
A lot of the secrets in the book belong to other people. Austin is, in many ways, kind of a normal guy (for a billionaire philanthropist). But I think his biggest secret is what he really craves from a sexual partner. He was even lying to himself about it! Until Katy.

What does your hero love most about your heroine?
Her strength. She's been through hell and never stops pushing, never stops pursuing justice for her sister, and a better life for her brother.

What does your heroine love most about your hero?
I think Austin restored her faith in people. And in love.

Which of your *Fifth Avenue* characters would you most like to meet and why?
I'll be very simple and say Austin. Who doesn't love a hot man in a suit?

HPQA0614TR

IT wasn't the first time a man had propositioned her. But it was the first time she'd felt a burst of flame lick over her when he did, and she was terribly afraid he knew that, too. That he felt the same slap of heat.

She couldn't let that happen, it was impossible, so she shoved it aside.

"Is that caveman code for 'sleep with me so I can put you back in your proper place'?" she asked, cool and challenging and back on familiar ground, because she knew this routine. She could handle this. Jason Treffen had taught her well, one painful lesson at a time. "Because you should know before you try, dragging me off by my hair somewhere won't end the way you think it will. I can promise you that."

Hunter looked intrigued and his head canted slightly to one side, but that wolfish regard of his never wavered—bright and hot and knowing. Reaching much too far inside her.

"I don't want to drag you off somewhere by your hair and have my way with you, Ms. Brook."

The smile on her lips turned mocking, but she was more concerned with the sudden long, slow thump of her heart and the heavy, wet heat low in her belly. "Because you're not that kind of guy?"

There was something more than predatory in his eyes then, hard and hot, a dark knowing in the curve of his mouth that connected with that deep drumroll inside her, making it her pulse, her breath, her worst fear come true.

"I'm absolutely that kind of guy. But I told you. You have to ask me nicely."

He smiled, as if he was the one in control. And she couldn't allow it.

"No," she said, furious that it came out like a whisper, thin and uncertain. His smile deepened for a moment, like a promise.

"Your loss," he murmured, and that aching fire swelled inside her, nearly bursting.

And then he laughed again, dismissing her, and turned to go. Again. For good this time, she understood, and she couldn't let that happen.

Zoe had no choice.

"I wouldn't do that, Mr. Grant." She didn't know why the dryness in her mouth seemed to translate into something like trembling everywhere else when she'd known before she'd approached him that it would probably come to this. She made herself smile. "I know about Sarah."

* * *

*The second step to revenge in the **Fifth Avenue** trilogy.*
Hunter has the money...
July 2014

HARLEQUIN®

Presents®

Glamorous international settings...
powerful men... passionate romances

Harlequin Presents stories are all about
romance and escape—glamorous settings,
gorgeous women and the passionate,
sinfully tempting men who want them.

From brooding billionaires to untamed
sheikhs and forbidden royals,
Harlequin Presents offers you the world!

Eight new passionate reads available
every month wherever books and
ebooks are sold.

HPBPA2014TR

Harlequin Presents welcomes you to
the world of **The Chatsfield;**
Synonymous with style, spectacle…and scandal!

SHEIKH'S SCANDAL by *Lucy Monroe* (May 2014)

PLAYBOY'S LESSON by *Melanie Milburne* (June 2014)

SOCIALITE'S GAMBLE by *Michelle Conder* (July 2014)

BILLIONAIRE'S SECRET by *Chantelle Shaw* (August 2014)

TYCOON'S TEMPTATION by *Trish Morey* (September 2014)

RIVAL'S CHALLENGE by *Abby Green* (October 2014)

REBEL'S BARGAIN by *Annie West* (November 2014)

HEIRESS'S DEFIANCE by *Lynn Raye Harris* (December 2014)

Step into the gilded world of **The Chatsfield!**
Where secrets and scandal lurk behind every door…

Reserve your room!
June 2014

HPCHATSTR

Love the book you just read?

Your opinion matters.

Review this book on your favorite
book site, review site, blog or your own
social media properties and share
your opinion with other readers!

Be sure to connect with us at:
Harlequin.com/Newsletters
Facebook.com/HarlequinBooks
Twitter.com/HarlequinBooks